# A Director's, Cut

Also by Simon Parke

*Pippa's Progress: A Pilgrim's Journey to Heaven*
*A Vicar, Crucified: An Abbot Peter Mystery*
*A Psychiatrist, Screams: An Abbot Peter Mystery*

# A Director's, Cut

## An Abbot Peter Mystery

*Simon Parke*

ABBOT PETER
A **HABIT** FOR
**CRIME**

DARTON·LONGMAN+TODD

First published in 2014 by
Darton, Longman and Todd Ltd
1 Spencer Court
140 – 142 Wandsworth High Street
London SW18 4JJ

The right of Simon Parke to be identified as the Author of this
work has been asserted in accordance with the Copyright,
Designs and Patents Act 1988

ISBN 978-0-232-53061-2

A catalogue record for this book is available from the British
Library

Phototypeset by Kerrypress Ltd, Luton, Bedfordshire
Printed and bound in Great Britain by Bell & Bain, Glasgow

For Hilary Mantel,
who has raised the bar for us all

My thanks to Shellie Wright, Elizabeth Spradbery and David Moloney who all gave precious time to read and reflect on the manuscript along the way; to all at DLT who have kindly kept on believing and stirring; to Marisa Bouman for lending me Hilary Mantel's wonderful *Bring Up the Bodies*, during the final stages of editing this manuscript. It was both kind friend and sharp instructor. And to every kind reader who has muttered appreciation in my ear at one time or other; such gift along the way.

*'In the end, I think theatre has only one subject: justice.'*

Edward Bond

# *Act One*

*In the modern media age we are rarely surprised by what we see. Whether it's on television or film or in the theatre, everything is so advertised, so trailed, that most entertainment is merely what you thought it was going to be like.*

**Rowan Atkinson**

# One

✤

## *1310, Paris*

*He wore a white tunic and scapular hat, black cloak and hood. It was the familiar dress of the Dominican Order, and the Dominicans had brought the woman here. From a distance, he was nothing special; just one more monk watching a heretic scream and burn.*

*And it was a skilful fire, skilfully made on the orders of William of Paris, which meant a progressive burning of the condemned, no premature death by choking or suffocation, but rather, a steady and deliberate sequence, moving from calves, thighs and hands to torso and forearms and then upwards, heavenwards some would say, to the breasts, upper chest and face until final death from heatstroke, shock, blood loss or simply the thermal decomposition of vital body parts... burnt meat. Sadly for the condemned, you didn't die of screaming.*

*The fire-making was a craft and determined the nature of the spectacle. Some victims died from suffocation with only their calves on fire, which was hardly appropriate, too easy a path down to hell. The journey to hell should be hell itself, this was the accepted orthodoxy, though the duration of the journey varied. When the wood was damp or ill-stacked, victims could take over two hours to die tied to the stake, and for some in the Inquisition, ill-stacking was itself a craft. In many burnings – not so common here in Paris, but not unknown – a rope was attached to the convict's neck and passed through a ring on the stake, by which means they were strangled and burnt simultaneously.*

*The crowd today was not baying however, whatever the churchmen said about her evil writings; indeed, chroniclers would record how on this day, the crowd were moved to tears by the calmness of*

3

*Marguerite Porete as she faced her scorching end. The man in the white tunic and hood – who currently shared a house with her chief persecutor, William of Paris – could not show his tears.*

*Or not yet – or he too would join her.*

# Two

'There's nothing like a good show,' said the Abbot, who, for reasons unknown, always approached theatre with the highest of hopes.

'And this is nothing like a good show,' she replied.

It was an old joke, but allowed.

'It's called pro-am theatre, apparently,' said the Abbot.

It was the half-time interval and he hadn't seen his companion for a while; weeks had become months, though maybe not a year.

'And we all know that that means,' she said.

'We do?'

'Professional ticket prices, amateur performances.'

'Ah.' She was being negative and a challenge was in order; negativity did need challenging. 'But then on reflection, Tamsin, I don't remember you paying.'

It was true, she hadn't paid, not a penny, it was his treat. But she could still muster resentment.

'I may not have paid in cash.'

'True.'

'But I did have to clear up after a children's party, prior to the show – so I think I earned it.'

'To be accurate, which is important, we'd have to say *I* cleared up after the children's party ... that's what I remember, at least.'

'I was there as well.'

'Yes, you were there but not cleaning; present but ineffective, looking supercilious in the corner, drinking a cup of tea ... while I cleaned.'

'It was disastrously weak.'

'What was?'

5

'The tea.'

'The tea was weak.'

'Pale as a death mask.'

'The tea which I also paid for.'

'It was still weak.'

'But free.'

'Why do people make weak tea?'

'The world is full of mysteries.'

'I mean, if you want milky hot water have milky hot water – but don't call it tea.'

'My tea is always stewed.'

'Then consider yourself excused.'

'Thank you.'

'On this occasion.'

'Though in the monastery – now, that was appallingly weak tea, so weak it could hardly crawl out of the urn.'

'So who was to blame?'

'We probably don't need to blame.'

'There's always someone to blame.'

'The desert tea delivery was sporadic, too much sand and not enough tarmac, so Brother Teilo was always a little sparing with the leaves, it brought out the hoarder in him.'

'You had a monk called Brother Tea Low looking after the tea?'

'Teilo, yes. Named after the sixth-century Welsh saint, obviously.'

'Obviously.'

The curtains are moving and the audience murmur stills. Perhaps they'll swing open, it looks like they might. Something is happening backstage, definite action … rather noisy movement, to be honest, which isn't what you want. But then the stagehands are all volunteers, none of them paid and probably doing their best; and of course this isn't the West End, it's Stormhaven for God's sake! The lead stagehand today, as Abbot Peter knows, works in the chip shop by the church, where she presents a relentlessly cheerful face through the grease and vinegar of business – and the dull 'chip on your shoulder' jokes. So if she knocks the curtain occasionally when moving props, is it really the end of the world?

And, as it turned out, the curtains didn't open, they settled again, it might have been the wind, but they stayed where they were, protecting the mystery until the mystery was ready … which allowed more polite conversation in the stalls.

'You may not have noticed the high heels.'

'I'm sorry?'

'My high heels,' said Tamsin, pointing down.

6

She was returning to the children's party, unfinished business, explaining her actions, or rather lack of them … she hadn't done anything to help clear up because of her high heels.

'I did notice them, Tamsin.'

'So you'll understand.'

'What I most noticed was your toppling gait … you moved like a ship's mast in a storm.'

'And of course you saw a lot of ships in the desert.'

'But they're very nice,' said the monk. 'The shoes, I mean, they're very.'

'Very what?'

'Well, they look very uncomfortable, which presumably means expensive.'

'You can't clear up after children in high heels.'

'You don't know until you try.'

'I was expecting a night out.'

'A night out was the idea, believe me.' Poor girl, it hadn't been her idea of fun. 'But Hermione rang me and asked if I could just get here a little bit early and "be a real godsend".'

Hermione. Tamsin needed to ask about her. She was the 'theatre director' here, whatever that was.

'You know her?' she asked.

'Not really.'

'She just picked your name from the phone book?'

'We met at the Stormhaven W.I. last week.'

'So you do know her.'

'I know her a little. When can you ever say you know someone?'

'The Stormhaven W.I.' Said with distance and disdain.

'I'd just given a talk there on the ancient Egyptians.'

'Who said they were stuck in the past?'

'I was talking about Egyptian attitudes towards death.'

Tamsin dusts the sleeve of her dress with her hand.

'So an afternoon of much hilarity.'

'Well, actually, there were some lighter moments.'

'But also the moment when Hermione thought, "Here's a sucker I can use. I know – he can clear up after the kids next week!"'

'Are you being personal?'

'She got you to clear up, Abbot, because she couldn't be bothered to employ enough staff.'

'It's how the theatre makes money.'

'Manipulating the vulnerable?'

'Needs must. And I'm not the vulnerable.'

Tamsin raises unconvinced eyebrows.

'But children's parties?' she said.

'It can't be cheap to keep a show like this on the road.'

'So why bother?'

Why bother to keep a theatre going? The question needed asking and Tamsin hadn't a clue. Peter ignored her.

'So I suppose it's space for hire,' he said.

'And staff for free.'

Abbot Peter was taking his niece Tamsin to the theatre. And here in Stormhaven on England's breezy and white-cliffed south coast, if you didn't fancy the Theatre Royal in Brighton, you were left with the Bell Theatre in Cliff View Road, a venue which had no right to survive, no right at all, but somehow had done just that. But for how long? It was a secret well kept, Hermione was keeping it to herself, but these were difficult days, with a growing chasm between money in and money out, this is what she suspected. She feared a close look at the books; they were a dark cave, forbidding and cold, in which a monster called painful reality may well lurk.

And sadly, there was no benefactor called Bell in the theatre's history, no large endowment to protect against difficult days, and more was the pity. Instead, the theatre boasted the real thing in the adjoining tower, the bell tower. There in the belfry hung four tons of reverberating metal which provoked upset and delight in equal measure. Not everyone appreciated its melancholic chimes at 3.00 p.m. every day. Some thought they resembled a death knell across the town, or a warning of danger from the sea, an invasion by the French. And had it been the fourteenth century, it might well have been, for the onion hordes had regularly put this proud port to sword and flame back then; massacre and pillage with a Gallic accent. Yes, Stormhaven knew much terror when young; and like the human body, the rocks don't forget.

But, by the twenty-first century, things had changed: the French came less often, school trips mainly, dreaded but not fatal; while the port that once brought wealth and prestige had moved two miles down the road to Newhaven – new and still resented by the Stormers, six hundred years on. Stormhaven, with its one hotel and derelict seafront, was left to make its own fun ... not that anyone would call the Bell Theatre's current production 'fun'.

'So what did you think of the first half?' asked Peter.

The play hadn't been his choice. Hermione insisted they come for the theatre's thirtieth anniversary night: 'Come as my guests!' she'd said. 'Complimentary tickets!' Yet she still made him pay. Was it only in the desert that guests came for free?

'Am I allowed to be honest?' said Tamsin.

'The world may survive.'

'A bit depressing.'

8

'That's your verdict?'

The play, called *Mother's Day*, had been unremittingly bleak, two women at war, trapped in a relationship that seemed to be destroying them both. But bleak was not the same as depressing; or not for Peter at least.

'Very depressing,' said Tamsin. 'Airless.'

'Some relationships are.'

'Tell me about it.'

Her venom did not surprise the Abbot. Peter knew almost nothing about her past, but could see the outcomes and noted its continued power in her life. She was like the unexploded bomb recently found in the high street ... dangerous until defused.

'And I didn't feel the two actors liked each other very much,' she added.

'I think it's called acting, isn't it?'

'No, I know they don't like each other in the play. I just felt they didn't like each other away from the play either.'

'Intriguing.'

'My guess is they're not sharing a laugh and a joke right now back stage.'

For Tamsin, the interval was generally the best part of the theatre experience – twenty minutes in which to find some wine, stretch her legs and look critically at other people, before returning for the second half, which tended to be shorter, a truth she was clinging to now. The play tonight, and indeed for the whole of the summer season, was a new work by a playwright, who – as she whispered in the Abbot's ear ten minutes into the show – 'clearly didn't have a happy childhood'.

And Hermione, the theatre's director, had warned Peter, as he was sweeping up after the children's party.

'It's not a comedy, Abbot.'

'So no custard pies?'

'All very intense, I think you could say, yes, pretty intense – definitely not a comedy.'

'I'm getting the idea. If there's a laugh, someone must have forgotten their lines.'

And sadly so far, no one had forgotten their lines.

'Hermione told me it was specially commissioned for the theatre's thirtieth anniversary celebrations,' said Peter. 'He's a young local writer.'

'That doesn't mean he has anything to say.'

'Everyone has something to say.'

'Or that we should have to watch it.'

'I enjoyed the first half.'

9

'So let's have the dirt on Hermione.'

'No dirt, as far as I know.'

'There's always dirt.'

'Hermione Bysshe-Urquhart, MBE.'

'My Big Ego.'

'Sorry?'

'MBE'.

'Oh.'

The Abbot was not moved to defend the honours system. But he would at least speak up for his new friend.

'She's the creator of all this really. Everything you see around you has been her vision.'

'The pillars?'

'No, the building used to be a church, but no one came, or not enough, so they sold it to Hermione and Nicholas, her husband, to turn it into a theatre, a place for dressing up and performance.'

'So no change of usage then.'

'And credit where it's due, she's stuck to her guns through thick and thin ... including his death, of course.'

'Nicholas died young?'

'He did, yes. So she's a determined lady, Hermione, dedicated to Stormhaven having its own theatre.'

'And is this her self-publicity or your considered opinion?'

Peter smiled.

'Maybe more of the first; as I say, I don't know her well. We all present a mask above our troubled selves.'

'You'll be telling me all the world's a stage in a minute.'

'No,' said the Abbot ... though the phrase had come to mind.

Tamsin watched as the seats filled around them. It was about two-thirds full, which was disappointing for the thirtieth anniversary night.

'I can't really get into the world of greasepaint,' she said.

'You don't say.'

'I just can't see the point.'

'The point?'

'I spend my time wondering which actor is earning the most, who failed which audition, who beat whom to which part; and who's jealous of whom.'

'I think I just watch the play.'

'How boring for you.'

'And in this play, there's professional and amateur working together, something they often do here apparently. So can you spot which performer's the professional?'

'No. But I do know which member of the audience is bored.'

And now the lights are going down, a hush falling, so Tamsin whispers:

'I just can't believe it, that's the thing; can't believe what's happening on the stage, can't get beyond the contrivance of it all … that's my problem with theatre.'

'Well, just suspend disbelief for the next fifty minutes.' She was beginning to sound ungrateful. 'Imagine yourself there now, on stage, in the scene.'

The theatre is dark and quiet. Gentle piano music plays as the curtains of the Bell Theatre open for the second half of *Mother's Day*, a new play by the young playwright, Paul Bent. On stage, the light reveals a chair, face-to-audience, on which the lone figure of a middle-aged lady sits, a new character. She doesn't look out, but looks up. Bathed in creamy light, she gazes heavenwards, head thrown back, dramatic pose, looking up at the lights, mouth open in motionless wonder. Her body pushed forward and her head yanked back, simultaneously, separating the vertebrae, as the pathologist would later say. And her throat cut, a mess of blood.

'Who's this?' says Tamsin. Why kill a character the audience doesn't know? This was her first thought.

'It's Hermione,' says Abbot Peter. 'Or rather, it was.'

# Three

## *Tuesday, 3 August*

'I suppose this makes the case yours,' said Chief Inspector Wonder.

He sat behind his large desk at the police HQ in Lewes, Storm-haven's posh neighbouring town, ten miles and several pay scales away. Tamsin wondered why men needed such big desks ... and it was men, men with big desks, desks they didn't really use, except to sit behind. Were 'big desk' and 'big car' syndrome the same de-ficiency at play? Tamsin chose to ignore the size of Wonder's man-hood. Today, she wanted him on side.

'It would seem to make sense,' she said, casually.

Detective Inspector Tamsin Shah wanted this case. She would enjoy pulling back the curtain, scraping off the make-up and reveal-ing all at the Bell Theatre.

'She's an MBE, of course,' said Wonder, tense.

'I know.'

'You knew her?'

'A friend knows her – knew her.'

'Hermione Bysshe-Urquhart, MBE.'

He said it with relish, lingering on the 'MBE' as though it were chocolate cake.

'And that makes a difference?'

'An honour from Her Majesty the Queen?'

'Do you want me to curtsey?'

'In the real world, Tamsin, yes, that makes a difference.'

'And the difference is, what – you sweat a little more freely dur-ing the investigation?'

Tamsin said it with a smile, which drew Wonder in – an insult that somehow made him feel better about himself, made him feel understood and therefore charmed. He was easily charmed by the attractive Tamsin; and irritated by the fact. It's no good being charmed by your staff, no good at all, because then they run rings round you, he knew that, he'd seen it … and that wasn't going to happen on his watch.

He hadn't helped himself, he wasn't stupid, because … well, yes, he had made one or two comments to her in the past, which he now regretted, obviously. Comments concerning her appeal, her female appeal, nothing inappropriate, well, slightly inappropriate possibly, but under the influence of drink, which isn't the same, you can't judge a man when he's drunk. You say things at office parties, it's just banter, doesn't mean anything; but of course it does, not at the time as the beer flows out your armpits, but the following morning, that's when the meaning dawns. It's a truth drug, alcohol, that's what makes it so dangerous, Wonder had told many a young constable that, you may speak the truth when drunk, dangerous … and then of course his home life was a rather distant affair these days, not that he brought his private life to work, much too professional for that. And while he'd never been to the Bell Theatre himself – he lived in the village of Cuckfield, another direction, towards Haywards Heath – Wonder did think of himself as a theatre man, liked the odd visit to a show, not Shakespeare obviously, but classics like *The Mousetrap* or a good farce like *A Bit of How's your Father!*, which had to be the funniest show of all time, bloody hilarious, with all that in-and-out-of-the-bedroom-wardrobe stuff in the second act. He had literally wet himself with laughter.

'Shame you missed the second half,' he said, reflecting on the night before.

'You obviously weren't there,' said Tamsin.

'Well, not my sort of play.'

'Not anyone's sort of play. After the first half, the murder was a relief to us all.'

But Wonder wasn't listening.

'I once saw *A Bit of How's Your Father* at the Theatre Royal in Brighton, and I was laughing so much I was hurting' – he wouldn't say 'wetting himself' – 'begging them to stop, quite literally begging for them to stop!'

'My thoughts last night.'

'You don't mean that, Tamsin.'

But Tamsin did mean it and now sat here the morning after the murder because, as well as being Abbot Peter's niece, she was also a Detective Inspector in the Sussex police force, where she was more ambitious than Stalin and much better looking. Her boss, Chief Inspector Wonder, had supported her fast promotion, part father figure, part sad old lecher, but she'd never thought to be grateful in return – disdain rather than deference was her starting place in the relationship.

'It's a sad day, of course,' he said, as though somehow it was required.

'How do you know it's sad?'

'A death is sad, traditionally.'

'It's quite possible no one liked her.'

A lot of people were profoundly disliked in Tamsin's experience, a truth sometimes forgotten when they died.

'But to be executed like that.'

'It was efficient,' she agreed.

'Torso pushed forward, head jerked back, vertebrae shattered – almost military.'

'Why do you say that?'

'Oh, I did my time with the big boys, you know.'

'The big boys? Was this at primary school?'

She knew it wasn't.

'I was two years in SOU, Tamsin.'

She nodded. 'Special Operations Unit' to the uninitiated and DI Shah was meant to be impressed.

'And we'd be sent up to the Hereford camp for training days with the SAS johnnies.'

'Useful?'

It was a withering question. As if the SAS had anything to do with policing.

'That sort of execution, vertebrae work, very much their line.'

Wonder half-mimed it.

'So you were taught execution techniques?'

Wonder, afloat on a sea of bravado, missed the mockery.

'If I told you what we saw, I'd have to kill you!'

'I'm sure policing in Sussex has been much helped by your Hereford away-days, sir.'

'I like to think so.'

'I mean, who knows when a summary execution will be necessary?'

'Different days, different days,' mused Wonder, glad to have established his virility. 'But they believe she was dead before her throat was cut?'

He prided himself on a grasp of detail.

'It's yet to be confirmed; but yes, it looks that way.'

Tamsin had handled the shock and horror in the theatre with some brilliance. From moaning member of the audience, she'd been in her element, born to it, making her way up onto the stage, declaring it a crime scene, closing the curtains, stopping all movement as far as she'd been able, establishing those who'd had access to the stage, and in due course, letting all others go. Forensics had been there within half an hour and the seven suspects gathered in make-up.

And her opening line had been better than anything she'd heard that evening from the stage:

'We'll all get on much better if the make-up extends only as far as the face paint. Do you understand me? Making up stories during this investigation is a very bad idea.'

It hadn't been the kindest of starts but then one of those listening was a killer, which can affect your tone, you speak to that particular slice of scum, and the other six have to put up with it. But the other six had their own responsibilities. The small lies and evasions offered during an investigation wasted so much time and made her angry. She'd wanted to give them a warning:

'Lie to me, withhold information from me – and I really will come after you.'

But now, the morning after, sitting in police HQ, she had a request for her boss to consider.

'I'll want the Abbot working with me again.'

'The Abbot fellow?'

'Yes.'

'This would be the third case you've used him.'

'So?'

'Well, you might say this is becoming something of a habit!'

It was a joke, not that she laughed, but it was a joke: Abbot Peter still used the clothes he'd worn in the monastery of St James-The-Less in the deserts of Middle Egypt. Quite why he'd retired to the south coast of England three years ago, Wonder wasn't sure, and couldn't pretend to be interested. Monks were another species, another world, even when they came out from behind their walls and tried to take part in normal life. But fair's fair; he remembered the Abbot had been used as a Special Witness on two previous cases, one involving a crucified vicar, the other, a murdered psychiatrist … and now a dead director. What was happening in Stormhaven?

But a good manager responds rather than reacts. He knew this from a waste-of-time training course two weeks ago … or was it the other way round? Should he react rather than respond? Anyway, he'd play the wise man and hear her out: DI Shah wanted the Abbot on the team. In some ways, of course, it was a compliment to Wonder, and he liked compliments, needed them more than people knew – and a compliment because he'd been a prime mover in the development of the Special Witness scheme in the Sussex force;

a scheme which brought in a local individual to help in murder investigations. They were to 'provide local insight and help earth the investigation in the community'. It was a move away from the 'Them and Us' policing which could prove unhelpful; this was the new thinking. The individual chosen had to be of good reputation, obviously – you wouldn't enlist the Kray Twins – and possess special knowledge of the crime scene.

'We see what we see because we ride on the shoulders of others,' said Tamsin.

'I beg your pardon?'

'The Special Witness scheme is one of your great legacies, Chief Inspector.'

'Oh, I see! Well, you know – .'

The real wonder was that she managed to speak the lines without choking.

'A towering achievement.'

'Well, thank you, Tamsin. It was a battle, I can tell you!'

She hoped he wouldn't; really hoped he wouldn't. He had a penchant for self-aggrandising stories, stories which she had to listen to when she wanted to get on ... and Tamsin always wanted to get on. Why sit around when there was work to be done? He was now on her side, though, that's all that mattered, which should mean a successful outcome.

'Is it true he's your uncle?' asked Wonder.

'We did discover that connection in the course of our first investigation together.'

This was not a conversation she wished to have.

'How can you not know close family?'

'Because we're not close.'

'But you're family.'

'We're distant family.'

'But he's your uncle, for God's sake!'

'That doesn't mean we're close.'

'But how could you not know?'

'Can we save my family tree for another time?'

'I've always known all my nieces.'

'Congratulations.'

'And my uncle. Uncle George. Strange man, always used to wear his pyjamas under his trousers, never knew why ... and never felt I could ask.'

'Tricky.'

'You just accept things when young, and then it's too late, they've died of a heart attack and you don't want to raise it at the

16

funeral. Who'd want to raise the whole pyjama thing at the funeral? You don't, do you? You want to remember the good times.'

'I want Abbot Peter on my team,' she said, slowly and steadily. 'He knows the theatre, knew the deceased – and doesn't hate actors quite as much as I do … '

# Four

'I've been here since eleven,' said the frustrated patient.

It was now midday in the doctor's surgery.

'And I've been here since 8.30 a.m.,' replied Janet.

Janet Lines was lead receptionist at Stormhaven's Wellness Medical practice. Dr Elsdon had given her this title to head off requests for a pay rise and it seemed to work.

'It's your job,' said the patient, leaning forward on the desk.

'And it's your free service, Mr Sykes. You should be grateful.'

'It's a free non-service so far.'

Mr Sykes could be difficult, but then he was a builder.

'You're only here because of a cancellation, Mr Sykes.'

'I'm here because I've sliced my hand.'

It was a mess.

'That's as maybe' – she wasn't interested – 'but you'll understand that readjusting Dr Elsdon's schedule is not an exact science.'

'But me losing my job is - if I'm not back on site by one o'clock.'

'I can hardly be responsible for that.'

'It's like the land time forgot round here.'

'Dr Elsdon is much in demand.'

'That's because he never bloody sees anyone.'

'Perhaps you should just go back to your – .'

'And what's with the magazines?'

'I'm sorry?'

Remain calm, Janet, remain the ultra-professional that you are, … remember last year's 'Handling Difficult People' seminar.

'The magazines here,' said Mr Sykes.

'Another service that's free.'

'For women.'

'I beg your pardon?'

'The magazines – they're all for women.'

'They're not all for women.'

'*Woman's Own*, *Women's Weekly*, *Women's World*, *Knitting World*, *Good Housekeeping* – .'

'I think you'll find – .'

'I think I'll find there's nothing for men, nothing about films, Formula 1, football, drills or politics, nothing for the lads. Do you not have any men patients?'

'It simply isn't true what you say, Mr Sykes.'

It was true.

'Is it because you're all women?'

'I beg your pardon?'

'That's it, isn't it? Doctors' receptionists, you're always women, so I suppose we get your old magazines when they're three months out of date. Is that how it goes?'

'I may, out of the kindness of my heart – .'

'So what about Dr Elsdon's old magazines.'

'I hardly think, Dr Elsdon – .'

'Bit naughty, are they? Not quite suitable? Or does he buy women's magazines and all?'

She'd cancelled his appointment on the spot, of course, because that sort of rudeness can't be tolerated from anyone, there were strict NHS guidelines, a small man – yes, Janet felt she could call him that – a small man, Mr Sykes, with little appreciation of how medical services worked, the long and demanding hours of doctors, paid well but, my God, they earned it, and the sheer professionalism and people skills required of receptionists … now where was she?

'He does have a point,' said Molly, when everything had calmed down and Mr Sykes had finally left, threatening all sorts as he stormed out. Molly was Janet's young assistant, an artificial blond, whom Janet was training up … and there was some way to go.

'He doesn't have a point.'

'About the magazines, I mean.'

'The magazines are quite adequate,' said Janet.

'But they are a bit, you know … for women.'

'Molly, I fail to see how a copy of *Playboy* or some silly football magazine is going to be therapeutically healthy.'

'I suppose.'

'And have you seen how much those football players earn?'

'Nearly as much as Dr Elsdon, apparently.'

Molly laughed, which Janet didn't feel was appropriate at all. What did Dr Elsdon see in this large-breasted airhead?

# Five

*'You seem to lack the courage of your convictions, Abbot.'*

This was the opening line of the letter which Peter now held in his hands as, fifty yards away, the green sea reached the foamy high point of the Stormhaven shingle. The Abbot lived in a small house at the end of the beachfront, before the white cliffs began their chalky climb up to Stormhaven Point. Beyond that, three windy miles on, was Beachy Head, popular with determined walkers and those in despair; with ramblers who loved a bracing wind and with those who wished only for the wind-rushing drop onto the rocky sea below.

The house required work. The peeling paint of the exterior walls – an easy metaphor for his 61-year-old body – spoke of salty proximity to the corroding westerlies and a simple lack of funds. He'd worked all his life, in a manner; but had never learned how to make money. How do you raise money to put new paint on the exterior walls?

And then the letter continued in rather more intimate fashion:

*'There is some discussion, Peter – may I call you Peter? – about which way you hang, so to speak. Local gossip I'm afraid, and when was gossip about anything honourable or heart-warming? It prefers the seamier side of life, we all know that. But I know, Peter, I know – your sexuality is no mystery to me. In fact, I know all I need to know from how you looked at me. I like reading, I often read before sleep, and I read you like a book! So isn't it time you stopped just looking? My pages could be for turning ...'*

It was at this point that the Abbot looked for the name at the end – and found none. Well, he wouldn't own up to this drivel either. He put the half-read letter down as the phone rang.

'Hello, Tamsin, and what can I do for you?'

# Six

✦

## *1327, a journey from Cologne to Avignon*

*He wore a white tunic, scapular hat, black cloak and hood – and he was walking. His clothes hadn't changed since his Parisian days, how could they? He was a member of the Dominican Order for life, there was no other way, no other path to tread. But his body had changed across the years, certain aches and pains more keenly felt, for it was sixteen winters since he'd left the fine university in Paris, and he was now a man of sixty-six years; almost senile enough to be the Pope he was on his way to meet. And as a monk with no money, spirit but no gold, he was walking the five hundred miles from Cologne in Germany to Avignon in the South of France, where the Inquisition lay in wait for him … as well as the senile Pope.*

*Yes, popes traditionally lived in Rome, ever since St Peter's execution in the city, the first of their number, the first Bishop of Rome and the origin of their authority. But these days, popes didn't live in Rome, or not only in Rome, they had a choice of accommodation. They'd learned that sometimes it pays to relocate, in order to protect and accentuate their political power; for popes were now political currency for kings and emperors, this is what they'd become, pawns in the games of the world. And, put brutally and simply, if you didn't like the Pope in Rome, you created another one somewhere else, one who agreed with you, and put him somewhere like, well – why not Avignon? The Pope in Avignon currently had bigger armies than his counterpart in Rome.*

*'I will be acquitted,' he says to Henricus.*

*Eckhart speaks with confidence, as if no other outcome is possible.*

*'We must hope so.'*

21

*They walk a little in silence. Monks do not find this difficult, though Henricus is more tested than Eckhart.*

'How can they claim that I preach beyond the confines of the faith?' *Eckhart is mystified, he finds the idea preposterous.*

'The Inquisition can claim anything they like,' *says Henricus.* 'They hold all the cards – and a few nasty tools.'

'They were set up to seek the truth. Or am I guilty of nostalgia?'

'That was a long time ago, Eckhart, a different, kinder world.'

*Eckhart doesn't appear to be listening.*

'They were set up to seek the truth,' *he repeats, as if saying it twice would make it so.*

'But have become an instrument of terror,' *says Henricus.* 'Read their charter.'

'It lacks comedy.'

'In which, as you will know, the benefits of communal fear are declared more precious than the benefits of an individual discovering the truth. This means – .'

'I know what it means, Henricus. It means they want people scared. It means that the burning of flesh, the breaking of bones and the tearing of ligaments becomes a virtuous act, creating godly terror, godly fear.'

'That's what we face in Avignon, Eckhart, so we need to be careful.'

'It's what I face, Henricus. I'm not sure you face it.'

*Henricus was a time-server, as frightened as a lamb caught by wolves. But Eckhart was not as disturbed as a sensible man should be.*

'They may accuse me of heresy, Henricus – my God, my own Order has even accused me of these things!'

'Not quite true.'

'But they'll not be able to prove it, this is the thing, for it simply isn't so – as you and your choking friends found out.'

*Eckhart looked at Henricus de Cigno, Provincial General of the Dominican Order for the region of Teutonia. He'd been sent to accompany Eckhart on his journey to Avignon to face charges of heresy. He was part Father-in-God to Eckhart, part friend, this is what he hoped, though probably more of the former than the latter, for friends are chosen and Eckhart had not chosen Henricus and why would he? No one would choose Henricus as a friend unless seeking a companion with a backbone made entirely of the desire for self-preservation.*

'They weren't my friends,' *spluttered Henricus,* 'as I think you well know.'

*He said 'as I think you well know' as though it were self-evident, something clear for all to see, but neither was true. Eckhart had been questioned by his own order, the Dominicans, concerning the nature of his beliefs. His own order! And though Henricus claimed no part*

*in the proceedings, most believed he'd been the busiest of the Do-
minican hierarchy in minding his back, by throwing Eckhart to the
investigative lions. And there was a reason for this. Like two inse-
cure siblings, the Dominican and Franciscan Orders were fighting for
the patronage of the Pope, and as with most sibling rivalry, it wasn't
pretty. Dominicans longed for Franciscans to fail and Franciscans for
Dominicans to fail. So when the Franciscan Archbishop of Cologne
smelled heresy on the breath of Eckhart, the Dominicans had been
quick to respond, starting their own investigation, as if to say: 'We Dominicans can do our own Inquisition! You bastard Franciscans think
you're hot on heresy? Then we're hotter still!'*

*'You seemed to huddle with them a great deal,' said Eckhart, re-
membering the investigation.*

*'Then you misconstrue.'*

*'I misconstrue?'*

*'We weren't accusing you of anything.'*

*Eckhart laughed. 'Then I most certainly misconstrue.'*

*This was Eckhart being angry, quiet ridicule, and Henricus felt dis-
comfort, felt the sweat of shame. He hadn't wished to speak of these
things on the way to Avignon.*

*'We were simply clarifying matters,' he said, 'so the Pope could rest
more easily.'*

*'I think the Pope rests easily enough in his fine bed, don't you?'*

*'They do say Avignon is not lacking in comfort.'*

*'And if he doesn't sleep well, he is troubled by his own conscience
rather than mine.'*

*There is a pause, before Eckhart reflects further, still incredulous:'My
own Order doubting me – would you believe it?'*

*This had troubled him more than the Inquisition's relentless pur-
suit; to be pursued and questioned from within.*

*'No wonder I take God more seriously than you, Henricus. God
wouldn't dream of treating me like that.'*

*'I'm here to support you, Meister, you know that – here on behalf of
the Dominican Order to support you.'*

*'To support me in my acquittal.'*

*'We must hope you will be acquitted, yes.'*

*Eckhart was quick to pick up on the doubt.*

*'You sound unsure.'*

*'I just cannot be sure what you will say, and your words will
matter.'*

*'I know well enough what I will say.'*

*'You know what you will say in fair debate, yes. But in extremis?
Since 1256, as you well know, inquisitors have received the Church's
absolution for using instruments of torture.'*

'I am aware.'

'Though the Pope in his mercy insists that they are not allowed to draw blood.'

'Mercy indeed. They can burn the body, tear its ligaments, break its bones – but they cannot draw blood.'

'Quite.'

Eckhart smiled and spoke: 'And after such gentle questioning, then what? You think I will be burnt at the stake?'

'Well, one doesn't like to – .'

'Always better to speak it, Henricus.'

Henricus was a nervous man, as nervous as he was round, with an inclination to expect the worst, to expect everything to go wrong – and he seemed intent on Eckhart expecting it too. They walked in silence for a while.

'You're thinking of Marguerite Porete,' said Eckhart.

'Of course I am!' exploded Henricus, who'd had trouble holding it in. He hadn't wanted to mention the name, unpleasantness obviously, deep unpleasantness, burning flesh, unholy screams – who is of a mind to mention that?

'Who wouldn't think of her at such a moment as this?' he continued. 'Especially you, for you were there, there in Paris at the time of her burning. I'm told you even watched! We haven't spoken about that.'

Eckhart had been in Paris at the time of her burning. He'd held the Chair of theology at the famous university, where he acquired his title, 'Meister' or 'Master'. But then his illustrious career in the Dominican Order had brought him many senior posts; honourable positions all over Europe including Saxony, Bohemia, Strasburg and most recently, Cologne … though Paris had been the intellectual pinnacle, the ecclesiastical cherry, no question of that, his position of greatest status. And he'd held this position not once, but twice – an honour granted to only one other, the great Thomas Aquinas himself!

But away from such titillation, he'd always been happiest behind monastery walls, pastoring those who found it difficult to live inside their skins, not always helped by the religion they followed.

And he preached well, everyone said that, even if they didn't like what he said, they had to listen, for he spoke not as others did, in distant Latin – church language – but in the people's native German, which rather marked him out. He still remembered the angry monk who complained about this, saying that if Latin was good enough for God, it was good enough for him.

But Eckhart continued to speak in German, not the language of the Church but the language of life, difficult life, and there were many in his monasteries who found it so. Yes, some were fresh-faced novices,

24

boys still waiting to be men, just starting out; but many had been soldiers, and not kind soldiers, not knights in shining armour, but soldiers who'd killed, ransacked and raped their way across France and Germany and now sought some kind of peace, some sort of hope for their brutalised souls. These were men who hated themselves, and, some would say, with good reason; but men who, above all else, needed to rediscover their origins in the divine, their union with the divine. This is what Eckhart spoke of, and this is what the Archbishop of Cologne called heresy, and hunting heresy was the Archbishop's passion – along with hatred of Dominicans, alcohol and the sound of his own voice. Indeed, he loved the sound of his voice so much, especially after wine, that among Dominicans, Henry of Virneburg, the Archbishop of Cologne, was known as 'The Fishwife'.

'We haven't spoken about that,' he said.

'I'm sorry?'

Eckhart's mind had wandered.

'About Marguerite Porete. We haven't spoken about her.'

Henricus spoke as if this was a confidence that Eckhart had, so far, been too weak to mention to his spiritual father. Eckhart's understanding was a little different.

'With all due respect, Henricus – and what is due, I give you – there is much we haven't spoken of, given that we only met yesterday.'

'Hardly! We have met often at – .'

'The heresy hearings?'

'Yes, the, er, hearings.'

'The heresy hearings, yes. And as you say, I often saw your face there, and on occasion, you even supported me.'

'Always.'

'No, not always – sometimes.'

'When it mattered.'

'When it didn't matter, actually, let's be accurate … when speaking up for me in no way endangered you or the Order.'

'However things appeared, Johannes, I was always mindful of your soul.'

'Though perhaps more mindful of your back.'

Henricus looked shocked.

'But my point is this, Henricus – throughout it all, we never spoke.'

'Well, it wasn't always – .'

'We never conversed alone, never sat with each other in calm exchange and human warmth … until yesterday, when finally you joined me on my journey.'

'Yes, well, I have explained my tardy arrival, Meister – I do have matters other than your misdemeanours to consider!'

'Misdemeanours?'

25

*Yes, misdemeanours! Henricus had had enough of this, he needed to re-establish his authority. He was the Dominican Provincial after all, a man of some standing, some stature, a busy man of the world and he would not be talked to in this way, as though there was deficiency in him! It was Eckhart on trial, not he!*

*'You must not stir yourself, Henricus.'*

*'I'm not stirred!'*

*He was sweating again, steaming with the stuff, and he wished he wasn't, it could make him look stirred, and really, who wouldn't be stirred by his present companion? Not that he was stirred, simply that there was good cause to be. The Blessed Virgin herself would have struggled to stay dry.*

*'I merely explain why we have never talked of this matter before,' said Eckhart quietly. 'It's because we've never talked.'*

*They travelled a little further, ruminating, until waylaid by some passing devils, villains and clowns (such was their apparel, at least) who waved at these two monks, and possibly mocked a little. Henricus did not think their zealous applause genuine for one moment.*

*'At your service, sirs!' said one of the devils, bowing low. 'I do a lot of work for the Church!' Henricus hurried on with his head down, muttering imprecations, while Eckhart gazed in astonishment. He'd seen nothing like this in his life.*

*'Who were they?' he asked, when the strange band had passed.*

*'Actors,' said Henricus, as if that said it all.*

*'I have heard of actors,' said Eckhart.*

*'Nothing good, I trust.'*

*'People who play a part other than themselves.'*

*'A truly desperate way to earn a living.'*

*'Though attractive if you're not fond of yourself, which is the way with some.'*

*'And I'll tell you one thing, Eckhart: we're losing them!'*

*'Who's losing whom?'*

*'The Church is losing the actors.'*

*'But we just found them – and when we did, you hurried on by.'*

*'And what – you think I should be conversing with devils, villains and clowns?'*

*'But they're acting, as you say.'*

*'And why would anyone wish to act a devil or a villain? Tell me that. Are the gospels not good enough?'*

*'The gospels are full of devils and villains.'*

*'I tell you, Eckhart, this century will be remembered – mark my words – this century will be remembered as the time the Church lost control of actors, lost control of theatre.' This matter clearly exercised him much. 'My son – .'*

'What of your son?'

Eckhart didn't know of a son, an unusual possession for a Dominican.

'We will not concern ourselves with my son.' Why had he mentioned his son – the shame of his life and the apple of his eye?

'He is a performer?' asked Eckhart gently.

Henricus acknowledged that possibly it was so.

'They used to perform miracle plays, liturgical dramas, godly performance on stages outside churches – but these days? These days the town guilds pay them instead and suddenly we have what they call "farce".'

'Farce?'

'The ridiculous, the absurd and the perverted!'

'Any churchman would recognise that; it's what the Church is made of.'

But Henricus wasn't listening, he was raging, raging at the new plays: 'With allusions, Eckhart – and this is how far we have fallen – with allusions in their performances to bodily excretions, fairies – fairies! – And even …', and now his tone hushed for fear of being overheard, 'even relations between man and woman.'

'They refer to such relations in their plays?'

'They do.'

'But is this not how you were conceived?'

'That's theatre for you, Eckhart! That's what's happened to the Miracle plays of old. While you've buried your head in your monasteries – .'

'I don't think my head has been buried, Henricus. Considering different things, perhaps.'

'Dress it up with your clever words, Eckhart, but that's what's been happening outside! It's the end of the world, mark my words. Sorcerers and devils run free these days. We may deliver our sermons, but it's Satan who covers our gloomy earth with his wings – and they say no one has entered paradise since the schism, since one pope became two.'

'I'd leave paradise to God. He's keener on the idea than the Church.'

'And now, as you've just seen, Satan has bought the theatre. The theatre is in the unholy pocket of Beelzebub! And you wonder why I passed by on the other side?'

And because he was still angry – angry with the change and decay around him and the collapse of former things; angry with Eckhart for not responding as he should, for not caring enough; and perhaps above all else, angry with himself for mentioning his illicit son – Henricus de Cigno, the Dominican Provincial, decided on a question for Eckhart that might create a little discomfort:

*'Did you ever meet Marguerite Porete?' he asked.*

*It seemed to hit the mark straightaway. A shadow of regret dark-ened Eckhart's calm. He seemed to fear this question more than the Inquisition. Would he have to remember again?*

# Seven

*Four months before the killing of Hermione*

'So d'you want the bad news, Hermione – or the bad news?'

It was a bright April day, though little light managed its way through the window. Hermione's office sat next to the bell tower and deep in its shadow.

'I want the good news, Bill.'

'The good news?'

'I always want good news.'

'Well, that won't detain us long.'

'You can take as long as you like.'

'The good news is me.'

Pause.

'And that's it?'

'That's it.

'So Bill is the good news?'

When under attack, sound like the Queen: professionally interested but cool.

'The fact that I'm here, Hermione, sorting this place out – that's the good news.'

'I see.'

'I hope you do.'

'And the bad news?'

'The bad news is everyone else.'

'I hope you haven't been nasty to anyone.'

Hermione was concerned this might happen. She wanted the omelette with no broken eggs, as her mother would say.

'I don't like nastiness, you know that,' she added. 'And everyone's doing their best.'

29

'Then the bar is pretty low.'

She did find the middle-aged Bill Cain an attractive man; at least his power, which came from his money, that was attractive.

'So what have you been doing?'

'I've just been looking, Hermione, just looking.'

'And what do you see?'

Bill sat himself on the edge of a chair, like a kestrel preparing a strike.

'What do I see as I gaze on the innards of the Bell Theatre?'

'Slightly melodramatic.'

'I see a bunch of dreamers and freeloaders about to sink on the rough seas of financial reality.'

'Does that include me?'

'Oh, I haven't gazed on you yet, Hermione. I wouldn't be so forward. But should you insist – .'

Bill smiled cheekily.

'Dreamers and freeloaders?'

Bill nodded, while Hermione neither affirmed this assessment, nor responded to his flirting. She didn't really have time for that now.

'To wake them up might just be the kindest thing to do,' he continued, standing up again, and talking on the move. He liked to be on the move when he talked.

'Bill, we have survived as a theatre for thirty years,' she said firmly. 'Amazing, but there we are. Thirty years without Bill Cain, how did we do it?'

'You haven't done it.'

'I think we have.'

'You're deep in the brown stuff and sinking fast.'

Bill Cain couldn't do softly-softly; just bull-in-bloody-china-shop. And Hermione had known this, had known the impact he'd have on the place … yet still she'd brought him in. He was a brute, but a brute in a suit, apparently conceived in a boardroom, happiest in that setting and he did sort things out, Hermione was aware – and things did need sorting out, most definitely. The theatre was in choppy economic waters – no, rough and dangerous seas – as the recession deepened, and yes, things had been allowed to drift. What had once appeared an exciting and energetic venture, successful without really trying, now looked dangerously disengaged – though she wouldn't be telling Bill that.

'So tell me, Hermione: here at the Bell Theatre, who gets paid?'

Pause.

'Who gets paid?' said Hermione, surprised by the question.

'Yep.'

'I'm not sure.'

'Okay.'

How could an intelligent human being run an organisation without knowing which of the staff got paid?

'So who does and who doesn't get expenses?'

Another pause.

'I grant you, Bill – I'm a little confused about the financial arrangements. I used to be more on top of them.'

'So who handles the finances now?'

'I do.'

Bill breathes in deeply. He likes Hermione, he's known her for years over various expensive soirees, which in Stormhaven meant the same ten people every time. But nothing had prepared him for the financial chaos he'd witnessed over the last two days ... and he'd seen some chaos in his time.

'And the Bell Theatre is pro-am, I'm told.'

'Very much so.'

Hermione felt a friendlier wind in her sails.

'And what does that mean in the real world? I mean, is it a for-profit or a not-for-profit organisation?'

'A bit of both really.'

'And how does that work?'

'We aim to make a bit, of course, and then – well, aim to lose a bit, I suppose.'

'You aim to lose a bit?'

'Does it matter?'

'It does on planet earth. It's not a great business model. Why plan to lose?'

'Because not everything that's good makes money!'

Oh dear.

'Let's put that another way, Hermione: whatever makes money is good.'

'You'd reduce all art to box office?'

'I come from a mill town, Hermione, those are my roots, not the soft south, and the great thing about being brought up in a mill town, unsophisticated you'd call it, is that nobody ever said this is good music or this is bad music, because nobody knew that there was a difference. There was something dark and mysterious called Highbrow but that didn't concern us; that was for snooty people. All the rest was music, judged by the effort put in by the performers and by the enjoyment of those listening. In other words, music was for pleasure. Good music was music people enjoyed in my town and a necessary escape from our dreary world of coal lorries, cotton, heavy machinery, linoleum, public baths and Sunday

School. And that's perhaps where the Bell Theatre should start from. Theatre as entertainment, theatre as escape – because life can be bleak, Hermione, life can be very bleak.'

'Very moving, Bill – you'll be telling me you appeared in a Lowry painting next.'

Bill was to be the theatre's first managing director, three days a week, largely unpaid. He didn't need any more money, it came in like the tide every day from hard-nosed deals done down the years. But he still enjoyed the thrill of the game, slashing waste, turning businesses round, putting structures for growth in place.

'Which brings us to *Mother's Day*,' he said.

Could there have been more disdain in a voice? He might have been asking about a convention of paedophiles.

'What about it?'

For a moment, as Bill noticed, Hermione looked shocked

'Is that really the best you can manage for the theatre's thirtieth anniversary celebrations?'

'What's wrong with it?'

'How long have you got?'

'Paul is a young writer with a lot of talent.'

'For what? Basketball? Spoon-bending?'

'And he's local.'

'And what the blue blazes has that got to do with anything? The drunk who threw up over my car yesterday is local.'

'Well – .'

How could he put this? 'Hermione, staging a seriously depressing show might be fine for university types and *Guardian* readers. But if you want to attract normal people – people who don't have pointless degrees sticking out their arse – they want to be entertained.'

'We wanted to give contemporary theatre a go, honour a contemporary voice, a local contemporary voice.'

It had sounded good in discussions last year, the honouring of a contemporary voice, and from that dream had come the idea of a competition for local playwrights. But somehow it all carried less clout in the relentless presence of Bill Cain.

'I'm not paying to watch someone else's sadness,' he said. 'I get that for free at home.'

And then Hermione had a thought. '*Les Misérables* hasn't done so badly.'

'*Les Misérables*?'

'Sad yet very successful.'

Bill Cain snorts in derision.

'Excuse me, but have I missed the show-stopping songs in *Mother's Day*?'

'There are no songs in it, no.'

'Or the passionate love story?'

'I grant you, it isn't a love story.'

'I heard the rehearsals, Hermione – it's two depressed women having an extended argument! Makes *Les Mis* look like a romcom.'

'We did contemplate a Shakespeare.'

'Don't.'

'Why not?'

'No one understands Shakespeare.'

'Some of us do.'

'Not enough. I went to see *The Tempest*.'

'We've never done *The Tempest*.'

'Best seats in the house, but do you know what? I didn't know what was happening from beginning to end. What's it about? It's in English apparently – but I didn't have a clue from start to finish.'

Bill Cain was determinedly lowest common denominator, perhaps Hermione hadn't realised this. It was beginning to sound as though he'd prefer bingo at the Bell to Shakespeare.

'Perhaps you should have done some research before going,' she said, sounding a bit matronly. 'Read up about the play before going to see it.'

'Drama shouldn't need a guide book, Hermione. *Jack and the Beanstalk* doesn't need a guide book. *Carry on up the Jungle* doesn't need a guide book.'

'They're completely different.'

'You mean they're enjoyable to watch?'

Suddenly a terrible noise shakes the walls. Bill Cain grabs a chair in shock.

'What's that?'

'It's the bell, Bill, just the bell.' Hermione hardly hears it these days, too familiar, like tasteless wall paper you just get used to. 'It always rings at three o'clock.'

'Ever thought of buying a watch instead?'

Hermione smiles.

'It wouldn't make any difference.'

'It'd be quieter.'

'The bell and the bell-ringer – they're both in the purchase agreement for the theatre, both in the contract.'

'What contract?'

Bill had a lifelong interest in contracts.

'Along with the graveyard obviously.'

'You have a graveyard? The Bell Theatre has a graveyard?'

'Coffee?'

'Is it decent?'

'And then I could give you a short tour of the tombs.'

# Eight

On that same April day, four months before the killing of Hermione Bysshe-Urquhart, there were other comings and goings at the Bell, other encounters and conversations. Margery Tatters and Millicent Pym, for instance, were just starting rehearsals for *Mother's Day* – the play chosen as the showpiece for the thirtieth anniversary celebrations.

'Have you done a two-hander before, Melissa?' asked Margery.

'It's Millicent.'

'Millicent, yes.'

On this first day of rehearsals, Margery felt every inch the professional, every inch the seasoned performer as she considered her young partner, who was an amateur ... someone unpaid for her work. They were paying Margery for her performance – well, of course they were paying her. And this said something about both status and talent: 'Amateur theatre's for the family and friends; professional theatre, for the rest of the world.' Isn't that how the saying went?

The Bell liked to combine the two, professional and amateur cheek by jowl, and why not? It was quirky but not without merit, so thought Margery, 'community theatre' and all that. And whatever one's private thoughts – and thank God no one saw those – one had to support it publicly. But community theatre should also be good theatre, quality theatre, so standards had to be maintained, this was the thing, and it was up to the professional to ensure that they were ... and the professional here was Margery, with the young waif Millicent the amateur.

Yes, she was older and stockier than Millicent, as you are in middle age. You can't be lithe for ever, hell will come and find you, you can be sure of that. A few brief years of youth and then hell comes ... unless, like Dorian Grey, you have a picture in the attic. But Margery had never been like Dorian Grey, never been lithe, never been a waif, unlike Millicent with her wisp of a body, clear skin and elfin eyes. Margery was always 'buxom' or 'comely', though she'd been called 'The Tank' at school and was still in recovery from that, not a moment of purgatory forgotten. Geraldine and Bernadette – called 'school friends' for some reason – had a lot to answer for, because she hadn't recovered at all, still holding the grudges and the names, every grudge and every name, lodged in her body because the body never forgets. The mind forgets, slips into denial and rationalisations but not the body, everything lodges there; and so Margery hid hers beneath baggy clothes, baggy top, baggy cotton trousers, no body to be seen ... but standards to be maintained.

'So no experience of two-handers?' she said.

'I don't think so,' said the waif, uninterested. Margery found her tone undermining, as Millicent sort of hoped.

'Nothing to be afraid of,' said Margery.

'I'm not afraid.'

'I'm just saying.'

'No need really.'

'As a professional to an amateur.'

Pause. Millicent was looking out of the window.

'It's a big break for you, of course, Milly.'

'*Millicent.*'

Don't acknowledge that, don't back down, Margery never backed down.

'It wouldn't be a surprise if you were feeling the nerves.'

'Well, I'm not. Does that disappoint you?'

Margery is irritating Millicent.

'You say you're not,' says the older woman with a know-all smile. 'We all do when we're starting out.'

'I say I'm not, because it's the truth. I hardly ever feel nervous on stage actually – hardly ever. I enjoy it too much, enjoy the attention. Is that allowed?'

Margery shrugs, Millicent continues:

'People shut up and listen to me, it's great! Who wouldn't want people to shut up and listen? I mean, when do people ever listen to you, Margery, apart from when you're on stage?'

'Or in front of the camera.'

She'd done TV and not just *The Bill*.

'Being listened to is everyone's dream, isn't it?'

It was Millicent's dream and she sat down at the battered piano in the corner, which could have done with tuning. She began to play, a simple piece, precise and ordered, which could have been Mozart, but simple Mozart, pieces he wrote for his young piano pupils when no one wanted his other music. Millicent liked Mozart, the fragile, brilliant, unwanted performer and composer, pretend-

36

ing he liked his parents, trying to keep smiling, always smiling. And so different from Margery, this heavy presence, determined to play the old pro to Millicent's nervous amateur, so obvious. But really, what was the difference between them, in terms of ability? There was no difference as far as Millicent was concerned. Okay, Margery had played that cow of a nurse in *Holby* – which Millicent never watched, because what was the point of all that heartache? And yes, she'd also been the irritating neighbour in *That's My Wife* ' – some tired sitcom for middle-aged suburbanites, but so what? Having now met her, Millicent could see Margery was playing Margery in both shows. Was that acting? Was it acting if you were just playing yourself? Actors were meant to play other people, weren't they, people other than themselves?

'And don't be overawed by me,' said Margery, standing too close to Millicent, who didn't like people close. Why was she standing so close? Millicent stopped playing the piano and got up. She was slightly taller than Margery.

'I don't think I am,' she said, escaping back to the window.

How do you say that politely? Millicent didn't mean to be impolite but her quick tongue went ahead.

'TV credits are fine,' continued Margery, 'and I have my share – oh, I could tell you some stories! But you can't take your success on stage with you. When Margery Tatters or Meryl Streep or whoever it is – one day you perhaps, Millicent Pym – when we go on stage, no matter what we've done or what accolades we've received, we start again.'

'There's no history on stage,' said Millicent, 'just the moment.'

She remembered her drama teacher at school saying that. It had seemed so cool, and perhaps a rule for life as well. Imagine living without your history! But Margery didn't want Millicent's theatre wisdom, she preferred her own, proper wisdom born out of experience, refined in the school of hard knocks, that was the purpose of this, to pass on the wisdom of experience, professional to amateur … to maintain standards.

'The secret of the two-hander,' said Margery, seating herself again, 'and take it from me, this is how it is – whether Shakespeare, Brecht or the strange little Paul Bent, bless him – is to remember the see-saw.'

'The see-saw.'

Millicent was feeling oppressed again, feeling trapped, wishing Margery would stop giving her advice, stop passing on the benefit of her non-existent wisdom. And when was Timothy coming? And why was he always late? It was quite irritating. He'd been late for as long as she'd known him.

'Like all two-handers,' said Margery, '*Mother's Day* is a see-saw, a constant shift in power between the two protagonists. First I have the power, then you have the power and so on, back and forward, up and down.'

'I think that's all pretty clear in the text.'

It sounded rude though it wasn't her intention, or not all of it, intentions are mixed, but it was just so obvious – of course there were shifts in power! And Millicent hated being told the obvious, so hated it, being told what she already knew, as if who she was, and what she knew, was of no consequence ... but Margery rumbled on regardless.

'So remember the see-saw, Milly.'

'Millicent.'

'Any two-hander, it's all about the see-saw. You have power, I have power. I have power, you have power. It comes and goes ... though obviously in the end, the see-saw stops and one of us must win.'

# Nine

'A little lost boy in the foyer! Could I perhaps be of some assistance?'

Neville Brownslie was box office manager and lord of all he surveyed at the Bell – in his own eyes at least. He wore a smart suit, polished shoes and gold cuff links. Luscious hair like Oscar Wilde, late thirties, but he affected older, mid-fifties, a country gent in his suburban dreams.

'I'm Paul Bent,' said the lost little boy.

'Infinitely preferable to straight, dearie.'

An affected toss of the hair.

'The writer,' said Paul.

The little boy was in his early twenties, an urchin in tight trousers, pencil-thin moustache and trilby hat, a bright-eyed spiv, but not in speech, flattened middle class.

'The writer of what, dear boy?' asked Neville, in his headmasterly tone. 'The Argos catalogue, the twenty-third psalm, the Highway Code?'

He was being amusing and magisterial.

'I wrote *Mother's Day*.'

'Oh dear.'

'The play for the thirtieth anniversary celebrations.'

'And a crime against literature, but never mind. I'm sure the bard's early work kept the Stratford bin men busy.'

Neville hated the play. He'd been forced by Hermione to read the damn thing, it was quite atrocious. What sort of a choice was that for the thirtieth anniversary celebrations? Why not an evening of show tunes, something uplifting and fun? Instead of – well, how did one describe *Mother's Day*? A depressfest?

'Is Timothy Gershwin around?' asks Paul.

Timothy Gershwin was to direct the play, and quite a catch he was too. But Neville had his own theatrical tastes to expound:

'More a Noel Coward man myself – cheek and chic, pose and poise.' He preened a little as he spoke. 'I mean, whatever happened to a sense of style in theatre?'

What Neville called style, Paul called avoidance. He wished to enter the guts of human pain, explore the bleak terrain of abandonment and the psychological distortions abandonment brings. Not that his work was autobiographical, it wasn't autobiographical, not at all, he was a writer, he got inside other people's lives, that's what he did. So no autobiography, no, as he'd said to the journalist, who kept on about it. Why does everyone have to assume that what you write is autobiographical? It was just an area that interested him, a professional interest, nothing more. Of course, there's always a bit of autobiography in any artist's work ...

'I'm meant to be meeting him here this morning,' said Paul.

'Mr Timothy Bloody Gershwin, our artistic director for the season?' Neville's feelings about the appointment were not in any way hidden. He spoke as one on stage, making his emotions plain to the back row of the upper circle. Neville had not wanted Timothy Gershwin, he'd done a season here before, one of those Buddhist fellows, no fun at all – and, if one will forgive the bitching, 'Quite a long way up his own derrière, dearie.'

So he hadn't wanted him, and he'd said so, he'd stated his case – but then what was his voice worth at the Bell these days? Some way down the food chain apparently. Hermione was theatre director and that was very much that. 'Expect fireworks,' he'd warned, 'Damp ones, which fail to ignite!' That might at least give Hermione something to think about.

'I'm meeting him today,' said Paul, deciding Neville was gay. It didn't usually take people so long. 'He's directing my piece.'

'I know, I know. I may only be the humble administrator, but I am aware of that and, don't tell me – you desire an artistic conclave on the premises?' He turned and indicated to Paul that he should follow him. 'Well, I'm sure I can find you some open door and cosy space at the end of a long, dark passage.'

Neville would only allow himself to be gay if he caricatured himself, like his father used to caricature them, though he was nothing like his father, so help me God. But the boy was rather sweet in an irritating way. Perhaps the irritation could be smoothed over.

'Is he here?' asked Paul.

'Timothy is not present, I'm afraid,' declared Neville, as he opened his office door. 'Most unusual for a Buddhist.'

Paul looked quizzical.

'I thought Buddhists were always meant to be present,' said Neville. 'It's a joke.'

'Okay.'

Timothy Gershwin was well known for his Buddhism and for being late and Neville didn't like him, a poseur and way too pleased with himself, with his good looks and TV work. But somehow he'd ingratiated himself with Hermione – perhaps for those very reasons – and seemed eager for a second season here, God knows why. As a well-known TV director, he must have had better offers than the Bell, surely? He could hardly have had worse.

'Neville Brownslie, Mr Bent, Mr Bent, Neville Brownslie, good to meet you.' Neville offered a handshake, slightly limp, across his desk. 'Administrator stroke Front of House – but only if Front of House is good!'

Paul found him quite repulsive, this was his first impression. There was something creepy and controlling about Neville Brownslie and the strange feeling – and where did this come from? – that here was a man who, if threatened, would do anything necessary. And Paul remembered these things as he left the close confines of the office and went off to find Timothy Gershwin, the Buddhist who was always late. Who could tell what would be useful and when?

But most important was the play: it had left his pen – but what would it become in this strange little theatre?

# Ten

'Ladies, ladies!' declared Timothy Gershwin, as he gazed in surprise on the scene before his directorial eyes. And quite a shock it was too! He'd walked into the room, glad to be out of the spring snow, and found two women at war, literally, face to face in physical struggle. Margery had Millicent hard up against the wall of the rehearsal room, this was how he found them, in grunting combat – and it was clearly no rehearsal.

'I'll have some respect!' shouted Margery, breathless and sweaty. 'Some respect!' She did sweat, always had, something else they'd laughed about at school. But Millicent had crossed a boundary, and street-fighter Margery was making her point, a forcible point, hands round throat, that sort of a point, when Timothy Gershwin entered the room ... late.

'Amateurs!' muttered Margery, pulling swiftly away from the violence like a disturbed hyena. She was watched with shock and amazement by Millicent.

'Artistic differences?' asked Timothy, who looked smooth and cool, like Richard Gere. Manly hair burst from the top of his open-neck shirt, and there was a sense of tan about his skin, it always seemed tanned, even when there hadn't been sun for months. The cold spring in Stormhaven had followed a wet winter, with no sun on bones for months; not good for a small town, not good for anyone. But somehow Timothy's skin remained tanned.

'Meditation has remarkable effects,' he'd say to a sceptical friend.

'Meditation under a sun lamp?'

You had to put up with scepticism. But right now, in the face of this particular crisis – and who knew the cause? – he simply said: 'This is going to be very helpful, ladies.'

'What's going to be very helpful?' asked Millicent, adjusting her top, her elfin eyes still stunned by the attack. Was Margery mad?

'The violence,' said Timothy.

'You think that's violent?' muttered Margery. That wasn't violent.

'Or rather the rage behind the violence,' said Timothy. 'The simmering shame and hostility that violence reveals … these things are going to be very helpful. Believe.'

'She bloody assaulted me, Timothy! I don't find that helpful – no way do I find that helpful!'

Timothy smiled, indicating with his hands that everyone just needed to calm down, girls, girls, girls! And that he had something important to say.

'We're going to use this energy in the play,' he said, putting down the large folder he carried. 'I just need you both to Be. Here. Now. Yes? Be. Here. Now.'

'Where else do you think I am?' said Margery. She did know what he meant, she'd heard about him and his hokum, heard about his Buddhist stuff, be here now and all that poppycock, like he was some maharishi, only she wasn't The Beatles and she wasn't going to sit wide-eyed at his feet; wasn't going to make it easy, because why should she?

'I mean, Margery, that I need you present,' he said, making a peace sign with his hands. 'I mean, that we allow these feelings to arise, to fall away and then to pass through us. How does that sound?'

'Or we could call the police,' said Millicent.

'We don't need the police.'

He could be firm.

'She just assaulted me.'

'We don't need the police!'

He could be very firm. Millicent returned to the window, looking out, seeking distraction. Her sense of injustice was total, a feeling of not being heard. Again.

'We don't need the police,' he repeated, like a mantra, calmer now. 'We don't need the police.' He'd lost it, but now he was calming himself. 'We just need to centre ourselves.'

Centre ourselves? This was too much for Margery:

'Timothy, I don't want any of your self-help nonsense. Get me? I've been around the block a few too many times for all that.'

'There is no block, Margery. There is just now.'

'Let's just get on with the play, shall we?'

And at that moment, all three became aware of the figure standing in the doorway. How to describe her?

# Eleven

The figure in the doorway was respectful and accusatory; subservient and judging. Late fifties, mousy hair cut short, prominent jaw, sharp eyes, prim clothes, smart but not fashionable. And then she spoke:

'You wished to speak about costumes, Mr Gershwin.'

Enter Janet Lines, stage left, and Timothy wasn't pleased. Maybe he'd said that, he may have said something to her about costumes, he couldn't remember. But he didn't wish to speak to her now, not at this particular moment. She was a doctor's receptionist, wasn't she? He'd probably said to her 'We must talk sometime', but he hadn't suggested a time, it wasn't what he did, he didn't do time, or not specific time. The time would arise but it wasn't the time now.

'It's going to be pretty simple, Janet,' he said.

'Simple?'

These were not the first words she wished to hear from the director. They were words which suggested costumes were not going to matter in *Mother's Day*. 'It's going to be pretty simple'? You might almost imagine – and this wasn't Janet being far-fetched or jumping to conclusions, it was a considered response and quite rational – that if the costumes weren't important in the show, if costumes mattered as little as his tone suggested, then Janet also mattered little. That was how it felt as she stood alone in the doorway, with a tightening jaw. She felt like a little girl who'd been told off.

'Perhaps I'll be the judge of that,' she said, 'as the theatre costumier.'

A frozen pause, as Timothy puts down his man bag.

'What I mean is, Janet, the play's contemporary. It's a contemporary piece.'

'A contemporary piece of nonsense,' thinks Janet.

Timothy speaks with a smile, heavily laced with patience. 'They're playing themselves really. Not literally, obviously – .'

Now Margery's taking offence.

44

'Meaning?' she demands.

'Meaning it's not *Aladdin and the Arabian Nights*, Margery!'

A slight raising of the Buddhist voice.

'I have read the script,' says Janet. And in those simply enunciated words lay an avalanche of feeling about the Bell Theatre's latest venture. And she'd witnessed a few.

Janet Lines had been responsible for costumes at the Bell for the last twenty years. She was lead receptionist at a Stormhaven's Wellbeing medical practice, but when she wasn't protecting Dr Eldsdon from ailments invented by patients, she brought her methodical presence to managing the theatre's surprisingly large wardrobe … thanks to Nicholas Bysshe-Urquhart's endless West End connections.

'I think costume is going to need a lot of thought,' said Margery.

Her earlier violence was now receding from the agenda. She had perhaps overreacted a little, she'd make it up with Millicent; no harm done but a marker laid down. 'Come for them before they come for you' – this is what she'd learned down the years. And was there something between them, she thought so; something between Timothy and Millicent?

Margery was quick to sense connections.

# Twelve

It was a garden residence, but no nineteenth-century summer house, where daughters of the rich wrote poetry and dreamed passionate dreams in long flowing dresses. Instead, here was a small green caravan, apparently abandoned, driven here and dumped, unwanted, here in the graveyard, single berth, never a beauty, painted in green but nothing natural or calm, a slightly neon overcoat to another colour, possibly beige, circa 1970, with an early attempt at a chemical toilet inside. And stuck on metal legs, this caravan had come to stay, come to stay here beneath the overhanging evergreen, its number plate for travel painted over, no need for that any more, travelling days done – a mobile home that was mobile no more. And like the graveyard company it kept, you sensed this rest house had come to the end; had come here to die.

It was a day of wet snow around headstones and caravan; the wet snow of late spring, snow becoming rain, becoming snow, becoming sleet; ice and crocus in strange union, the daffodils heavy with the white stuff, confused to their roots, the last gasp of winter, trees still bare, thin spindly fingers in clear silhouette against the grey sky, the seasons at war, winter and spring, both trespassing on a time that wasn't theirs, and a cold wind and slicing chill … but the graveyard doesn't care.

This place has no cares, the gravestones in lazy ranks, some upright like soldiers, some leaning like the elderly – they do begin to lean, gravestones crack and buckle with age, like the bodies beneath, as tree roots shift the earth. But beneath it all, peace … here is a picture of peace, our graveyard scene, a silent repository of death, no worry or concern on display as the snow flurries in the cold sea air. These discarded bodies, they'd passed beyond such things, been there, done that, passed beyond worry, passed through those fiery hoops, the fire-filled hoops of stress and fear, they could not touch them now, neither sadness nor despair, all left behind in the fleeting world, for every day here is quite perfect;

though not for the weather-hit face which now peers from the caravan window.

He is the graveyard's only living resident, the living among the dead. The caravan windows are plastic, not proper glass, and scratched plastic, so the image is unclear, like the markings on the Turin shroud; but it was a face, an elderly face. A visitor's first thought might have been of a homeless tramp seeking refuge for the night; and in a way, they'd be right, though every tramp has a story, none was born a tramp, it's not a label given out at birth. And unlike the dead who surrounded him, a homeless tramp can have concerns, very particular concerns, as the weather-beaten face at the plastic window reveals. And he isn't homeless, not in his mind, he has a caravan, single-berth, with a working chemical toilet – he no longer has to pee in the street or sleep in shop doorways … the caravan is his luxury home.

And the graveyard? A theatre with a graveyard was puzzling at first and attracted its own comedy:

'Actors do talk of "dying" on stage,' said Neville to Bill Cain. 'So we're a one-stop shop really.' To which Cain replied, 'From the shows I've seen, it'll need a bloody big graveyard.'

But it made sense once you knew, this is what Hermione had found, because the story wasn't complicated … odd but not complicated. When the church sold the building to the Bell Theatre Company, the maintenance and upkeep of the graveyard was part of the deal. It remained consecrated ground, and the bereaved still had access, coming with memories and flowers – some of them at least. It was hardly busy, not many came, because people moved away or moved on; this is why graveyards are quiet, particularly in Stormhaven, where people always move on if they can.

But some bereaved souls made the journey to stand awhile or kneel; they'd sometimes kneel. And some would speak, spill their hearts to the dead, telling them about the week they'd had, about how things were going, the ups and the downs, sometimes to say sorry, sometimes a thank you, and how they missed them, how they missed their hug or their smile or their company watching TV, and how it would be better if they were here, much better.

And then they'd stoop, place flowers by the headstone, scrape away some of the mould – a headstone only looks fresh for a while – and then return to the world of the living, return to the changes and chances of this brief life; but always a part of them here in the graveyard of the Bell.

There was even the occasional burial. Not many, mostly cremations these days, and cremations were in Eastbourne, enough elderly there to sustain a very good trade. But sometimes a burial here at the Bell, a robed figure appearing outside the scratched caravan windows, a local priest with the funeral men, four with the coffin and an overseer, a huddle of mourners and talk of dust to dust and resurrection hope as the seagulls screeched overhead.

But as time went by, and family history faded like old ink, such moments were increasingly rare. And the dead who remained were looked after mainly by mower, scythe and wild flowers. As every headstone knows, one day the visits must cease.

And now the door of the caravan opens and an old man appears, razor-head and short, but strong in body, with working arms. And he has electricity, the caravan has light, thanks to Neville ... the old queen isn't all bad, he's quite good really, not a bad sort – and it was better than the bus shelters he'd known. He could share his home with the garden tools, the shovels and rakes, which lay across the shelf at the end, by the caravan's front window. And caravan or not, he had to be here, here in this place, for he had no home now but the Bell and the ghosts who lingered here. He would find out more, as much as he could, and then he'd be on his way, though maybe he'd stay. But first he had to find out.

So this morning the graveyard resident would mow the grass, grown long over the winter months. And he'd do some weeding, trim around the headstones. And later, in the afternoon, he'd walk across to the tower and ring the three o'clock bell, this is what he's thinking, with no hint of what is to occur, no suggestion that today a discovery will be made which will change everything, or at least change much; a discovery that will set his heart beating and his mind racing ... and this is how it happened.

It was halfway through the morning, trimmer in hand and snow still wet; the grass had not cut well, he'd wait for a drier day. And then he saw them, words which both disturbed and delighted him or delighted and disturbed him, because like the chicken and the egg, he didn't know which came first and which most lingered. Was this the happiest news of his life? Or the most shattering? He'd been sitting on the bench with his thermos of coffee, he liked coffee from a thermos, always had. Memories: when he'd been a street-sleeper, people would buy him coffee from one of those coffee places. You did see them nowadays, and rather fancy they were. Not in Storm-haven, you didn't see them in Stormhaven, because the town didn't have any. But in other towns and cities he'd seen them, they were all over the place and passers-by would buy him a cup, sometimes the most unlikely folk. But he'd always pour it into his thermos when they'd gone. He wouldn't drink it from their cardboard cups but from his thermos, because he preferred coffee from a thermos.

And that was when he saw them both. How had he missed them before, sitting right in front of him?

Had the clue been sitting unseen in front of him all these years? The graveyard dweller must have the conversation now.

# Thirteen

'It's not that I don't like the man, Hermione.'

'It is that you don't like the man.'

How could Neville be so unaware of what everyone else could see? He hated the man.

'I have no feelings about him, God's honest truth, neither good nor bad, no feelings at all. Why would anyone have feelings for such a little shit?'

They sat in Hermione's office, as spring snow hit the window in chunks.

'So you don't like him. It's not a crime.'

'I don't take to him greatly, if that's what you mean – but then what is there to take to?'

'Thank you.'

Hermione liked feelings out in the open.

'But like or dislike doesn't enter into it,' said Neville, returning to denial.

'I think it might enter into it a little.'

'Not at all.'

'You despise him, Neville.'

'And what if I do? He's just not the right man for the Bell Theatre, simple as.'

'Sadly, I think he is the right man,' said Hermione, removing her glasses as a statement of intent and to make herself absolutely clear on the matter. Glasses removed, she said: 'Do I make myself absolutely clear?' She'd once seen it done on stage and noted how authoritative it appeared.

'He's a brute, Hermione.'

'And we need a brute.'

'And he's upsetting the theatre's delicate eco-system.'

'You mean he's upsetting you?'

'Me? Oh no, I'm a big boy. I've brought down much bigger monsters than Bill Cain in my time. I'm thinking of the community here.'

'There won't be a community here unless we do something.'

'I can't work with him.'

There, he'd said it. Hermione paused and put her glasses back on.

'A little Sarah Bernhardt, Neville.'

'And what's more, Hermione, I don't think you should make me work with him, I really don't!'

And now the little boy was stamping his feet, tantrum on the way and Hermione couldn't be doing with that, he had to take responsibility.

'I'm not making you work with him,' she replied, casting her eye over a letter sitting on the desk. She was losing interest in Neville; she had more issues on her plate than his stupid tantrum and he needed to understand that. Sometimes he forgot he was just the administrator.

'What are you saying?'

'I'm saying the choice is yours, Neville. Times are changing at the theatre.'

'And not for the better, Hermione.'

'It could be for the better. Who knows what's for the better?'

Stay silent, Neville, silence is the better way, this is what he was thinking, don't give her any ammunition.

'No one knows anything from where I'm sitting,' she continued. 'They just know what suits them and push for that.'

Pointed.

'If Bill Cain is the "better", Hermione, then, well, believe me – something's amiss in the kingdom.'

Off with her glasses again.

'Neville, I've been here long enough to know that things go in cycles.'

'What's that supposed to mean?'

'And perhaps you're a bit cosy here.'

'Cosy?'

This was preposterous.

'It's what happens. People join up to serve the cause, but once their feet are under the table, they want the cause to serve them. Most stalwarts in institutions are parasites, don't you think?'

'If you're saying what I think you're saying – .'

'The theatre isn't here to serve you, Neville – you're here to serve the theatre.'

There was a shocked pause, shock at the cruelty, at the complete lack of gratitude and Neville did whimper a bit and how he hated himself for it.

'And I hope I do, Hermione, one does one's best. And I don't remember any complaints' – he remembered a few – 'and we've always worked as a team, all for one, one for all!'

That wasn't remotely true – but say it anyway.

'Life brings hard choices sometimes, Neville – choices which we just have to make.'

'You're beginning to sound like a weasel-faced politician.'

'Neither choice makes us happy, that's the trouble – but we still have to choose.'

She was determined to be heard and knew the truth of her thoughts.

'You're saying I should like it – or leave? Is that what you're saying, Hermione? After all these years, you're delivering an ultimatum – like it or leave?!'

'No, Neville, I'm simply offering you a choice.'

# Fourteen

And long before any of these events and conversations, many years previously, when the bright young couple had only recently arrived in Stormhaven, a newspaper story truly gripped its reader.

The story concerned Nicholas and Hermione Bysshe-Urquhart, West Enders come south from London to the south coast, to open a new theatre in Stormhaven. Londoners usually came south to Brighton, all gaudy and gay, but Stormhaven? Never Stormhaven ... yet it was just along the coast from where he sat.

He didn't usually read the papers. Newspapers were mainly for bedding as far as this reader was concerned ... and an arse wipe when necessary. The stories themselves did not concern him, and why would they? They described another world, a parallel world, close enough in a way, one that walked past him each day here in Worthing – but a distant world for those with no front door. Maybe he'd get back to that world, he certainly couldn't stay here. Worthing welcomed careful drivers but not vagrants.

But the theatre story was interesting. He'd taken the paper from a bin, a mattress of pages between himself and the cold stone of the shop doorway. And then there was that name, in the by-line, not one you forget, Nicholas Bysshe-Urquhart.

And apparently he'd arrived in Stormhaven, which wasn't far from here.

That's how you come to live in a theatre graveyard.

# Fifteen

*Tuesday 3 August,
the day after the murder of Hermione*

'So who wants to kill a saint, Tamsin?'

'It might be quicker to ask, "Who doesn't?"'

They were walking along the sea front towards the house at the end, Peter's house, called Sandy View, which was lies, all lies. There wasn't any sand for miles.

'You have a cynical streak,' said Peter.

'And you don't?'

'I do, but I have other streaks as well, a variety of streaks to choose from.'

'And my range of streaks is more limited?'

'This is not a streak competition.'

'But if it were?'

'I merely suggest that your cynical streak is given much honour in your life, bowed to and revered on a daily basis.'

'And you have a problem with that?'

'I'm not sure a cynical streak should receive quite such praise.'

And then wishing to change the subject, she said:

'I've never felt those rocks looked right, you know.'

Looking east towards France, she sought distraction in the white cliffs ahead. They did look odd to the newcomer.

'How very perspicacious, Tamsin. You're gazing on one of Storm-haven's most ridiculous attempts at self-improvement.'

'What was that?'

'The reason for the rocks not looking right.'

'You mean human hand played a part?'

'Human explosive.'

'Was this in the war?'

'Sadly, they don't have that excuse. It was 1850 and the idea was to create a breakwater in a split second, to protect the town from the encroaching sea.'

'Their first mistake: Stormhaven should have been drowned long ago. Kindest thing, put it out of its misery.'

'One day you will appreciate this town.'

'Please shoot me when I do.'

'But to return to the point, the local powers decided to blow up a sizeable part of the eastern cliffs.'

'These ones?'

'Yes.'

'But how would that help?'

'It was judged, unwisely as it turned out, that the fallen chalk would give the town all the protection it needed at minimum cost.'

'A cheap victory over the waves.'

'That was the plan.'

'And then?'

Peter told the story of a very public disaster – recounted graphically in the *Sussex Silt* in their *Barmy but True!* section. The blasting of the cliff had been widely advertised and keenly anticipated – what else was there to do in 1850? – and on the explosive day, 19 September, large numbers from the area gathered as near to the cliff as they dared. 'A special train even brought people down from London,' said Peter.

'An early rock concert.'

'Sorry?'

'It's a joke. The rock – .'

'Seven tons of gunpowder were used,' he said, passing over the comedy. 'Huge explosion and around two hundred thousand tons of chalk came crashing to the ground. It must have been quite a sight and quite a sound.'

'The Rolling Stones.'

Peter watched the fracturing again, the noise and the falling, the screaming crowds …

'So Stormhaven was protected,' said Tamsin.

'Well no, it wasn't. In fact the outcome was the opposite of the one they desired: the downsizing of the cliff actually made the town more exposed to the sea, gave the waves freedom to get closer, because within weeks, most of the fallen rock was washed away by storms.'

Tamsin laughed.

'Has Stormhaven done anything right?'

'Eventually the place had to be protected by the sea wall we walk along now, built in 1881. The cliffs were murdered for nothing.'

'Which brings us back to saints – and their killing.'

'From one murder to another.'

'Quite the eco warrior, Abbot.'

'I like rock.'

'But saints can be seriously irritating – and don't pretend you don't know that.'

'I won't defend the indefensible.'

Saints could be a nightmare.

'But Hermione does seem to have been a good woman,' said Peter. 'On the face of it.'

'How so?'

'Inspirational leader of a community theatre that has somehow lasted thirty years – that's a good definition of "worthy", surely?'

'All inspirational leaders are phoney.'

'I'm sorry?'

It was a strong wind and words were easily lost.

'I said, all inspirational leaders are phoney.'

Peter smiled.

'A heart-warming thought, Tamsin.'

'And true.'

'Remind me not to book you to speak at the National Bravery Awards.'

They reached his peeling blue front door, both keen on some coffee in the shadow of the abused chalk cliffs.

The best-laid plans …

\*

It was the morning after the murder of Hermione Bysshe-Urquhart at the Bell Theatre and Abbot Peter was on board. This was why they'd been walking along the sea wall. He'd agreed to be Special Witness, and without the usual prevarication. With the previous two cases, involving the murders of a vicar and a psychiatrist, he'd had to be persuaded. He'd insisted on discussing the matter, which was tiresome for Tamsin who didn't like unnecessary delay, a waste of everyone's time. Yes, he was also her uncle – a discovery made recently, and a shock to them both – but that didn't make her any more tolerant; in fact, it made her less so. Family should know better than to inflict their indecision on her. They should just say 'Yes' when she told them to.

But there'd been no hesitation this time from the Abbot. Even as they'd stood on stage in the theatre last night, as scene of crime officers got to work around the executed figure – vertebrae broken and soft neck scissored – he'd said to her:

'You'll need me on this one.'

'We'll see,' she'd said in non-committal fashion.

She did need him, but he didn't need to know that. Police work was always undertaken on a 'need to know' basis; and no one needed to know that Tamsin had needs.

She had a murderer to find ... everything else could wait.

# Sixteen

He was furious, and with good reason.

'Have you any idea – any idea at all? – how this is all playing out for those around you?'

The voice on the phone was incandescent, close to screaming, perhaps he was screaming, despite the dog collar and purple episcopal shirt. The voice on the other end was mocking:

'You mean you're worried about how you're going to look, Father?'

Father. It could be such a cold word.

'Nothing could be further from the truth, Paul.' Dig in, Stephen. Don't get caught up in the boy's hysteria.

'It usually comes down to that, I've noticed,' continued the voice down the phone. The voice was twenty-four years old now, Paul Bent, the playwright … but always aged twelve to his parents.

'It usually comes down to what?'

'The issue of how you're going to look.'

'Oh dear – not this again, Paul.'

He was so weary of this conversation.

'That was my only concern at school.'

'What was your only concern at school?'

'That I might make you look bad, I was really frightened of that.'

'Really.'

'And I wonder who put that fear in me, Father?' Give me patience, Lord, thinks the Bishop.

'I'm not saying I'm perfect, Paul. God knows I'm not perfect – but really, I can hardly be blamed for what you thought at school!'

'I think you can, actually.'

'Oh, of course, I'm to blame for everything, aren't I? Everything wrong in the world is down to me!'

'A childish response, Father, and we won't go down this road again, because we both know where it leads.'

'I don't know what you're talking about – never have.'

'It leads to you being right and me being wrong, that's where every path leads with you.'

Paul's grubby little play was bad enough for the Bishop – I mean, why write it? What was the point of writing a play like that? Who could possibly be helped by such a destructive take on family life? You take the rough with the smooth in families, everyone knows that. And Paul could at least have told him what he was doing, or that a story was about to break ... that might have been thoughtful! But not Paul, no! Instead, the Bishop had learned of it from Martin Channing of all people – Martin Channing! Editor of the *Sussex Silt*, the despicable local newspaper, which everyone hated, and with good cause ... yet which everyone seemed to read. The Bishop even glanced at it himself on occasion, in a research capacity, and was always appalled. Always.

It was true he'd once considered writing a weekly column for the *Silt*, and it hadn't been a vanity project, as some suggested, quite the opposite in fact. Like Jesus, he simply wished to spread the word, and with a readership of nearly half a million, where better to put his words than in the pages of the *Silt*? It was important for the Church to be in the marketplace, to be where people were, and if it happened to be his name at the top of the column, then so be it – but that wasn't what mattered, not at all.

As it happened, Martin Channing had proved himself to be something of a deceiver in the end, and the column never worked out. And that was the last he'd heard from the dreadful man until the phone call last week:

'Stephen, glad to have caught you. Martin Channing here.'

The Bishop had felt some excitement, it was true. He'd wondered if perhaps Channing wished to return to the column idea, with his name at the top; wondered if this might be the start of something.

'Always at your service, Martin – and I don't just mean your funeral!'

It was a good joke, he'd heard another priest use it, and the Bishop hoped it struck the right note and would be heard in the right way – blokey banter but with an element of threat and aggression.

'I won't be at my funeral, Bishop, so it's of little consequence whether you are.'

Touché! And you had to be ready for this with Channing. Channing played hardball, Stephen couldn't relax ... it was very much 'wise as a serpent' time.

'No,' continued Channing casually, 'I was just wondering whether you'd like to comment on your son's play *Mother's Day*, opening at the Bell Theatre next week.'

What was this? Episcopal sweat broke out across his body.

'Well, I don't think I do have a comment to make,' he'd said, stalling for time. He had no knowledge of the play. How could he have? He hadn't heard from Paul for months.

'Oh come now, Stephen, we respect each other too much for "no comment"! I'm on your side here.'

Martin Channing was never on your side, the Bishop knew that. Neither did Channing respect anyone. If he met Achilles, he'd write a damning piece on his heel.

'From where I'm sitting, Stephen – in my rather swanky Lewes office by the River Ouse – we have two interesting story lines: first, a son who changes his family name. You do you know your son Paul writes under the name Paul Bent?'

He didn't know that. Paul Bent? A ridiculous attack on his family name, of course. He'd grown up as Paul Straight.

'Still there, Stephen?'

'I'm still here.'

'And the second story line, a Bishop's son who writes a controversial and, some would say, damning, play on family life, when the Bible says we must honour our father and mother and all that.'

The editor of the *Sussex Silt* quoting scripture at him ... he'd heard it all now. Still, perhaps silence was the best plan here.

'Now, I'm not saying they're right, Bishop, it's not for me to have an opinion, it's for the public to decide, they are the jury here – but people, for good or ill, are going to put two and two together. And it's not adding up to a good story for the Bishop of Lewes.'

Stephen was aware of that already.

'Are you ambitious, Stephen?'

The Bishop was ready to explode; of course he was ambitious. What a damn stupid question! I mean, obviously you don't speak of ambition as a bishop, not publicly. Or if you do, you laugh at it, mock it and talk instead of servanthood and community and things like that. (He had deliberately chosen the title of Bishop *for* Lewes rather than Bishop *of* Lewes. He felt it sounded more humble.) If pressed on the subject when an episcopal vacancy arose – he'd been 12 to 1 to be the next Bishop of Coventry – you say, 'Let us leave the future to the good Lord. It's best in his keeping.'

So no, as Channing well knew, he didn't want to stay Bishop of Lewes all his life; it was a beginning not an end, a rung on the ladder, with plenty of rungs above. You had to be looking at Winchester, Durham, London, and yes, York and Canterbury, why not? Those were the real bishops! And a brief stay in Liverpool on the way there perhaps, for credibility. But what hope of that now? His career could be wrecked by all this.

In the end, he'd told Channing he needed to think about it, anything to get away from his smooth insinuations. But that was before the latest disaster, before things got a great deal worse with the murder of Hermione Bysshe-Urquhart. Now his son's grubby little play was wrapped in a murder investigation, and Channing would publish with or without him, no question of that; and, whatever the angle, it wouldn't be nice. So yes of course he was worried about how he was going to look. Why was that idea so strange to his disappointing son Paul?

'It's not about how I'm going to look, Paul, believe me,' he said. 'I have absolutely no concerns on that score.'

'Really?'

'No, it's about your mother's feelings – that's what it's about.' Alter the line of attack. 'But then why change the habit of a lifetime, Paul, and care about those?'

Yes, turn it back onto him, let the smug young man feel a bit of the heat for once.

'Who's that on the phone?' asked Margaret, the Bishop's wife.

'No one.'

'Who is it?'

'Paul.'

'Paul?'

'We were just talking.'

'Let me talk to him.'

They hadn't talked in months.

'I want to talk with him,' she said.

'He rang off.'

The Bishop held out the phone to prove his words.

'He rang off?'

'He's in one of his moods.'

He hadn't rung off, Bishop Stephen had cut him off as soon as Margaret came in; she didn't need to hear this, and as for Paul, if you haven't got something nice to say, don't say anything.

'What was he saying?'

'Usual drivel.'

'Is he all right?'

Perhaps she ought to hear the truth; it wasn't as if he should take the blame alone.

'He's written a play called *Mother's Day*, Margaret, and it's the centrepiece of the thirtieth anniversary celebrations of the Bell Theatre.'

Pause.

'They do good work there,' she said.

As if that was relevant!

'They did do until last night, when the Director, Hermione Bysshe-Urquhart, MBE, was murdered on stage.'

'Murdered on stage?'

'Yes.'

'Oh.'

'Well, that's one response.'

And then a worried look on her face.

'Paul wasn't involved, was he?'

'Paul?'

'I mean, he wouldn't be, would he? He wouldn't be involved with murder?'

# *Act Two*

*It is brilliant going to the theatre and being forced to sit and listen and think about life. It can be almost a near-religious experience.*

**Emily Mortimer**

# Seventeen

'So who do we have in the frame?' she asked.

They sat in Sandy View, Abbot Peter's simple house on the sea front, so called because it looked out on shingle. If you wanted less irony and more sand, you'd go to Camber or Bournemouth and, let's be honest, most people did; Stormhaven's sea front had the footfall of Mars ... except when the chalk cliffs were blown to pieces for no good reason.

But set a road's width back from shingle and sea wall was Sandy View, boasting one comfortable chair, left by the previous owner, and an old wooden herring box, rescued from the sea by Peter. It was as an extra seat when visitors came, an occurrence he tried to avoid, solitude being his preference.

But one of life's ironies is that hermits attract company. Remove yourself from the world and the world becomes ever more eager to find you, as Julian of Norwich discovered in the fourteenth century. This unknown and unvisited individual sealed herself in a cell in the town and suddenly became the most known and visited of all. And so it had been for Peter, as time and tide brought people to his door, people like Tamsin, for instance, who wanted him to help her solve a crime, and now sat in the comfortable chair, with a cup of coffee in her hand and a rejected digestive on a plate by her side.

'We must hope biscuits don't have feelings,' said Peter.

He didn't like it when people rejected his biscuits.

'I've never eaten a biscuit you've offered me.'

'No.'

'You should have seen the pattern.'

'I have seen the pattern.'

'Then why continue to offer them?'

'Because I don't want to get trapped by the pattern ... or assume that you and your pattern are one, because of course you're not, you're more than that, more than your pattern.'

Never ask Abbot Peter a question. He might give you an answer.

'Suspects?' said Tamsin.

Time to move on from biscuits.

'Well, there seem to have been eight people with access back-stage last night,' said the Abbot. 'I did write them down some-where.'

He felt in the deep pockets of his habit, which is where he put everything he didn't know what to do with; but without immediate success.

'It's not a filing system unless you can find it in two minutes,' said Tamsin.

Peter sighed.

'From memory,' he said, 'a back-up filing system, there's Bill Cain, Managing Director; Neville Brownslie, Administrator/front of house; the two actors, Margery Tatters and Millicent Pym.'

'Who don't get on.'

'That was your observation in the interval. I thought they might be acting.'

'They don't get on,' repeated Tamsin.

'Well, we'll soon find out. Who else?'

'Paul Bent, the young writer of the play, who wears his damage like a crown and should get a proper job; Timothy Gershwin, the laid-back Artistic Director – never trust anyone who presents as laid-back; Janet Lines, the costumes person who clearly makes ev-eryone feel awkward; and of course strangest of all, the bell-ringing Quasimodo, who must be seventy, if he's a day.'

'I'd rather you didn't call him that.'

'What's wrong with Quasimodo?'

Peter makes a despairing face.

'Okay … the weird old man.'

'It's not a crime to be old.'

'But it is to be weird. And he smells like a chemical toilet.'

'There's a reason for that.'

'Not a good reason.'

'And his name is Boy.'

'Boy?'

Peter nods.

'Not his real name, presumably.'

'I don't imagine it features on his birth certificate.'

'So what was written on his birth certificate?'

'It's just what everyone calls him apparently.'

'Boy.'

'Yes.'

'What did you make of him?'

'I – .'

'I thought he was a bit freaky, a bit weird.'

'It's traditional – .'

'A failure, he stank of failure to me. I found him depressing. What were you going to say?'

'That it's traditional to wait for an answer if you ask a question.'

'Didn't you think he was freaky?'

Peter breathed deeply.

'He looks after the graveyard,' he said.

'My case rests.'

'Which case?'

'The weird case.'

'And he rings the bell at three o'clock every afternoon,' said Peter.

'I never did discover why.'

'It was part of the contract of sale.'

'Quasimodo was part of the contract?'

'There were originally eight bell-ringers in the church, but when the church went, so did the bells, bought by a parish in Dorset. Or rather, seven of them were bought. The tenor bell, which is the largest, remained.'

'The tenor bell?'

Tamsin is surprised by this accuracy of knowledge. A bell's a bell, isn't it?

'Yes.'

'And how do you *know* the tenor bell is the largest?' she asked, with some frustration.

'I've always taken a keen interest in campanology, Tamsin.'

Peter is listening to the waves outside, gentle today, but still smacking and sploshing on the stones, wearing them down, one cold wash at a time.

'And why can't you just call it bell-ringing?'

'Because I have a rich and varied vocabulary.'

'So how many words do you know for "smug"?'

'And also because a monk at St James-the-Less, in a previous life, rang in Liverpool Cathedral, which features the heaviest bell hung for full-circle ringing in the country.'

'Now this is getting odd.'

'It weighs over four tons.'

Some interest awakened.

'Four tons? How do you ring a four-ton bell?'

'It can be safely done by an experienced ringer – and he was. We used to call him Big Ben.'

'He was Brother Ben?'

'No, he was Brother Anthony. And he wasn't big, either – he was tiny. Big Ben was a nickn– .

The comedy was dying as the words left his lips.

'The hilarity of monastic life,' said Tamsin.

'Oh, we did laugh a lot in the sand,' said Peter wistfully. 'Strange, isn't it?'

And it was strange, the strangest thing about the desert – so much death in the air, so much nothing, yet so much laughter. And Peter was suddenly aware that he hadn't laughed like that for a long time … aware that he wasn't laughing like he used to.

'Does comedy in the cloisters require papal permission?' asked Tamsin.

'It's more about skill than brute force, bell-ringing. Big Ben the bell is bigger, of course – thirteen and a half tons of metal ringing out across the Thames. But then no one rings Big Ben – it's mechanical.'

'I'm losing the will to live.'

'And we started down this path' – Tamsin did sometimes behave like a child – 'because the bell in the Bell Theatre is in fact the second largest tenor bell in the country, after Liverpool Cathedral.'

Pause.

'And that knowledge helps the murder investigation because?'

'It's not all about outcomes.'

'I like outcomes myself – which may explain why I'm an inspector and you're unemployed.'

'Not at present.'

'Temporary jobs don't count.'

'It tells us that Boy, whoever he is, is an experienced bell-ringer.'

'Which I think we knew.'

They did already know that.

'Though Paul Bent hates the bells,' added Peter, 'and wishes Boy would "stop his bloody ringing and crawl down a hole, a long way away".'

'What it is to be appreciated.'

But the question remained: Who was Boy? And why on earth was he here?

# Eighteen

✤

*The rat looked at him in the moonlight, a quizzical look, before am-*
*bling back with his scaly tail towards the rough skirting from whence*
*he came. Next to him – next to Eckhart, not the rat – the large body*
*of Henricus was snoring, alcohol sleep in this rough hostelry. But Eck-*
*hart used the night hours to remember.*

*Paris, 1310 – yes, he'd been there when Marguerite Porete was*
*burned. He'd been about to take up his post at the city's fine univer-*
*sity. 'Master of Theology' had been his title which seemed grand at the*
*time, if rather grating now. A Master is merely someone who knows*
*how much they don't know – and is that really mastery? But yes, he'd*
*been there in 1310, greatly honoured no doubt, and held in high es-*
*teem. Yet the talk on the street had not been of him and his great*
*mind, but of Marguerite Porete, an educated and dangerous woman;*
*dangerous to the Church, that is, and condemned accordingly. And*
*yet … and yet right in all she believed, this was Eckhart's view. She'd*
*been burned for the crime of being right at the wrong time.*

*He hadn't known her well, perhaps no one did, for she was furtive*
*about herself, as if her story was of no consequence; but as clear as*
*the papal pond in her rejection of church authority. She refused to*
*speak with William of Paris or any of his dull inquisitors during her*
*imprisonment; and then when, after much investigation, charges were*
*finally brought, she refused to recognise the validity of the court, and*
*spoke only of her innocence. What can you do with such a woman?*
*As William had said at the time, in his experience, an incapacity to*
*recognise one's own guilt was a very feminine trait.*

*It was her book that did the damage: 'The mirror of simple souls'.*
*Eckhart suspected this was the nub of the complaint. Written in the*
*1290s, it had gained quiet popularity without a word of protest from*
*anyone. But then in 1306, for reasons unknown, it was suddenly*

*declared heretical and the world fell in on her head. Presumably its popularity was the thing that did for her. No one minds a heretical book if no one's reading it – but if everyone's reading it? Heretics should pray for poor book sales.*

*But still the question: why had Marguerite been picked on? She was no different from many other female mystics at the time, yet these women remained untouched by the torturing Church, un-tied to the stake and quite un-burnt. They all said the same things – just not to so many, perhaps. And dear William, not usually a vindictive man, William of Paris, Eckhart's host at the time, so eager to bring her down, and employing every academic and lawyer in town to achieve this aim. In those feverish months, the condemnation of Marguerite Porete had been an industry providing employment for every bankrupt theologian in the district.*

*She wrote like an angel, of course, which didn't help – didn't help the Church who prefers its followers stupid. But hers was the most beautiful prose in Old French, which everyone could understand, prose in which she called on the reader to give up reason as a means of experiencing God. 'Reason, you'll always be half-blind,' she declared. Instead, she said, believers were to become annihilated souls, souls so destroyed, so dismantled by God's love that a union is formed which transcends the contradictions of the world.*

*This was truly dangerous talk because a believer's oneness with God left the Church redundant, which was an unwise place to leave it. Talk such as this left the Church like a large whale on a beach, this is how it could appear. The teaching of Marguerite Porete left the Church with no fear to play on, no forgiveness to deal out, and no indulgences to sell to lessen time in purgatory. So yes, Eckhart remembered her well.*

*And now the rat was back, looking at him again, undecided about something. Henricus turned over, his vast bulk repositioned on the urine-soaked mattress, after which the snoring resumed. But Eckhart remained awake, remembering ... for he himself had developed these ideas, he'd said similar things to Porete, emphasised the divine oneness of God with his creation. As he'd said at his Dominican hearing, and to some consternation: 'The eye with which I see God is the same with which God sees me. My eye and God's eye is one eye, and one sight, and one knowledge, and one love.'*

*But while they'd burned Porete, they'd called him 'Meister'. So why did they pick on her? And why was he so haunted by their conversation, the night before she was cooked in the Parisian flames?*

*When he looked at the rat, did he look at himself?*

70

# Nineteen

The Reverend Ainslie Meddle was eighty-two, fit for his age, but having to be careful. He couldn't stand for too long and sadly – and this *was* sad – losing his sense of taste; so yes, his life was different now. No more for him the cut and thrust of parish life, that was long gone; the needy knocks on the door, flower festivals and suicides – so pressing at the time, but passing things. To lose the taste of scrambled egg felt a more painful letting go.

And amid loss was gain, for he felt freer now, a man more free, free in his life beyond the Church, liberated you might say. Experience no longer had to be turned into a sermon, which meant he lived it more wonderingly. Things just were and they were better unexplained, much better. These days, it was enough to potter in a kindly fashion through the village ... through the mid-Sussex village of Henfield, where daddy bought horses for his daughters, golf clubs for himself and a Pilates studio in the garden for his wife. Oh, and everyone ate organic vegetables, without a glance at the cost. Henfield was 'rather well-to-do', as his mother would have said, 'very top-drawer'.

And neither was it new on the scene. There'd been a church here since the eighth century – 'just before my time' he'd joke with people, and it was here, in this ancient Sussex settlement, that Reverend Ainslie lived, just off the high street, No 4, Cowfold Close, in a house he'd called 'Dunpreachin' – one of a small row of cottages with front gardens which had to be diligently maintained. It wasn't written down that this was so, just assumed. Maintaining the front garden, visible to all who passed, was not a choice in Henfield – it was simply expected by demanding neighbours who were guardians of their patch. They say there's much gas under Sussex, and large quantities of oil, Ainslie had heard this. But which energy company would take on these people and win?

When not forced into gardening, he'd offer cheery words here and there, an absent-minded wave to people he couldn't always recognise, eking out his pennies which weren't piled high and wondering increasingly what his life had been about, when everything was considered and weighed? And would it be weighed? Were there really divine scales in which good and bad were placed? The belief did seem a trifle fifteenth century, but you do wonder later in life, of course you do, the matter's more pressing; and it was particularly pressing today after reading the *Sussex Silt*.

You shouldn't read the *Sussex Silt*, no one should, but there's brief if soiled pleasure in seeing others exposed, ridiculed and shamed. And of course having read what he read, he was haunted again by those headstones. Would they never go away? And heaven forbid, but might it happen that he was the next man named and shamed in the *Silt*?

He didn't feel good about it, his part in it all, but what else could he have done? She'd been such a nice girl and so full of energy, so well intentioned – it had been difficult to say 'No'. Well, he couldn't have said 'No', surely? On what grounds could he have said 'No'? Yet it had been a strange request all the same, with an unsettling quality that had never quite left him down the years, even here in organic Henfield, with its three flower shops. You can buy a new house and buy a new bed; but your old self moves in, and your old self dreams restlessly at night.

Some things you forget; so much of the past consigned to the oblivion of unremembered matter. But other truths linger, like predators in the dark, hidden but there, always. And it was the headstones that had lingered for the Reverend Ainslie Meddle; he'd never quite escaped them. And now here they were again, and troubling him again, with news of the terrible events at the Bell Theatre.

Was the death of Hermione connected in some way with what he'd done? Or rather, with what he'd *allowed* to be done all those years ago? There was no particular reason to imagine it to be so, no reason at all; in fact it was ridiculous. But then sometimes there doesn't have to be a reason, just a sense that bad seeds sown in the past have become a present harvest of harm. And the thing was, it was making Ainslie feel like a murderer himself; like a man on the run, a man on the run from unfinished business – and he didn't want to feel this way.

Of course, he'd known Julie Dicks a long time and that's how he still thought of her, the struggling actress. But then she'd met Nicholas Bysshe-Urquhart and a change occurred. Nicholas was a theatre man through and through, older than Julie, but thoroughly decent, a beacon in the West End and behind many new shows – before being smitten by the young thing and married to her. And then they'd run away to Stormhaven on this mad adventure, to create a theatre by the sea, the Bell Theatre in the ashes of St Augustine's ... where Ainslie Meddle had been priest.

Julie – or Hermione as she became, cutting her links with the past, as if the past never was – was the one everyone noticed, everyone admired. People imagined that she was the energy behind everything, but it was Nicholas who oversaw the running and development of the theatre; he was the visionary and the guide, until his most sudden death from bowel cancer at the age of forty-three. They'd been married for ten tears and their only child was the theatre and its reputation for both quality and integrity. People came from all over the county to see the shows, which was unusual for Stormhaven. People usually travelled there because they had to – a visit to their ailing mother, a meeting of the Sussex Beach and Shingle Society or a strong need to throw themselves off the white cliffs that rose so magnificently at the town's edge. This was why people came to Stormhaven, not to see something interesting. If you wanted interesting, you got the bus to Lewes or Brighton – or if rich or royal, to Glyndebourne and the opera house there. But Stormhaven as a beacon of artistic excellence? That was a joke and a slightly bitter one ... until the Bell Theatre, which in the hands of the great theatre manager Nicholas Bysshe-Urquhart had bucked the trend, reversed the tide.

But after his sad death – as sad as a death could be, apart from that of a child – while the theatre had carried on, it was a wounded and weakened creature. Hermione had kept the place active, children's parties had become a new source of income – but distracted. As a former parishioner said to Ainslie, 'There's a lot going on, Reverend, but nothing much happening, not like it used to.'

People noted somewhere in their psyche an increasing fragmentation at the Bell, of various empires working in something less than harmony, this is what they said: 'Can't put my finger on it, but something ain't right.' The greater good was exchanged for personal goods, with theatre director Hermione a juggler of many balls, but a holder of none. He didn't ask for the gossip, Ainslie, it just came to him, people assuming interest, interest which he didn't really have. You let go slowly when you leave a place, and then you lose interest, this is how we part ... until the shocking news of the murder, of the death of Julie, of Hermione Bysshe-Urquhart. And onstage would you believe? That was a mean stunt, he reckoned, and heavy with vindictive irony: the same stage that had built the theatre's reputation, now threatened to bring it to its knees.

And he knew what he must do, without any doubt: he must go back there, a couple of bus rides, first to Brighton, and then along the coast, that's all it was. The decision had been made in a moment. He must tell someone … not confess, because what was there to confess? There was nothing to confess as such. Well, perhaps there was dishonesty to confess, but his conscience was clear, as clear as anyone's is clear. How can anyone have a clear conscience – unless it's a conscience with selective memory? He didn't know if his conscience was clear, he just needed to tell someone.

The Reverend Ainslie Meddle needed to make a confession. After a gap of seventeen years, he was going back to the Bell Theatre.

# Twenty

## *Two days before the murder of Hermione*

'Paul, I'm sorry, but – and there's no gentle way to say it – I'm going to be a complete bitch and pull the play.'

It wasn't gentle.

'You're what?'

'I'm going to pull the play, close it down ... end the run.'

'I don't understand.'

And Paul didn't understand, the news had come from nowhere.

'The last performance will be our thirtieth anniversary night,' said Hermione briskly.

They sat in her office, theatre director and playwright, power not equally shared.

'You mean in two days' time?'

Hermione nodded.

'But why?'

'No one's coming to see it, Paul, if you hadn't noticed.' That sounded a little harsh, so she tried to soften the blow. 'It doesn't mean it's a bad play, it's just that no one wants ... to watch it.' That probably wasn't an improvement.

Paul says: 'These things take time, you know they do,' and she replies that it's all about momentum, Paul, all about momentum, and *Mother's Day* doesn't have it.

'It could have.'

'No, it has the opposite of momentum ... it's slowing down, like a car running into sand.'

She hadn't meant to say that, not the bit about the sand, she'd hoped for it all to be nice, but Paul was making it hard and, to be honest, she was angry about the play, angry about its failure, so why shouldn't Paul catch some of that, because he wrote the damn thing? He should just accept it, let it be, instead of looking so bemused, so little-boy shocked – because how much of a surprise can it have been? And anyway, he should be grateful, what did he have to moan about? She'd given him his first break, hadn't she? This is what she was thinking. Most playwrights never get this far, never find a theatre foolish enough to showcase their precious little creation.

'This is Bill Cain talking,' he said.

'It's reality talking, Paul.'

'Reality?'

Hermione sighs as Paul's mood darkens.

'I didn't realise you and reality were such close friends, Hermione – I haven't seen you talking much before.'

And that was that for Hermione. She didn't like to hurt people, she wanted to be kind … but once she'd decided on a course, then it made complete sense, to her at least, and from then on, whoever was hurt and however badly, her only irritation was people being slow to accept it – people like Paul.

She'd decided to axe the play and now she wanted to move on. What was his problem?

# Twenty One

'Oh, hello, Margery – I thought you'd gone.'

Hermione had poked her head into the rehearsal room, expecting to find it empty; and there was a sedentary Margery, not unusual, staring out the window.

'I haven't gone,' said Margery, without turning round. 'And I don't particularly feel like going.'

'You can't just sit there, Margery, taking up space.'

Margery thought about being fat all the time, or most of the time, and comments like that didn't help ... always thinking about it, catching her reflection in shop windows, turning away, thinking about whether her arms were wobbly, or about the lift or the bus sinking when she got on. Was that her, did they sink downwards with others, was that normal and what were people saying? When she stood and when she moved, were they thinking 'She's a bit tight in that dress?'

She'd lost four stone in drama school, they'd been kind to her really, the other students, very kind; helped her to eat more healthily when she didn't know what healthy eating was. They helped her to see that not everyone ate like her 30-stone father whom she'd gone to when her mother threw her out; and he hated himself for it, that was the thing, hated himself for being fat, but carried on eating, because what was the point in stopping? 'I could lose five stone and no one would notice – so why bother?' he said. And it was hard to argue.

But the drama students were different. They helped her see that you can't go on putting cake in your mouth, there are consequences – 'Five Bakewell Tarts in a day is too many, Margy.' But she wanted to put cake in her mouth, she liked it, so while she thought about being fat all the time, she also wanted her butter as thick as her bread, like her dad, because who'd notice if she lost a few pounds? Not that Margery was anywhere near 30 stone and never would be, that wasn't going to happen, but she was putting a little back on at the moment, since the sacking, from a size fourteen to sixteen, since she'd left *Holby* … not that she needed the money yet, she had some put away. But she needed work or she could regress, needed purpose, structure to the day, she could easily slip back … even now she was sitting too much, sitting and staring, the creeping laziness, the dark cynicism that asked 'What difference does a few pounds make? Well, what's the point of anything?'

'Welcome to my world,' as her dad would say.

But back in Stormhaven, Hermione is reminding her that the children's entertainer will be here soon and Margery sighs.

'Was that why Timothy cancelled the afternoon rehearsal?'

'I don't know. I did tell him the space wasn't available. There's a children's party. He's known for a while.'

Margery didn't move but she did speak:

'And there was me thinking Timothy just wanted to work on Millicent's lines … if you know what I mean.'

Hermione did know what she meant, everyone had heard the rumours.

'People's private lives are their own,' said Hermione.

Why did people get involved in other people's lives? Hermione had never wanted anyone sticking their noses in hers, and she kept out of theirs; unless there was a good reason, a correction to be made or whatever.

'But now it appears I'm being uncharitable,' said Margery, in a vague and to-no-one manner.

'And that wouldn't be a first,' thought Hermione. Margery could be extremely negative, a heavy presence, just the worst sort.

'Because the real reason why there isn't a rehearsal, it transpires, is because there's another children's party … the third in the last two weeks?'

Hermione heard that as a dig.

'How do you think we pay you, Margery? It's not as if your star appeal is pulling them in.'

The posters had made the most of the *Holby* connection. The lure of the TV star did work in local theatre … but it didn't seem to be working here.

'You never could stick at anything, could you?'

Margery looked out the window as she spoke.

'What the hell's that supposed to mean?' said Hermione. 'And it's polite to look at someone when addressing them.'

But Margery didn't look.

'Even when you got your West End break, you just couldn't hack it, found it all a bit too much.'

'I got married, Margery. Someone wanted me.'

Harsh.

'No, you were "little-girl-lost" long before that. Nicholas was hardly your first relationship with an older man, was he? So why did you really give up that part and disappear?'

'I got bored.'

Margery laughed, derisory and pitiful.

'I got bored of saying the same lines eight times a week,' added Hermione.

'It was Drury Lane.'

How could a young actress, at the start of her career and with everything to play for, get bored at Drury Lane?

'It was still the same lines eight times a week.'

'It's called acting.'

'No, it's called dying.'

'Where's your staying power?'

'I've stayed here. Now, are you going, Margery, before we fall out?'

They'd already fallen out, both knew that; it was about limiting the damage. And then the Tank fired again: 'You couldn't handle that part.'

'The part you wanted.'

'And then you had a breakdown, because that's what we're talking about here. Acting was a little tougher than you thought.'

'How little you know, Margery.'

'Perhaps that's what Nicholas saw in you – someone he could save.'

'You're so bitter.'

'Never has "your better half" been more apposite.'

'You need to get over *Holby*, Margery.'

'There's nothing to get over. It was my choice to leave.'

'Of course. I'm sure you were begging them to end your contract in a street explosion from which there was no return.'

'I was, yes; that's exactly what I was doing. I'd taken the part as far as I could.'

Hermione couldn't hold back a laugh.

'Hah! Where have I heard that before?'

Margery blushed, a hot flush of anger.

'I think you're taking yourself a little too seriously, Margery. You were playing yourself, for God's sake – a bitter old cow!'

Margery had still not turned round.

'Anyway, you'll need to leave, my dear. The party booking arrives at four.'

'Cutting-edge theatre at the Bell,' said Margery. 'A children's entertainer with a flower that squirts water. Nicholas must be turning in his grave.'

Ignore it, Hermione, ignore it. 'At least he's an entertainer the audience enjoys,' she said.

'I mean, why not call the Bell a party venue and be done with it?'

A pause ... and then Margery turned round and engaged the eyes of Hermione for the first time. She knew a little about drama.

'You do know that you'll always be Julie Dicks to me – Julie.'

But then so did Hermione:

'And very soon, you'll just be a memory for me.'

'I'm afraid you've got me all summer, Julie.'

'Well, it's funny you should say that.'

And the first sign of fear in Margery's eyes, like a child caught out.

'What's that supposed to mean?'

'There was something I haven't mentioned, a decision I took today.'

And so it was that Margery heard of the imminent termination of her contract, and the end of the summer run of *Mother's Day* – with effect from the thirtieth anniversary night.

Two days away.

# Twenty Two

Typical!

Bill Cain was chatting up her assistant, Molly. This was why he didn't notice Janet, why he never noticed her. He was too busy flirting with pretend-blonde Milly-Molly-Mandy who was an office liability in Janet's book.

Some were surprised he was there at all; surprised that the wealthy Bill Cain still stood in this particular queue, when he could have gone private, could have paid for receptionists who showed some respect and where he got appointment times that suited him, rather than times that suited an occasionally open surgery. Instead, however, this local boy-made-good still used his old quack because he liked it that way.

'Good enough for my dad, good enough for me,' he'd say, because although he wanted to screw people, he also wanted to be one of them, one of the people, a regular bloke. And he was fond of a pretty receptionist, as Janet had noticed. He couldn't help himself, could he? What was it with men? And she must be half his age, he could be her father! As far as Janet was concerned, Bill Cain was just a small boy with a big bank account.

'I need to see him today, Molly,' said Bill.

'There aren't presently any spaces, Mr Cain.'

'I need to hear that without the negative.'

Janet so wanted to intervene. She wanted to tell Bill Cain to get over himself, perhaps she wouldn't use the phrase, but that was the idea, and come back another day like everyone else had to. 'Dr Elsdon's time isn't elastic,' she'd say. But she knew there'd be trouble if she opened her mouth. Molly had actually complained about Janet's interference to Dr Elsdon; and while he'd been privately supportive of her – they'd known each other a long time and she was his lead receptionist – he had said that she must be careful:

'Molly's young, Janet, needs to be allowed her head!'

'She's too indulgent.'

'Patients like her.'

That hurt. Did that mean they didn't like Janet? Not that she cared, she was a professional with a tough skin and doctors' receptionists weren't there to be popular, it wasn't a popularity contest. Receptionists were there to protect the doctor from wasters who thought only of themselves and their imaginary illnesses.

'*Men* like her,' she'd said in reply. 'They like fake blondes with mascara. The women see her for what she is.'

Janet saw her for what she was, with her fluttering eye lashes and rather contrived breasts.

'Janet, we must move with the times.'

Now what was that supposed to mean? Move with the times? This was a doctor's surgery not a space research centre! Or a brothel ...

And then Dr Elsdon had said, 'Surgeries aren't what they were, Janet, the whole matron thing, it's a thing of the past.'

Janet had breathed deeply, felt her innards heaving and posed the question: 'What do you mean, "the whole matron thing"?'

'Your approach.'

Bill Cain got his appointment. He wheedled his way into Molly's deficient decision-making, left her laughing, flattered and finding him an appointment time at 5.15 p.m., as long as he was on time.

'Oh, I'm never late,' said Cain. 'I always come on time.'

Disgusting.

'I'm sure you do!' said Molly.

'You should work for me,' said Cain, 'I'd pay you more.'

'Then how would you get your last-minute appointments?' she said, giggling.

'Good point, Molly,' said Cain, who just held back from glancing naughtily at Janet. 'Stay right where you are. I'll pay you a retainer!'

Janet felt sick as she listened and saw only intruders in her surgery, behind and in front of the desk. She looked out on the queue, waiting faces, and decided on an adventure of her own.

# Twenty Three

'Back in the day, I was one of those.'

'What, a knuckle boxer?'

Simon nodded sagely.

Simon and Jamie were talking as they worked ... which this morning was painting tiny figures, with war games in mind. This is why lonely souls would drop by later; why they'd loiter round the large table at the centre of the shop space in *Onslaught Games*. The forces of darkness were marching, the un-dead emerging from their graves, cosmic clashes in the air ... with Simon and Jamie as their hosts.

'Yeah, I used to punch trees to condition my fists. Me and the guys, we'd be out giving the trees grief.'

'Classic martial arts technique.'

Jamie admired Simon, because he was so savvy; but he could at least try to appear equal.

'Yeah, but we didn't know that at the time,' said Simon. 'We just did what we did, warrior intuition, doing our own thing, self-made fighters.'

'I saw a gypsy bare-knuckle fight once,' said Jamie. 'Savage.'

'You've seen that?'

Some respect from Simon.

'No quarter asked or given ... mad men.'

'Where was that, then?'

'Secret location ... Newhaven way.'

'I mean, I was in London for two years,' said Simon, who needed to take charge again. There was no way Jamie had seen a gypsy fight, though Newhaven had its dark side.

'London?'

'Mean streets,' said Simon.

Jamie nodded like he knew them well, as Simon reminisced:

'Different kind of action going down in London town ... went back to my old street-fighting techniques.'

'Different moves, street fighting.'

'I mean, this guy comes up to me, no lie – it's three in the morning, no one else around, some sink estate in Peckham and it's "Yo, lemme get your cigarettes, man, yah wallet, yah phone".'

'You took him out?'

'I'm a peaceful guy.'

'Sure. But peace don't make da streets safe. Only war makes da streets safe.'

It wasn't something he'd said at his public school, where the two met.

'I had no beef with the guy,' said Simon, putting down his little brush. 'To me, he was just a dick with a knife.'

'He was tooled up?'

'Tooled up and acting tough and I was laughing – no, I was, couldn't help myself, and then two of his mates appear from the shadows.'

'And you're, like, in warrior mode.'

'The guy with the knife came first.'

'Dead man walking.'

'Well, running, yeah, but a dream come true as I kick him in the gut.'

'Bring it on.'

'And he was down, getting all choky, throwing up like a girl, drops his knife, job done, and then the other two rush in, and were working me pretty good.'

'You were taking the blows?'

'You learn how, you roll with it, and then I got an opening, and head butted the taller one and he dropped like a jelly-legs.'

'Two down, one to go.'

'And then the other guy jacked my jaw, but it didn't bother me … all the hits I took when I was younger.'

'Battle-hardened.'

'You could say.'

'And you made him pay?'

'He paid in full, mate, with interest, when I threw a straight jab into his face and placed a kick to the side of his knee.'

'Classic moves.'

'And then the first guy is up again, and he's picked up his knife – and that was a mistake, serious mistake, because that makes me upset, I'm upset now, and I'm walking towards him, trying to reason, I try to reason and he charges me, so I throw my arm up and jack his jaw and he tries with the knife, but I have his hand, and that's when his wrist goes snap, oops, but now the other guy whose

84

nose I broke, he jumps in, gives my head a beating, and that's when the little prick stabbed me.'

'He had a blade as well?'

'Yeah, and as soon as I felt that knife hit my chest, the game was over for them, it was real now, no more playing, no more Mr Nice Guy.'

'It was gloves off.'

'I was angry, and you don't want to see me when I'm angry, I'm a destroyer when I'm angry, and at this point, it's been about two minutes, right?'

'Right.'

'And I didn't use a knife in what followed, they weren't worth it, but the two guys that were standing then, well – they weren't standing by the three-minute mark.'

'Thank you and good night.'

'And the other guy who got up and tried to have one more whack at me, I just kicked him straight in the face and watched him drop like a bag of shit.'

'Have you finished the painting yet, boys?'

It was the boss.

'Er, nearly Mr Brownslie,' said Simon, picking up his little brush again.

'You're not still on the un-dead, are you?'

Neville liked these lads, always polite and always on time, but he had to keep an eye. It was a business after all, one of his stranger hobbies away from the theatre, and he needed the new figures for his 'Dead Flesh Festival' display in the window.

'We're getting there, Mr Brownslie,' said Simon.

'Just waiting for them to dry,' said Jamie.

'Perhaps less street fighting tales until the job's done?' said Neville.

'Certainly, Mr Brownslie,' said Simon.

And from then on, there was silence inside *Onslaught Games* … silence and the careful painting of zombies, some way from the sink estates of Peckham.

# Twenty Four

The Reverend Ainslie Meddle, of Henfield in Sussex, enjoyed travelling by bus, as you do when you're not in a hurry. He took the Number 17 from Henfield to Brighton, and then the 12 from Brighton to Stormhaven, a very reasonable service, just over the hour and time to think, time to remember, given the disturbing events at the Bell. And as the Sussex countryside passed by outside – neat cottages, open barns and sprawling heaps of manure – he was remembering the dying man's call to his bedside. Nicholas Bysshe-Urquhart had been in a hospice for his last few days on earth, wonderful staff, quite unafraid of death, and perhaps Nicholas was too ... but he was troubled. He hadn't been a man at peace.

'Ainslie, can I speak plainly with you?' This is what he'd said, and Ainslie hoped he always had spoken plainly. He felt their relationship had been honest, in the limited way men are. But if a social mask needs to be removed, a hospice is a good place to do it.

'Of course, Nicholas. Plain speaking is good.'

With permission granted, Nicholas paused. Where to begin?

'Hermione and I, it's been a good marriage,' he said.

'It has.'

'No regrets, none at all, absolutely none.'

'I'm glad,' said Ainslie, waiting for the regrets.

'No children, of course.'

'No.'

'Hermione didn't want them, a woman's right and all that.'

'Of course.'

'So no quibbles there.'

'Did you want children, Nicholas?'

'Me?'

'I was just wondering.'

'Oh, well, since you ask – yes, I probably did actually … haven't really considered it but it might have been nice.'

Ainslie remained quiet.

'But she was quite sure – Hermione, I mean. And really, given my condition now, maybe it's all for the best that we didn't.' Nicholas attempted a smile. 'It would have been sad for them. Though who knows, perhaps they could have reminded her of me – you know, when I'm gone?'

'I don't think she'll ever forget you, Nicholas.'

'No,' he said. 'No. So no regrets … which is good.'

'So you're a man at peace.' It was halfway between a statement and a question; like a festering boil, there was still something more to come out.

'Well, I am and I'm not, Ainslie.'

'Welcome to the human race, Nicholas.'

He smiled.

'You've achieved great things here in Stormhaven,' said the Reverend. 'The Bell Theatre is a remarkable creation – you leave behind a great legacy.'

'It is, isn't it, yes, I think so – pretty good, though I say it myself! Not Drury Lane – but not bad!'

'But part of you has still to find peace?'

Pause.

'She's hiding something from me, Ainslie.'

There, he'd said it, straight out.

'Hiding something? Who, Hermione?'

'Yes, Hermione. She's hiding something. I don't know what it is, and she doesn't need to hide anything, that's the thing, I could cope, broad shoulders me. But she's hiding something and I don't know what it is. Do you know what it is, Ainslie?'

Ainslie pondered his next words. Something stirred in him, knowing Nicholas was right. There was a secret, something withheld by Hermione, and withheld from him, as well as from Nicholas … though maybe Ainslie had more clues. But then Nicholas was dying of cancer, a flickering candle in a gusty wind, so what good would such knowledge be to him? What do the dead do with knowledge? And he couldn't be sure anyway, couldn't be absolutely sure what it all meant. So really, what was there to say?

'I don't know of anything,' he said, gently. 'I only know of a wife who loves you very much.'

'She's hiding something,' he said, firmly, before starting to choke. And now Ainslie felt like Judas, a betrayer of a dying man who simply wanted the truth.

'We're all hiding something, Nicholas. I suppose we must allow everyone their secrets. Can I get you anything?'

Nicholas then took the clergyman by the arm.

'What's Hermione's secret, Ainslie?'

# Twenty Five

Also on the bus that morning, a different bus, travelling from Lewes to Stormhaven, was Stephen Straight, the Bishop for Lewes. He'd decided against bringing the car, this being a visit of a more private nature, unofficial you might say ... though how that made sense was open to question. It wasn't as if he had a chauffeur, like some of the more elevated bishops – the Canterbury, York and Durham brigade. It was all right for them, swanning around the highways and by-ways with their butler behind the wheel! Inequality could make Stephen fume. So it was good to travel by bus, this was Stephen's view, good to see real people going about their daily lives, you missed these things as a bishop, floating from one ceremony to another, that could be the perception, and Stephen was a man of the people, very much so, called himself 'the people's Bishop'... none of this posh nonsense, and they loved him for it, this was his feeling. Of course a lot of people were stupid, without doubt, and others behaved in a despicable fashion ... people like Martin Channing at the *Sussex Silt.* So the Bishop was a man of the people, but not of *those* people obviously, you had to draw a line.

And right now, he had a son who was proving a headache. First, Paul secretly writes this dubious play about family life, which is then offered an airing at the Bell Theatre – what are they thinking? And then the boy finds himself caught up in a murder enquiry. I mean, he wouldn't murder anyone, not Paul, he wasn't that sort of a boy; but Martin Channing would love this story. He loved it enough before the murder, anything to embarrass the Bishop – but now?

So it was time to sort a few things out; no more the purple-shirted doormat. Not that he regretted asking Paul to leave the family home six months ago, not at all, there was only so much Margaret and he could take. The boy had been insisting on a 'family meeting' – that sounded ominous – to talk about the past, his childhood, nonsense like that. Stephen had turned the suggestion down flat, saying he refused to put Margaret through such an ordeal.

'You must stick together, is that what you're saying?'

'It's called the sanctity of marriage, Paul.'

'Sounds like the collusion of marriage to me; collusion terrified of truth.'

One day, and let it be soon, Paul would understand how marriage worked. It was true, the boy hadn't been born into the happiest of homes, but then marriage was a work in progress, a labour of love, though with more labour than love and they'd tried to shield him from the worst, and done a good job, this was Stephen's view. Certainly no need for Paul to start asking questions now, no need for 'family meetings', he had nothing to complain about. He should try growing up in the Congo, then he'd see what hardship looked like! The conversation had ended shortly after, and since that time they'd had no contact with the boy, his choice.

No, it was definitely time to act, time to sort a few things out; time to pay Paul a visit at his precious little Bell Theatre.

It was Judgement Day.

# Twenty Six

Everyone should have a little book, a place where they write everything down, all the stuff, year after year, even the nonsense, because who knows what's nonsense at the time? At the time, you don't know what's what, it's just life, unfiltered … and then one day you might be able to make sense of it, if you read everything over again, you might see a pattern or a thread, 'a thread of gold' someone called it, a thread of gold running through your life, like a river runs through farmland, quietly watering the soil … this is what Boy thought.

And he had such a book, which he'd kept down the years, though sometimes winters would pass with no writing, hands too cold or the heart too hard, so the book would stay safe in supermarket bags, wrapped tightly with elastic bands because damp could hurt books, rot the binding and crinkle the page … and this was his only one. Yes, Boy's library contained only one book and he'd written it. No Shakespeare, no Dickens – just himself.

And now with the death of Hermione, and the presence of the police, and the things he knew, or suspected he knew, he'd write some more nonsense, get it down in the book and this he was about to do – oh, and God bless Neville for the electricity this morning! It was a cold one again and the kettle was the kindest truth on earth … he'd have warm fingers soon, warm enough to write, when through the caravan window he saw a figure in the graveyard that he hadn't seen before.

He decided to go out; he'd find out what they wanted, this mystery figure, outlined through the scratched plastic, wandering among the tombs. A short chat couldn't harm, even if it was cold, and Boy was glad he did, glad he stepped out, because what followed proved most revealing, unforgettable really.

There had indeed been deceit, as he suspected. But what joy and excitement in the learning of it!

# Twenty Seven

✤

## *1310, Paris*

*'They have put me next to the men's latrine,' said the condemned woman, deliberately.*

*'Not an act of kindness,' said the monk.*

*'Believe me, no.'*

*The stench in the cell was sick-making and he'd barely arrived. To breathe this air day and night could make burning appear the sweeter way ...*

*Meister Eckhart sat with Marguerite Porete. With her burning set for the morrow, and appropriate arrangements made – scaffolding, brushwood and the sacraments – everyone hoped for fine weather. Rain was not anyone's desire, particularly the one tied to the stake ... the condemned wished for dry wood, not wet.*

*'The Dominicans – they waste their time with insult.'*

*She looked at him as she spoke, and her eyes set his Dominican habit on fire. The cloth became a burning thing, terrible against his skin, this is how it felt. He'd been in the Order since the age of fifteen, entering the Dominican priory in Erfurt, but never been shamed by it. He'd only praised his Order, only revered it – until now.*

*'They have not, well, hurt you in any way?' he asked. 'The inquisition – .'*

*'They publicly burned my books in Valciennes,' she said. 'In my presence. I think that was designed to hurt.'*

*'I did hear.'*

*There was a silence. He was the enemy, after all – a Dominican. He wore the clothes, had prospered through their power and now shared lodgings with the man who had hunted her down and pros-*

92

ecuted with such venom. Anything but awkwardness and distance in this cell would have been surprising.

'But you continued to speak your ideas.'

This could have been an accusation, though Porete heard it as praise.

'You can't burn an idea,' she said, and there was almost a smile.

'They are rather free things,' admitted Eckhart, 'for good or ill.'

'And I circulated my books!'

There was such fire in this woman, not a phrase to use in the circumstances, but Eckhart felt the fire, the determination.

'After the burning at Valciennes, you continued to circulate your books?'

'Why would I not? What is unorthodox about my writing?'

'Unfortunately, I am not your judge.'

'But if you were?'

While Eckhart pondered his reply, she continued:

'The respected Master of Theology, Godfrey of Fontaines, he approved the book.'

'Indeed he did. But then William of Paris found twenty-one other theologians in or around Paris who disagreed, and declared it heretical.'

'And you, Meister?' Never had his title sounded less convincing. 'What do you declare it?'

She was trying again, seeking out the colour of his soul. He should have realised this query might arise, this swinging mace of a question.

'Of course, if you confessed and pleaded guilty, you would face only imprisonment.'

'Is this why you have come?'

It wasn't why he'd come. He had come for himself not his Order.

'You have refused to speak with any of your accusers,' he said.

'Why would I speak with those who cannot hear? Would you show stained glass to a blind woman?'

'No doubt they hoped you would speak with me.'

'I won't.'

'I confess they were not sad I was making the journey, your silence makes them uncomfortable.'

'Little people make their own hell.'

'Little but powerful.'

'Little people cannot receive, that is how they are discovered to be little.'

'And that is why you do not speak with them?'

'Hollow people, Meister – their voices too weak to be heard in heaven.'

'And so too weak to be heard by you?'

93

'I might as well listen to the thoughts of straw.'

They sat in silence for a while, Eckhart liking everything about her; but fearing her question, the question evaded twice.

'I simply say we are united to God through love,' she said. 'Is that so bad? That through love we return to our source, become our source and find the presence of God in all things. Do you condemn me for that?'

For the third time, he was asked the question, like the apostle Peter, asked three times if he knew the condemned Christ. What did Eckhart think? Did he condemn her?

'I can only agree,' he said.

'You speak quietly.'

'This is not the cathedral.'

'So you will raise your voice in the cathedral, call them to silence and in a strong voice tell them you agree with Marguerite Porete?'

'Would it help?'

Porete smiled.

'Tonight in your prayers, Johannes, thank God he did not make you a woman – or you might be sitting here with me … and facing the flames tomorrow.'

Eckhart sat in silence. What could he say?

'Instead you will be the Master.'

'I will.'

The title and position were quite rinsed of glory now, in this cell which adjoined the latrine.

'But when they come for you – .'

' I will remember Marguerite Porete.'

'No, remember yourself, Johannes, remember who you are and from what yeast you are brewed, divine yeast.'

And sixteen years on, on a walk of 500 miles from Cologne to Avignon, Eckhart did remember. He had such decisions to make before the papal lair came into view …

94

# Twenty Eight

'And you have no idea who did it?' asked Tamsin.

'I am quite without a clue,' said Neville Brownslie, the mystified theatre administrator; and also a bit of an actor.

They'd finally tracked him down to a small shop off the High Street called *Onslaught Games*. Peter had not seen the likes of it before, a shop dealing in the fantasy of dark forebodings; and games with names like *The Undead Expansion*, *Apocalypse Army* and *The Hordes of Devil Mountain*. Inside, they could see two young men with unkempt hair and large jumpers sitting in religious silence applying paint to plastic models: models of tanks, guns, cohorts of weird aggressors, monster figures, soldiers of Armageddon, coloured with loving care, licked into life with small brushes and careful hands and put up for display in the window, battle lines marching to inter-galactic war.

'What is it with the male species?' asked Tamsin.

'You may not be allowed in, of course,' said Peter.

'Like the Church then.'

'There are differences.'

'Not immediately obvious.'

'No steeple.'

'That's the thing with men.'

'What's the thing with men?'

'Everything comes down to destruction in the end.'

'As opposed to the heroic female virtue of clothes shopping.'

'At least no one gets hurt.'

'But they do get obsessed, which is hurt by a different name.'

'Shall we go in?'

'If the un-dead say it's okay.'

And there, in a dark corner, they found Neville, eyeing up a game called *Destruction Day*.

'My secret pleasure,' he said, covering his surprise at their arrival.

'Not that secret,' said Tamsin. 'The cleaner knew; she knew exactly where you'd be.'

'Fantasy games have been a love of mine since I was eight years old, Detective Inspector, and so *Onslaught Games* is as near as I get to a shrine in Stormhaven.'

'As long as we don't have to take off our shoes.'

'I even have a small investment in this fantasy. You're talking to management, you know.'

'Honoured, I'm sure,' said Tamsin with no hint of honour. 'But I'm afraid it's reality that brings us here.'

'How dull!'

'Sadly there's a lot of it about at the moment – in the world beyond, that is.'

'I think last night, we all had enough reality to last us a lifetime. Shocking, quite shocking – and Neville is not a happy bunny this morning.'

People who spoke of themselves in the third person were an irritant to Tamsin, and a case study to Peter.

'So you seek consolation in the peace and tranquillity of *Destruction Day*.'

'A decidedly cheap shot,' he said. 'Decidedly.' And then he sniffed a dismissive sniff. 'It's a classic.'

'A classic what?'

'The unbeliever must remain for ever stupid,' said Neville. 'For the unbeliever cannot see. Wouldn't you agree, Abbot?'

Tamsin says: 'Can we go somewhere more private?' and it wasn't a question.

'There's a room at the back,' said one of the un-dead, without looking up from the evil tecnotron he was painting.

'My name's Peter,' said Peter.

'Simon,' said Simon. 'And this is Jamie.'

Jamie nodded nervously and Peter smiled at them both … polite young boys.

'Your office?' said Tamsin, once they were wedged into the small store room at the back. It offered boxes of games, a grubby kettle, a jar of instant coffee, some turning milk and a collection of unwashed cups by the sink.

'What about my office?'

He didn't fit here, really he didn't. He didn't fit into this down-at-heel den with his smart green corduroys, V-neck jumper and cravat. And in the single light hanging from the ceiling, shadeless, he looked terrible.

'The break-in.'

'Oh, you've come about that,' he said.

'A little surprised that you didn't mention it to the police,' said the Abbot.

'And what would be the point in that?'

'If nothing else, context.'

'Context?'

It was dismissive.

'The morning after the night before,' said Peter. 'The morning after a murder, the theatre office is broken into. Your office is broken into the morning after the theatre director is murdered ... context.'

'I don't imagine the two are related in any way at all.'

'Was anything taken?' asked Tamsin.

'I couldn't begin to guess.'

'But have you at least tried – guessing?'

'I've tried many things,' said Neville. 'But guessing?'

'You discover your office has been ransacked, talk about it briefly with the cleaner – and then disappear to a fantasy games shop. It seems strange behaviour.'

The office was the administrative hub of the Bell Theatre. Neville's Niche, as it was known, and famously immaculate, not a paper clip out of place on his ever-clear desk. Even the bin was tidy, almost an auxiliary filing system, and the desecration seemed all the worse for this, an attack on order, a further attack, the morning after the murder of Hermione Bysshe-Urquhart.

'I think you'll understand if I didn't want to stay there unduly?'

'The computer is the most obvious casualty,' said Tamsin.

'Love 'em or hate 'em, we sure as hell need 'em!' Neville affected a Wild West drawl.

'I smelt alcohol?' said Peter, standing in the doorway of the store cupboard, because only two could sit.

'Now you mention it,' said Tamsin.

'Oh yes, I smelt it as soon as I walked in,' said Neville, 'As. Soon. As.'

He seemed very definite about this.

'And what did you conclude?' asked Peter.

'What did I conclude?' Neville had to turn slightly to speak with him. 'How very Sherlock! I always rather fancied Watson – the part, I mean.'

'And the answer?'

'Well, backs to the wall and arm twisted, I did wonder about a vagrant,' he said, lighting a cigarette in air that was already stale. 'I mean, one doesn't like to use the term, but really, how else to describe the homeless wasters who squat and pillage along the south coast? It's like the fourteenth-century French all over again!'

'Would the computer be interesting to anyone?' asked Peter.

'It's barely interesting to me! I mean, there's hardly a worn track to the data stored there.'

'But I notice they didn't steal it – they smashed it.'

'Luddites.'

'Our very own destruction day, Neville, which then made me wonder if perhaps it contained information that might be of concern to someone.' The Abbot paused. 'Perhaps you smashed it, for instance, fearing we'd find something?'

'You're saying I smashed it?'

'I wasn't saying you smashed it.'

'Well, what a rude Jude!'

'As I say, I remember a question not an assertion; a question opening with the word, "Perhaps".'

'Because if you were suggesting I smashed it – .'

'Yes?'

'Well, that would be very offensive, Abbot – and perhaps one day we'll find out why you're here, why we have an unqualified Abbot investigating these terrible occurrences at our wonderful theatre? There's my question to you. Not an assertion, just a question! Were there no professionals available?'

Tamsin watched him.

'So what information did it hold?' asked Peter casually.

Neville made a 'this is ridiculous!' gesture.

'Nothing to die for!' he exclaimed. 'Booking information, volunteer shifts – we rely on a lot of volunteers here – Friends of the Bell, people who fundraise for us, absolutely invaluable, couldn't continue without them, that sort of thing. It's hardly National Security material.'

'We'll fingerprint the room, obviously,' said Tamsin, 'and if it was a marauding vagrant, then no doubt some new sets of prints will appear.'

'Unless they wore gloves.'

'Vagrants don't usually wear gloves. And in the meantime, if you could let us know if anything's been taken – when you get back to reality.'

Neville nodded as Tamsin extracted herself from the store cupboard and, led by Peter, walked out of the shop, aching for sunlight and air, past the un-dead with their cold coffee and tiny brushes, and out into the balmy August breeze.

'Why do people make up battles?' said Tamsin.

'Because they can't cope with the real ones. This is a world they have control over.'

'But Neville? I wouldn't have had him down as one of those.'

98

'Oh, I think Neville likes power,' said Peter. 'He likes to be in control, especially when his inner world is collapsing. Then I could imagine him getting very controlling.'

'And his office?'

'I think what I most felt in that room was anger. The one who did this was angry.'

Back inside the shop, Neville remained in the store room, blaming himself; he'd been stupid. But then again, had he really been stupid? He was a risk-taker, always had been, Neville had to take risks to feel alive, to give him the highs amid the lows. Somewhat unwise decisions had been taken along the way – they could appear so to the world. But he had to do it, had to jump into the white water because he had to see, had to know the outcome – and if he didn't risk, he'd never know. Ruinous of course, entirely ruinous, because he'd left people he loved, done things he regretted, chased his own destruction, and why? Because he couldn't be doing with flatlining, living in some ghastly rut, playing it safe, dying safely, he'd had to take risks – just to see what would happen, that was the high! And Paul was a bad idea, but then that made him appealing, the little tart, and Neville was at least alive this morning, very alive.

He'd buy *Destruction Day*.

# Twenty Nine

Tamsin and Peter sat in Hermione's office for the interviews, sur-rounded by thirty years of theatre history on the walls – first nights, last nights, celebrity visits – was that really Prince Charles? Had he been here? Posters of old shows, hilarity in the rehearsal room, it looked a happy place, full of buzz, everyone having the time of their lives, smiling, laughing, hugging and holding ... though all the pho-tos fading slightly, they weren't the newest of shots, better days perhaps, when success was easy and the Bell Theatre had it all.

'I feel a bit dull sitting here,' said Peter. 'Feel as though I should break into song.'

'I think there were only nuns in *The Sound of Music*.'

'We had the video case for that in the desert ... but not the video itself.'

'You mean someone took it?'

'It's possible.'

'One of the monks took it?'

'There wasn't anyone else.'

'And what would they ... oh, I don't want to think about that.'

'It could all have been very innocent.'

'Anyway, at least you've come in costume.'

The Abbot raised his eyebrows.

'It's a monk's habit,' he said.

'Exactly. From the large wardrobe of religious theatre.'

'Working clothes.'

'But not common in the real world, so a little bit stagey, a little bit "Here-I-am-notice-me".'

There was an edge to Tamsin. Well, there was always an edge, but the blade sharper today, slightly desperate. And then the door opened and a trilby hat came in, followed by the thin body of Paul Bent.

'Do sit down, Paul, and thank you for making the time,' said Tamsin.

Paul nodded.

'A shocking event of course,' she added.

Did he find it shocking? He didn't look greatly shocked. A little haunted perhaps, but not shocked.

'First things first,' said Paul.

'Right where they should be.'

'I'm not my father.'

'I'm sorry?'

'So don't expect platitudes of sympathy.'

Tamsin had heard many denials, but never that one; never anyone claiming not to be their father, it seemed uncontroversial. But the Abbot understood, and this was about identity: Paul was the son of Stephen Straight, the Bishop of Lewes, whom both Tamsin and Peter knew. They'd had uncomfortable dealings with him in the past, in the crucified vicar affair. Neither of them had warmed to the man, remembering a rather self-righteous soul, eager for advancement. So perhaps they should be glad the apple had dropped some way from the tree.

'Your change of surname does suggest as much,' said Peter. "A statement", isn't that what they call it?'

Paul got out a pack of cigarettes.

'Do you mind?'

'I think so,' said Tamsin. 'It's a "no smoking" theatre.'

'Health and safety?'

'Something like that.'

Paul smirked.

'So what went wrong last night? Did someone forget to put the sign up?'

It was sneering, an attempt at dark comedy with aspirations to be clever, young man's clever, an arrogant assault on the plod and the monk sitting opposite, tied to their silly little list of dos and don'ts … instead of stopping real crime.

'Health and safety are always important,' said Peter. 'I'm for both, generally.'

'Bit late for your benedictions.'

'Really?'

'Hermione's new office is the morgue, if you hadn't noticed. And none of these fading pictures of lost luvvies to comfort her.'

'Perhaps where she is, she doesn't need comfort,' said Peter.

'And after the sermon, how about a hymn?' said Paul.

Tamsin couldn't help but smile. Not a believer herself – or rather, a believer in science rather than God, in chance rather than creation – she enjoyed seeing religious planes shot down. But the Abbot was remembering, thinking again of the body on the stage, gazing skywards above a broken vertebrae. The scissor in the neck had seemed almost incidental.

'The chaos needs holding back, Paul.'

'Or mere anarchy is loosed upon the world?'

The boy seemed eager to impress.

Peter thinks: 'You're looking for a father and a mother. But God help any applicants who let you down.'

Peter says: 'So you chose a different name, Paul?'

He'd decided to calm the intoxicated exchange. The initial sparring had only brief interest and it was time to travel on.

'So what?'

'Nothing.'

'Writers often change their names.'

'But Paul Bent?'

'What of it?'

'The opposite of "straight" – a name that took you rather publicly away from your parentage.'

'Maybe.'

'Like Van Gogh signing his pictures with just "Vincent". He never used the family name, Van Gogh.'

'I can understand that.'

'He had religious parents as well.'

'It's as natural as leaving home.'

'What is?' asked Tamsin.

'Changing your name. It's another way of being free.'

'And are you free?'

He didn't reply.

'You wrote *Mother's Day*? said Tamsin, failing to sound neutral. Paul nodded.

'So what's it about?'

'I thought you'd seen it.'

'Only the first half,' said Peter. 'So we're thirsty for resolution.'

'It's an exploration of what we mean by "family values",' said Paul.

Tamsin: 'And that's what theatre's for, is it?'

'Theatre's for anything we want it to be for.'

'It seems, from what I saw, that you don't value them very much.'

'What?'

'Family values.'

Paul laughed.

'There's no such thing.'

'Really?'

Now Paul shook his head.

102

'There's just a lot of families all living out different values – and most of them are sick. Terrible things are done beneath the banner of love.'

'Some families better than others, surely?'

'Politicians and the Church, they make me laugh.' The Abbot noticed that Paul wasn't laughing, that he was just very angry. In England, you say 'It makes me laugh' when you're angry, this is how the English proceed. Paul continued: 'They speak as though family values are somehow good – but it depends which family. Some families are concentration camps.'

'Oh, don't be ridiculous!' said Tamsin.

It just came out and surprised Peter. His niece rarely showed hysterical reaction in interview.

'Have I hit a nerve?' asked Paul.

Tamsin was silent … he had hit a nerve.

'And have you any idea who might have wanted Hermione dead?' asked Peter, improvising. It was a borrowed question, and meaningless, he knew that as it passed from his brain across his tongue and out of his mouth.

'It's not really something you go around wondering,' said Paul.

'Not before a murder, no,' said the Abbot reassuringly. 'But I suppose afterwards, after the event, it might make you think, perhaps? Might make you look around and wonder.'

'I'm an outsider here.'

'An outsider?'

Paul nodded.

'How's that?'

'I have no history here, these are not my people.'

Odd phrase, thought Peter.

'Who are your people?'

'Writers don't have people. They don't relate, they record.'

Tamsin was still absent, present but absent, and so Peter had to field this pomposity.

'I understand – even if I may not agree.'

'You're not a writer, so how would you know?'

'Fair point. I just feel you may be doing yourself a disservice, that's all. I mean, to the untutored eye like mine, you seem to get on with everyone.'

'It's my writing that is here, not me.'

Peter allowed this nonsense to pass through him.

'And the two are different?'

Paul is getting impatient.

'Look, I merely entered my play in their little competition. It won and so I've been in on a few rehearsals – but it's not like I'm part of

103

the scenery. I'm not a Friend of the theatre, or making marmalade to sell on its behalf. Who knows who killed Hermione – and frankly, who cares?'

'You don't?'

'Why would I? I don't have to wail and I don't have to care, because I don't have a public image to maintain.'

'You didn't like her?'

'I had nothing against her at all. She was always very decent to me. It doesn't mean I care.'

He wouldn't be mentioning their final conversation about axing the play. It would only get plod excited for all the wrong reasons.

'So you didn't kill her, you have no reason to kill her … and you have no idea who did kill her?'

'No, no and no.'

Peter seemed to have reached a dead end. What now? 'So where were you during the half-time interval when the murder took place?'

'I was having a smoke out the back.'

'Alone?'

'Alone.'

It didn't feel enough.

'If I'd known I'd need an alibi, I'd have invited two police officers and the Dalai Lama to join me.'

'You must tell us about the concentration camp,' said Tamsin, returning to the interview.

Paul looked at her sharply. She was staring straight at him.

'Why would I do that?'

'Sounds interesting.'

'Interesting?'

This was said with so much disgust Tamsin looked away.

'You've been very helpful,' said Peter, aware of distress at his side. 'We may need to speak to you again, obviously, but that's enough for now.'

Paul looked at Tamsin: 'I don't think it's my concentration camp you need worry about,' he said, as he picked up his trilby and prepared to leave. 'I know a fellow inmate when I see one.'

'Are you all right?' asked Peter, once he'd left and closed the door.

'Why wouldn't I be all right?' said Tamsin, who was breathing with difficulty.

'You disappeared.'

'I didn't disappear.'

'You did.'

'I just thought I'd give you a go … you need the practice.'

'Not true.'

'Quite true.'

'You disappeared … he wounded you. I haven't seen that before.'

'He wounded me? That's a joke!'

'But the comedy's passing me by. He's a damaged boy.'

'No, he's just a bad writer.'

'And as he says, he knows a fellow inmate when he sees one. Who could he be talking about?'

# Thirty

'Twenty years at the theatre, Janet?'

'Twenty years next weekend, I believe.'

'Having a party?'

'Not really the thing to do in the circumstances.'

'Oh?'

'The murder.'

'Ah.'

With murder so routine, so every day, Tamsin sometimes forgot it could be a shock for others. Not that Janet looked shocked.

'But you must have some stories to tell about this place,' said Tamsin, playfully attempting to relax the slightly stiff figure sitting in front of them; and it seemed to work.

'My lips are sealed,' she said with a mysterious smile. Janet liked knowing things that others didn't know, as long as the others knew that she knew. It gave her status, a sine qua none, made her a little enigmatic and Janet wished to be enigmatic, someone not easily grasped. She wished to be an enigma to people, a woman of some mystery. She was bored of the old Janet.

'And I don't suppose you miss much at the doctor's surgery,' said Tamsin, continuing the casual flattery.

Janet raised her eyebrows in surprise, searching for a reaction inside and locking her jaw, a habit of hers when faced by the unexpected; and this was unexpected, she hadn't expected this, hadn't expected to be asked about the surgery, that was different, she'd need to prepare a response. And it was hardly the matter in hand, given the terrible murder in the theatre last night.

'I didn't realise you wished to speak of the surgery,' she said, gathering herself.

'I don't particularly,' said Tamsin airily. She liked to jerk people around in interviews, force them to shift ground, away from their safe haunts, make them unsure of the next question, the next angle, distract them from their chosen path, their prepared path, encourage slip-ups and unedited reaction – particularly in Janet, who was a wary editor of every word, careful in every way about how she appeared.

'I miss nothing at the doctor's surgery,' she announced with some deliberation; but, all in all, happy to release this information. 'You can ask Dr Elsdon. I think he'll tell you that I don't miss very much.'

Was she in love with Dr Elsdon? She seemed strangely deferential.

'And likewise here?'

'I beg your pardon?'

'I suppose you see everything here as well.'

'Enough to make a virtue out of discretion,' said Janet.

More self-importance and a good start. Let Janet feel magisterial rather than a suspect, make her feel different, a keen observer of human frailty, a police helper and confidant, a psychologist of some perspicacity ... if Stormhaven knew what such a thing was.

'So if Janet blew the whistle on the Bell, a lot of people might be frightened, I'd imagine?'

'I have no time for whistle-blowers.'

A decisive reaction, and a sudden change of gear.

'You don't?'

'If you don't want to be involved in the organisation, you shouldn't join in the first place.' Janet readjusted her neat skirt, pulled back her shoulders and straightened her back. Posture seemed important as she added: 'Leave the company and then tell all – is that any way to behave? I wouldn't do that to Dr Elsdon.'

'You'd keep your mouth shut if you found malpractice?'

'I would at least handle it in an appropriate and respectful manner.'

A sprint start to the interview had run into a little sand, but no harm done.

'Do the rules change if there's been a murder?' asked the Abbot.

Janet sniffed.

'One must be cautious with blame,' she said.

How carefully she chose her words.

'What do you mean by that?'

'I would have thought it was fairly obvious, Abbot.'

Tamsin intervened: 'Then humour the elderly man in the habit and explain to me.'

Tamsin wanted her onside.

Janet sniffed again.'I'm merely saying that blame is not a productive pastime.'

'Is someone blaming you for the murder?'

'No one's blaming me for anything – not that I'm aware!'

Sudden panic; the exoskeleton of controlled reserve cracked for a moment.

'As if I would be blamed!' she exclaimed. 'And why are we even talking about it?'

Peter and Tamsin kept a pause, slightly shocked at the passion on display.

'It was you who raised the subject,' said Peter, quietly. 'You said we must be cautious with blame, so we're just following your lead, which feels important. You've taken us down an interesting path, Janet, and we're grateful for that.'

Janet looked down, the door now closed on the issue of blame.

'My brother was a policeman,' she said.

'Oh?'

'Yes.'

'Did he enjoy it?'

'I think he enjoyed it.' But there was nothing more to come on that subject.

'So where were you as the curtain opened for the second half?' said Tamsin.

Fresh line of enquiry, no mention of blame.

'I'd checked with Margery and Millicent.'

'What were you checking?'

'Their costumes.'

What else would she have been checking?

Tamsin nodded.

'There can be issues after the first act,' said Janet. 'A rip, a lost button, Margery is hardly the thinnest performer – though it's the fight scene in the second act that tends to cause the problems.'

'There's a fight scene in the second act – between the two women?'

Janet was surprised at Tamsin's lack of knowledge. You might have thought the detective would know about the fight scene.

'You haven't seen the play?'

Tamsin soured. Why would she have seen the play? She was a police officer not a bloody theatre critic.

'We've seen the first half – and then a murder interrupted things.'

Janet's face suggested incompetence rather than murder to be the problem.

'It's ridiculous, of course,' said Janet, brushing a non-existent crumb from her skirt.

'What is?'

'The play.'

'In what way?'

108

'How there could ever be a fight between mother and daughter is beyond me.'

'I see.'

'As if that happens in real families … but that's modern drama for you.'

'A son kills his father in *Oedipus,*' observed Peter.

'As I say, modern drama running out of ideas.'

'It's a Greek tragedy by Sophocles, first performed 429 BC.'

Janet was not to be knocked from her path.

'That doesn't make it any less ridiculous. There's a lot of old nonsense as well as new.'

'But their costumes were okay?' asked Tamsin, shifting the conversation back a little.

'Whose?'

'Margery and Millicent's? How were they when you checked them?'

'They were fine, yes.'

'So what then?'

'I told them to leave their clothes in the costume room at the end, folded neatly, they can be rather slap-dash, Margery in particular – just throws them down sometimes – and I was just returning there myself – .'

'Where?'

'To the costume room, to get my car keys, when I heard noises from the stage.'

'Why were you getting the car keys?'

'I was going home.'

'You were going home?'

'It's what people do at the end of the day.'

'But the day hadn't ended surely?'

'My day had. I don't always stay.'

'No.'

'There's little to be done if something rips during the second act. I can hardly walk on stage and sew it up for them!'

'No.'

'Any accidents in the second half and that's up to them … they can improvise. Isn't that what actors are supposed to do?'

'It is.'

'And really – and one doesn't wish to be critical – the further I am from that play, the better.'

Agreed.

'So you were off,' said Tamsin.

'Yes.'

'You didn't fancy staying – not even for the theatre's thirtieth anniversary celebrations?'

'The theatre's celebrations are not necessarily mine.'

'Though you celebrate twenty years here next weekend.'

'I do have another life.'

And Tamsin could believe that, though what it might be, she had no idea at all.

'And of course the scissors used in the assault were your scissors.'

'My scissors?'

'Your scissors and found sitting in your drawer, wiped but not entirely clean. Did you not think we'd look there?'

# Thirty One

✣

## *1327, from Cologne to Avignon*

*The substance of the matter was this: there'd been a hole in Eckhart ever since he'd met Marguerite Porete. There'd been a hole ever since he'd left her cell by the latrines, not the Dominicans' finest hour – and a sense in Eckhart of something unfulfilled. A hollowness certainly, but it was the nature of the hollow that eluded him.*

*It could be darkness or it could be light ... and how hard to know the difference. Was it a sense of guilt, a sense of deep-felt shame that he had not tied himself to the stake that day in solidarity with Marguerite? He could have insisted, and what would they have done then? So was this simply shame at his cowardice? Or was it something different, something more honourable, was this hollow within a holy space, space inspired by her courage, a cell of God's presence placed within him, free from the world's crowding concerns? Had Marguerite placed in him the liberating gift of space – a liberation that brought him now to his own hour of reckoning?*

*Guilty hole or liberating space? To declare it a hole made it something lost, a regret, a fracture unhealed; while to call it space described something wondering, spontaneous and free. So was this heaven or hell, hope or despair?*

*'We need to talk,' said Henricus de Cigno, who was enjoying their brief sojourn in a monastery. Less rats, more meat, more beer ... and more prayer, of course. One mustn't forget the prayer, prayer to the almighty for the right outcomes, for the protection of the Dominican name in Europe, and for papal exoneration – the only sort that counted – from any false accusations made against the Order. Oh, and prayer for Eckhart, especially if the Inquisition got their hands on him,*

111

*though really you're beyond prayer then, when the burning and the breaking starts, way beyond prayer ... that's not something to be said publicly, of course, or even thought. But you had to be realistic and Henricus was nothing if not realistic. Prayer had its limits.*

*Tomorrow, they would resume their journey to Avignon, more intolerable walking, but first they needed talk and he said this to Eckhart.*

*'We need to talk, Eckhart,' he said.*

*'And what will we talk about?'*

*Eckhart sensed a storm cloud in the air.*

# Thirty Two

'You're entering another world,' said Bill Cain, settling into the interview with the rude health of the sailing fanatic he was. Mid-fifties and a strawberry blonde ... not his description, of course, not masculine enough: what sort of a man is strawberry blonde? That's for the ladies. But a force of nature in the boardroom for many years.

'Luvvies, eh?' he said.

'You don't like them, Mr Cain?'

Tamsin liked the formality of that particular appellation, damning with indifference ... but Mr Cain didn't notice.

'I don't know what the collective noun is for a group of actors,' he said, 'but it should be an ego – an ego of actors!' He was used to people laughing at his jokes. 'Only interested in their reviews, that lot!'

Tamsin had taken an instant dislike to Bill Cain and it showed, because dislike always shows. How can it not show? He was much too like her father, which wasn't a good start.

'So you're the Financial Director of the Bell Theatre?'

'You know the story about John Gielgud, I suppose?' said Cain, ignoring her.

He leant forward, he was confiding, taking them into his confidence, pulling them aside with easy charm, before nailing the deal.

'Does he work here?' said Tamsin.

'Famous English actor,' said Peter.

'That's right, Abbot, keep the young ones up to speed.'

'It's more about struggling to be interested,' said Tamsin.

Mock shock on the face of Cain.

'Feisty! I like it.'

'Not a concern of mine,' said Tamsin, quietly.

'And John Gielgud?' asked Peter, guiding the businessman back on track.

'Married to the actress Peggy Ashcroft, right? Not sexist. They were called actresses in those days. And before that they were called whores!'

The Abbot smiled politely.

'You were telling us about Peggy Ashcroft.'

'Famous as well,' said Cain, 'very famous she was, Peggy Ashcroft, nearly as famous as her husband John, John Gielgud, and it's at the end of the war, the day after the bombing of Hiroshima.'

This sounded like another drinks party anecdote – but, love him or loathe him, he was a good raconteur.

'So it's the worst bloody day in the history of the world and all that, Gielgud arrives back at his theatre, holding the morning papers, right?'

'Right.'

'Shocking photos obviously, dead bodies all over Japan or wherever it was, world in trauma and he's looking troubled. So his friend asks what's the matter?

'Terrible news,' says Gielgud. 'Peggy's got the most frightful reviews.'

Bill Cain laughs for all of them, and Peter tries.

'Funnier than your talk on the Ancient Egyptians, Abbot,' says Cain.

'I didn't know you were a member of the W.I.'

'Sent the missus, didn't I? Getting on my nerves, she was, thought it would do her good. But she said she was asleep within five minutes of you starting.'

Abbot Peter did remember a couple of comatose figures, but Tamsin moved swiftly on. No one intimidates Tamsin, not even a boardroom brute, though he could try, and if he did try it would be war.

Tamsin: 'So if you hate them all, Mr Cain, as clearly you do, all these awful luvvies – when you're so wonderful, of course – what are you doing here?'

'What am I doing here?'

'That was the question.'

'Doing them all a bloody favour,' he said, sobering up. 'Have you seen the accounts?'

'Not yet. Are they interesting?'

'Make Hiroshima look like a small accident in the kitchen.'

He wanted more of a response than he got.

'And so you're their saviour, their financial messiah?'

Cain sensed the snide overtones.

'I know how to move a business from red to black, darling, from debt to profit. I don't know what your clean-up rate is, but mine's

114

very good … and yes, pretty profitable, can't complain, scrape a living. It's what I do. I may smash a few eggs, break a few hearts along the way – but I make a profit. I sort things, I solve things.'

'Oh, I solve things too, Mr Cain.'

'I'm sure you do, love.'

Mistake.

'And I'll find the murderer of Hermione.'

'I'll watch with interest.'

'Yes, do Mr Cain, because if it was you, I'll find you.'

'Steady on, my girl!'

'I'm not your girl.'

The Abbot noted the awfulness between them, a car crash in slow-motion.

'So where were you when Hermione was murdered?' Tamsin was circling again. 'Unless you were the one standing behind her, of course.'

Just then, the bell rang out, shattering conversation. It was three in the afternoon, and the large tenor bell sounded across Storm-haven's warm summer air, calling no one to prayer but maybe some to tea. The bell had always rung at this time and always would, so long as the last bell-ringer lived. It was there in the contract, as long as Boy lived – and Boy showed no sign of dying.

But then there are some corners you just can't see round.

# *Act Three*

*Unless the theatre can ennoble you, make you a better person, you should flee from it.*

**Constantin Stanislavski**

# Thirty Three

❖

'The trial has begun early, I see.'

'This is not a trial.'

Meister Eckhart looked up into the blue sky of Southern France.

'You will say it's an act of clarification, no doubt.'

'It is precisely that,' said Henricus, 'an act of clarification, very good.'

'It is an act of betrayal, my friend ... grievous betrayal.'

They had finally got round to the talk that Henricus thought necessary back at the monastery. He'd postponed it, of course, and then postponed again – he was called St Postponement when he wasn't in the room. But with Avignon close, he was wrenched from procrastination by the force of papal proximity. Eckhart, of course, was misunderstanding him entirely, this was the view of Henricus, just as he feared he would, and the reason he'd postponed the conversation. The Meister didn't like scrutiny from his own Order, and who does, no one likes it. But – well, the Dominicans had to get along with the Pope, had to show willing in the heresy stakes – unfortunate word in the circumstances, but it was the sensible way, Eckhart must see that? They had to be seen to be keeping order, had to show the Pope they were as zealous as the next inquisitor. Especially as the pontiff had the damn Franciscans bending his blessed ear night and day ... and it was well known the Franciscans hated the Dominicans. This was not quite the original vision of their order, but there we are: who has ever stayed true to their original vision?

And of course living proof of this Franciscan hate was the garrulous, alcoholic Archbishop of Cologne, Henry of Virneburg, a great hater of Dominicans – and bitterly keen that the Pope name Meister Eckhart for the blasphemer he so clearly was. In Dominican circles, *the garrulous, alcoholic Archbishop of Cologne was known as 'the Fishwife'.*

'It's just that, well— it is difficult, shall we say?'

'What is difficult?'

'Not for all, Johannes, I'm sure … but for some at least.'

'What are you trying to say?'

'That it's difficult, some might find it so, to see the difference between what you say and what the Porete woman said.'

'The Porete woman?'

'Yes.'

'You mean Marguerite Porete.'

'Quite.'

'Would you wish to be called 'the de Cigno man'?

*Henricus smiled. That was hardly going to happen.*

'And think of the implications of what you say,' said Henricus.

'Which particular implications?'

*This needed sorting out before they reached Avignon.*

'Well, a soul so united with God, a soul annihilated by the divine to the constraints of this world – which you and Porete both agree about – a soul so intimately sourced by and unified with the Godhead … well!*

'Well what?'

*Eckhart was struggling to see the problem. He could discern the glory, but not the concern.*

'It's as if we have no parent but God!'

*Eckhart wondered if he was missing something.*

'It would seem so, yes.'

*What else was there to say?*

'So tell me – .'

*He seemed to be stalling.*

'Say whatever you have to say, Henricus.'

'Well, what about the fourth commandment!'

*So that was his problem.*

'Remind me of it,' said Eckhart gently.

'The honouring of our parents! What happens to that commandment, I wonder!'

'Wonder is a good word in the circumstances. We must indeed wonder.'

'It will not be a good word with the Inquisition.'

'Which word?'

'Wonder. They don't like wonder. They like doctrine nailed down and fixed.'

'Almost crucified, you might say.'

'Don't say that to them either!'

*Henricus' eyes bulged with fear.*

*'And stay away from wonder.'*

*'I do not seek their advice when it comes to vocabulary, Henricus.'*

*'Then perhaps you should ... perhaps it would be a good idea, perhaps it would save your hide!'*

*And as they arrived at the top of the hill, there it was – Avignon.*

*At last they had reached it, papal residence since 1309, snug on the winding River Rhone. They called it Windy Avignon, scoured by the dry Mistral wind. Its city walls were weak, this was well known, and clear enough even from this distance. But also clear were the huge walls, eighteen feet thick they'd heard, that surrounded the papal palace itself – no turning of the other cheek here, nothing as stupid as that. And around the palace – and this became more apparent as the two Dominicans approached – such busyness and intent, like ants at work. For where popes settled, much else followed. Where popes settled, bankers piled money, money-changers eased exchange, caterers found remuneration, wine merchants drank to their profits and artists queued to offer immortality in paint.*

*Frescoes and finance, Avignon had flourished under the Romans, flourished again now and was not without beauty from a distance, this is what Eckhart thought as he gazed upon it – beautiful like a cluster of poppies hiding a snake.*

*He'd made it to Avignon. But would he ever leave?*

# Thirty Four

The interviews with the two actors, Margery Tatters and Millicent Pym, did not carry the case forward a great deal. Margery had been more animated about the death of professional theatre than the death of Hermione.

'The amateur theatre community devalues the art form,' she declared angrily. 'It damages the industry.'

Tamsin had cheekily asked her about the pain of performing with an amateur and discovered strong views, expressed in a posh voice that belied Margery's small-town, small-home roots. It was a voice she'd acquired, so she was always acting, that's the way it had to be, it was a posh profession. There were only so many parts for cockneys.

'How?' asked Peter, who'd never imagined amateur theatre to be harmful, and didn't mind if the interview wandered a little. Sometimes the crooked mile was the more instructive walk.

'How?' Margery was irritated by the very question. 'Through the promotion of unskilled performers, directors and crew, that's how; through the relentless lowering of standards – enjoyable for the family and friends of performers but not for anyone else. And that's all the Bell's good for now. Wasn't always the case, not when Nicholas was alive, but that's how it is now, good for nothing but family and friends. And children's parties!'

Strong feelings.

'But you're one of the performers,' said Tamsin. 'And you're a professional.'

'I'm an exception.'

'The jewel in their crown?' said Peter, smiling. Margery needed some affirmation.

'I suppose so,' she said with a pride, which annoyed Tamsin. As though Margery were some sort of queen, some sort of diva – when she was only famous for *Holby,* if famous was the word, a drama in which she played herself. And frankly, how difficult is that? Tamsin played herself every day – and did a proper job at the same time. But Margery was enjoying being the queen.

'It's a parasite.'

'What is?'

'Amateur theatre – it steals the audience from high-quality, professional theatre.'

'Really?'

'Ask any pro and they'll say the same.'

'That's your experience?'

'My drama teacher called it an institution that exists in order to give significance to "amateur dramatics".'

'Harsh.'

'A frivolous kind of amusement with no pretention to art, and more often than not' – and was her voice getting progressively posher? – 'nothing more than a show case for the dubious talents of the most popular or politically astute members of the group.'

It sounded like an audition piece, disdain dripping from every word and perhaps her best performance to date, because it wasn't Margery, not Margery at all, not small-town Margery, not Margery the survivor in a world where she was always second best, always fighting to survive. It was posh Margery, actor Margery, bitter dismissive Margery.

'Yet still you agree to appear here,' said Tamsin calmly.

'Oh, well, I have roots in this place,' said Margery, deflated and less posh now. She had poisoned roots here, thought Peter, roots still hurting the plant. 'My mother lives here, so I like to help out.'

Convincing?

'And I suppose now the TV work has dried up – .'

Tamsin left it there – but then you can if you've just shot someone. Peter stepped into the vacuum:

'And of course you can pass on your wisdom to the amateurs,' he said. 'Is Millicent a willing learner?'

Such an innocent question.

'Who knows what Millicent learns?' said Margery. 'Or how she was cast in the role in the first place – you can ask Timothy about that.'

'Well, I'm sure we will – but what are your thoughts?'

'I have no comment to make at all.'

'Okay.'

'But, well, you only have to use your eyes.'

'What are you saying?'

'I'm saying nothing; as I say, not my place – but if she got the part for her acting ability, then I'm Robert de Niro.'

'You think there's something there, something between them?'

123

'It would hardly be the first casting decision influenced by pecker pilot,' said Margery. 'The casting couch is not exclusive to Hollywood.'

Margery had not personally benefited from the casting couch, Tamsin sensed that. She'd had to fight for everything. But she then spoke of respect for Hermione, that's what she said, and yes, was glad of the work at the Bell Theatre, some said it was a step down, but acting was not a steady career, one had to adjust and take the hit of the endless failed auditions.

'That's life,' she said bleakly, but added that she'd been nowhere near the stage when Hermione was killed. She'd been alone in her dressing room.

'Millicent wasn't there?'

No, said Margery, she wasn't there, but Margery wasn't sure where she was, could have been the toilet, could have been in 'performance discussions' with Timothy. It wasn't unusual for her and Millicent to be apart at the break, they didn't generally converse at half-time, it wasn't that sort of a relationship, they weren't friends … at which point Tamsin couldn't help looking at the Abbot in brief triumph.

'So there isn't much acting going on out there?' said Tamsin.

'How d'you mean?'

'The curtain opens on two women at war – and that's how it is when the curtain closes as well.'

'There's no war between Millicent and me.'

'It feels that way.'

'We bump along, one or two collisions, but it's hardly a war.'

'We heard you had a real fight in rehearsal.'

A worried look in Margery's eyes, fleeting, before control is resumed:

'It was nothing.'

'Do you often fight about nothing?'

'A line drawn in the sand.'

'You attacked her?'

'There has to be respect.'

'Does she not respect you?'

There was a pause.

'No damage done,' said Margery, 'just a line in the sand.'

The line in the sand again.

'Rehearsals can be like this,' she said, the experienced professional again. 'They can be rough, nature of the beast; it's an unformed time, a time for exploration, for knocking off the rough edges.'

'But not a time for assault.'

124

Margery looked at Tamsin.

'There are many ways to assault someone,' she said. 'And the worst ways are not physical.'

Margery is suddenly close to tears:

'And she's always got Timothy to run to, hasn't she? It's not like she's alone.'

Whereas you are, thinks Peter. He offers her one of Hermione's tissues but she waves the offer away, wiping her eyes with her forearm, which isn't so posh. But there's another matter to deal with and Peter chooses this moment:

'And everything was healed between you and Hermione, it seems.'

Margery looks blank.

'I'm told she pipped you to a West End lead in your youth,' he continues.

No reaction.

'Which can't have been easy, especially when young and hopeful. It's difficult when we don't get what we long for, when dreams die.'

'It's life.'

Peter nods.

'I suppose it's about how we respond,' he says, 'what resources we have to recover.'

'You do what you have to do.'

Margery was keeping it simple, no fancy psychology, no time for that, just survival.

'But the experience set you on a downward path for a while?' says Peter gently. 'That's what I heard.'

He allows the pause, no pressure, no need. Margery looks blank again, nothing to say on the matter.

'You don't want to speak about that?'

Margery doesn't.

'Is there a reason?'

Margery sits quietly.

'And so in time, you put that behind you,' continues Peter. 'Perhaps you forgave her – or at least did whatever you needed to do ...'

Peter sees the grudge lodged in her painful body.

'Forty-seven episodes of *Holby* is a great aid to forgiveness,' says posh Margery, with a smile that doesn't quite reach her eyes ...

# Thirty Five

'It wasn't a job I was going to turn down!' said Millicent emphatically. It was a ridiculous idea that she'd turn the part down.

'I can understand,' said Peter.

'It's a good part – and chances like this don't come along so often, believe me.'

'I do believe you.'

And then Tamsin picked up the baton, like some drama student told to play 'interested'.

'So how does it work, Millicent? I need you to tell me.'

Even Peter was fooled.

'How does what work?'

'Getting parts in plays! Fascinating to hear how it actually happens. Never been into amateur dramatics myself – always found the jealousy levels dangerously high, but – .'

'Higher than in the police?' said Millicent drily.

'It's a fair cop,' said Tamsin, smiling. She didn't wish to battle with this young woman, there was a youthful innocence about her – though scarcely a youth in age. Early thirties, Tamsin was thinking. But somehow for ever young, that's how Millicent appeared. She'd keep that youth as the years passed by and Tamsin was briefly envious.

'So tell us how it happens, Millicent?'

'It's not complicated – it's like any other job.'

'Hardly!'

Acting was not like any other job. Apart from anything else, it's quite without purpose, this is what Tamsin is thinking, but she carries on playing interested:

'I mean, is Timothy on the phone saying, "Millicent, I've got this great new play called *Mother's Day*, it's a two-hander, and I think you'd be perfect for one of the parts"? Is that how it goes? And if it did go like that, how did he know where to find you? No offence, but it's not like you're famous.'

'Something like that, yes.'

'Something like what? He rang you up?'

'I had to audition of course.'

'So he didn't just say the part's yours if you want it, Millicent? Is that what he calls you?'

Pause.

'He calls me Milly … now.'

'So he didn't just say "Milly, the part's in the bag – but just for form, come along and do an audition"? He didn't say that? Do directors sometimes do that? Must be tempting if there's a bit of a thing between them and the actor.'

Another slight pause.

'No.'

'So it was a cold call?'

'Yes.'

'But he called you Milly.'

'He calls me Milly now. Some people are like that. Timmy's a very informal type of guy. I like that, he's not up himself.'

Abbot Peter raised a quizzical eyebrow at Tamsin … this was not a desert saying.

'He'd got your number from some local theatre group, presumably,' said Tamsin.

'I think he'd seen me in something.'

'Did he say what?'

'I don't remember.'

'I think I'd remember if a top director had seen me in something and liked it.'

'Then perhaps you're more ambitious than I am.'

'Everyone's ambitious, Millicent.' It was almost said as a threat. 'Some just hide it better.'

'Maybe everyone's ambitious for different things.'

Tamsin considered this, before moving on.

'But he did his research, didn't he? Timothy Gershwin, I mean. Dragged himself away from the murders in Midsomer, trawled church hall productions in the Stormhaven area – I'm impressed!'

Tamsin wasn't in the least impressed; she didn't believe any of this, not for a moment.

'And the audition process?' she continued. 'That must be fascinating.'

'It's okay. I quite like auditions, they're a bit scary but okay.'

'Having to sell yourself.'

'I'm not a prostitute.'

'I wasn't saying you were. Is that what others have called you?'

'No.'

'So what happens at the audition?' said Peter, stepping in.

'Well, you deliver prepared material.'

'What did you prepare for this one?'

'I read some Pinter.'

'I'm sorry?' said Tamsin.

'He's a playwright,' said the Abbot, 'famous for his flat dialogue.'

He warmed to the absence of anything happening in Pinter's plays which he'd read in the desert, before retiring to bed.

'And you can make a living out of flat dialogue, can you?' said Tamsin.

'If it's good flat dialogue.'

'Sounds like someone trying to sell bad breath to me.'

'You don't understand,' said Millicent.

'Really?'

Millicent shrugged her shoulders, which irritated Tamsin – more irritation, she was definitely getting too irritated on this investigation, Peter had noticed, and she was almost aware of it herself.

'Then explain yourself, explain what you mean,' said Tamsin. 'Convert me to the wonders of a dull play with flat dialogue, because at the moment I'm struggling.'

'Sometimes in plays or novels, the dialogue moves the story on.'

'One can but hope.'

'But that isn't really the purpose with Pinter, or not the external story anyway, it moves it inside, moves the story inside, inside the characters. It's only on the surface that nothing is happening.'

Peter would not have reckoned Millicent a Pinter girl, but she spoke on the matter with as much passion as she knew.

'Where were we?' said Tamsin, seeking movement, like a ship becalmed.

'Learning about Millicent's audition,' said Peter.

'And was that it?' asked Tamsin.

'I read Pinter because he's a very clever writer.'

'So you say.'

'And then some lines from the play itself.'

'From the meisterwork, *Mother's Day*?'

'Yes. And there's no need to be sarcastic about it.'

'And is Paul a clever writer?' asked Peter.

'I think he is, yes. He reminds me of Pinter in a way. I mean, nothing much happens in *Mother's Day*.'

'That was certainly my feeling,' said Tamsin.

'And then after the audition?' said Peter quickly. His colleague was proving graceless, which in turn made her stupid.

'Well, then you go home and wait by the phone, wondering if you'll get a call-back.'

'Nerve-wracking, I'd imagine,' he said.

'Yes, it is. I mean, some actors pretend they don't sit by the phone, pretend they just get on with life – but I don't believe them.'

'You sit by the phone.'

'Of course.'

'Perhaps one day you'll have the money to pay an agent to sit by the phone for you.'

'Maybe. But then I'd just be sitting by the phone waiting for their call. It wouldn't change much.'

'No,' said Peter smiling at this succinct dismantling of success.

'Timothy must have been impressed with you, though,' said Tamsin.

'I suppose so.'

'He'd obviously watched you closely in some production – we're not sure which – and then decided he must ring you.'

It was an absurd idea, but Tamsin proposed it as something entirely reasonable.

'Like I said, I think he'd seen me in something. Or heard good things.'

Vague. Millicent was a little flustered.

'A call-back means they want another look?' said the Abbot.

'Usually, yes – with perhaps two or three others.'

'So you met your rivals for the role?'

'Er, no, they must have been there at different times. It does happen. I'm sure there were a lot, though; a lot of people would want this part.'

'I'm sure a lot of people did,' said Tamsin. 'But it was you who got it.'

'I did, yes.'

'Timothy must definitely have liked you.'

Millicent blushed … it was hardly subtle from the detective inspector.

'I mean, he must have liked your portrayal of the character,' she followed up.

'He must have done, yes – or I wouldn't be sitting here now, would I?'

'And he must have liked you more than Hermione liked you.'

'Why do you say that?'

Millicent was suddenly defensive.

'Well, didn't she slap you in the face five minutes before she died?'

'Hardly!'

'We were told she did.'

'Who by?'

It was something Paul had let slip.

'We're told you had a little tiff in her office during the interval ... and that it ended in a stinging slap.'

'You don't want to believe everything you hear.'

'I don't believe anything I hear. That's why I'm checking up. Did something happen between you and Hermione minutes before she died?'

Millicent looks like a traveller at a crossroads, who doesn't know which way to go.

Tamsin speaks: 'I'll take your silence as confirmation that Hermione did indeed slap you five minutes before she was murdered.'

# Thirty Six

✤

## *Avignon, 1327*

*The question for Eckhart was simple: 'Guilty' or 'Not guilty'? Just how was he to describe himself?*

*The court would make its own decision, without reference to his. But his plea would set the tone, lay down a marker in his own heart. Eckhart gazed upon the papal court, as grand as one might have imagined, had one imagined ornate pillars, frescoed walls, tense faces and costumes dripping with gold. But more pressing than stressed magnificence was the need for a decision: guilty or not guilty?*

*The issue had been temporarily postponed, pushed down the agenda, while the court discussed the Church's divine calling to burn people. It hadn't been on the original agenda, not as a discussion point. After all, what was there to discuss when the answer was so plain? Where was the controversy? But when Eckhart foolishly suggested that roasting people in flames lacked the quality of love, it became necessary to allocate some court time to putting the heretic firmly in his place.*

*The prosecution focused on the merciful aspects of burning, on the merciful intent behind roasting people. This is how it must be seen, they said, a sweet mercy: 'A mercy as large as the stone in the papal ring!' That raised some smiles, aided by Pope John playing along and raising his ringed hand aloft: the mercy of God was clearly very large. And as the Archbishop of Cologne then kindly explained, and surely everyone knew this, in feeling the flames – as fine a foretaste of hell as could be imagined – while retaining their mental faculties, the condemned were magnanimously granted one last chance to repent, based on the best possible evidence. Do I want to feel this burning* pain for eternity? If the answer was no, you did what you had to do – you confessed your sin, or rather, screamed it, and then surrendered yourself to God's infinite patience with the lost. How was such an experience not merciful? It was almost too thoughtful.

There was nothing more to say, but that doesn't usually halt a churchman, and sure enough, a further member of the prosecuting counsel then rose, fully in support of the Archbishop's most insightful and beautiful words, words which had brought tears to his eyes, wishing only to add one further grace and benefit of burning and it was this: the licking flames and the roasting flesh were particularly cleansing for the soul, this was well known, enabling a profounder liberation for the sinner from their previously damned state. Tolerance of misguided opinions, in refusing to burn people, was cruelty in disguise, leaving them less purged.

And so with these truths confirmed to everyone's satisfaction – certainly those covered in gold – attention had turned to Eckhart himself, and the twenty-one charges of heresy that faced him: guilty or not guilty? And in a way, it wasn't a choice: he must plead guilty, and that was that. This was certainly the path encouraged by Henricus de Cigno, the Dominican Provincial for Teutonia, here to support and advise ... mainly advise. The Fishwife would have his man and that would be enough. The Church would be delighted at his repentance, and parade his contrite scalp around Europe for a while and then put him out to grass. Painless enough really. Eckhart would be hidden away in some distant monastery, the Dominicans a little shamed, and the Franciscan cause advanced.

'And the upside?' Eckhart had asked.

'You'll still be alive, Johannes, and we live to fight another day. It's a bad day for the Dominicans – but not Destruction Day, not Armageddon.'

'I might not be alive, of course.'

'I believe you would be; your surrender and our shame would be enough.'

That did seem the more peaceable way to Eckhart, to throw himself on the mercy of the Church, though there was an alternative, if you could call it that. Eckhart could plead 'Not guilty' to the catalogue of charges against him. Everything's a choice. But really, what would be gained? Brief but stupid heroism – heroism headstrong and foolhardy. They'd come after him in court with a terrible force and wipe him out, destroying him and his words for ever. They had that power, the Church, the power to define your existence in the world, to place you outside the circle of Christian civilisation – and what other civilisation was there? There'd be no mercy, and his life's work made as nothing.

*So guilty or not guilty? The simple plea of 'Guilty' would take the nastiness away and grant him peace at the end, the forgiveness of the Church, and embarrassment rather than shame to his order. Marguerite had said to remember his soul when they came for him, but he and she were different: she had been a free soul, without position or responsibility. But he was a man with both; a man under authority, the authority of his Order.*

*Eckhart looked around. Before him sat Pope John XXII, son of a shoemaker but now a prince in cushioned and bejewelled luxury; oh, and close friend of the French king. To the left of His Eminence sat Henry of Virneburg, the Archbishop of Cologne, for once silent. And to his right, the assembled theologians, numerous and learned, here to declare Eckhart in error. No further space was necessary at the front, no room for any defence, for he had no defence, no defenders to declare him without error, other than his frail self. His own Order was hedging its bets, neither for nor against, fingers in the air, testing the dusty wind in Avignon: which way would the holy breeze blow?*

*Here in the papal court, Eckhart felt alone ... as alone as he'd ever felt and sometimes the alone have to bow. And now the question is being put, clearly stated by the clerk:*

*'To the twenty-one charges of heresy read out in this court, does the defendant plead "Guilty" or "Not guilty"?'*

*'The charges are lodged out of jealousy and pursued out of ignorance,' says Eckhart. 'I plead "Not guilty".'*

*Let the shit fall.*

# Thirty Seven

'A very wonderful book, as I'm sure you know, Abbot.'

Timothy Gershwin, director of *Mother's Day*, referred to the copy of *The Power of Now* which sat on his lap. Tamsin was writing some notes, not yet fully engaged.

'I presume you've read it?' he asked Peter, as if there was hardly any need. Of course the Abbot had read it! Surely all spiritual souls had a copy of this remarkable tome on their shelf?

'No,' said Peter.

It was best to be honest, he hadn't read it.

'Oh?'

Timothy was bemused, almost an injured party.

'But I've heard only good things,' said Peter, to soften the blow.

This was a lie, less honest, the truth being that the Abbot had neither read it nor even heard of it. But then he had an aversion to spiritual books, particularly those recommended by others.

'Here's a book I just know you'll enjoy, Abbot! It's so you!'

Why did people presume such knowledge, when they were always wrong?

'It's definitely on my list,' continued the Abbot, the second lie always easier than the first.

'It's sold millions,' said Timothy, 'which must say something.'

'Maybe.'

'A publishing sensation and many believe – and perhaps I'm among them – the dawn of a new era of global consciousness.'

'I'm sure.'

'Sure of the new dawn … or sure that many people believe it might be so.'

'Probably the latter.'

'So you're holding something back, Abbot! I sense resistance.' The Abbot smiled. 'So out with it, out with it!'

'Well, I'm told Hitler could draw a very good crowd,' said Peter.

'What's that got to do with anything?'

'Very much the sensation of his time, great orator – with many women achieving orgasm during his speeches, as I recall.'

Tamsin was suddenly engaged, regarding him with a 'where did that come from?' face.

'Not quite the same, Abbot.' said Timothy. 'The author, Eckhart Tolle, is hardly Hitler.'

'I'm sure he's a very good man, and certainly a better man than I – who isn't? But it's a warning perhaps never to equate truth with numbers. Or truth with intensity of response.'

Timothy looked at Peter with some hostility beneath his pacific calm.

'And then Hermione Bysshe-Urquhart got murdered,' said Tamsin firmly. What exactly was the point of discussing some self-help book in the middle of a murder investigation? Self-help wouldn't help Hermione … and female orgasms? You don't want to hear about those from your uncle.

'A tragedy, of course,' said Timothy, focusing quickly. He was familiar with meetings, meetings of all sorts, pitching meetings, creative meetings, financial meetings, cast meetings, he understood how they worked.

'So how did your relationship with the theatre start?'

'Quite by chance and not particularly honourably.'

'How so?'

'Well, I was touting a rather disreputable comedy round every theatre I knew. It was called *Life's a Drag* – it was before I found my more spiritual self.'

'But life is a drag,' said Tamsin. 'It doesn't stop being true just because you've found your inner whatever.'

'Maybe I look at things differently now,' said Timothy.

Tamsin decided not to pursue this.

'But that was when you met Hermione.'

'Yes, Hermione liked it and so we did a short summer season, raised a few eyebrows and kept in touch after that.'

From performing disreputable comedies, Timothy had climbed the directorial ladder, cutting his teeth in commercials, including the famous army ad, involving authentic conflict footage and the tag-line 'Only for the extraordinary'. 'Though my last job was directing an episode of *Midsomer Murders*,' he continued. 'Six people killed before the crime was solved! I hope we don't have a repeat of that here.'

He looked knowingly at his two interrogators.

'It ended with the usual self-congratulatory scene and some half-cocked domestic jokiness – but it all felt rather hollow, with the families of the six dead all weeping their guts out somewhere. And it wasn't as if the murderer was hard to find – by the end, he was the only villager still alive.'

Peter smiled weakly as you do when someone describes a show you've never seen.

'But then I don't suppose you watch *Midsomer Murders*?' said Timothy. 'Busman's holiday for you.'

'I'd prefer root canal treatment,' said Tamsin. But there was an obvious question to be asked: 'So why on earth are you here, Mr Gershwin?'

'How do you mean?'

'A two-month season in Stormhaven's struggling Bell Theatre is hardly a career move for a successful director.'

'Depends on how you define a career,' said Timothy.

'I define a career as a climb up the ladder of success. And this is the bottom rung.'

'Then there we part company,' said Timothy. 'I see a career as a journey into nothingness.'

'Then Stormhaven is a good choice,' said Tamsin.

'My colleague is not the town's greatest fan,' said Peter. 'She thinks it's just fish and chips and the sea.'

'It is just fish and chips and the sea,' said Tamsin.

'And that's enough for anyone,' said the Abbot firmly. What else did people want?

'Fish, chips, sea and *theatre*,' added Timothy.

'But clearly there's something else that draws you here.'

'How do you mean?'

'Well, a summer season at the Bell, a seaside theatre in decline, offers you neither the kudos nor the wages of TV work.'

'It's the relationship, as I told you. Hermione gave me a break when I was less well known, and maybe I'm still repaying her.'

'It's a generous repayment.'

'I go with my heart, Abbot. I'm all about relationships, it's how humans are defined.'

'Speak for yourself,' thinks Peter, as Timothy adds, 'And of course I believe passionately in community theatre.'

'Even when your two leads hate each other?' asked Tamsin. 'Not much community in this theatre.'

Timothy waved the idea away, with amusement.

'Well, you may dismiss the idea, Mr Gershwin – .'

'Timothy, please!'

'So Margery and Millicent are the best of friends are they – Timothy?'

'Dark needs light, light needs dark, we are many selves.'

'And in English? You've lost me.'

'And maybe that's good.'

'Not from where I'm sitting.'

'Maybe it's good just for a moment to hear your lostness.'

'I'm hearing only pomposity,' said Tamsin.

All this 'stay with those feelings' stuff was fine with actors in rehearsal, they could explore their 'lostness' as much as they liked. But Tamsin had a proper job, she was a detective and that sort of talk made her feel ill. And then Timothy spoke again:

'It was the great fourteenth-century mystic, Meister Eckhart – the man who Eckhart Tolle named himself after – it was he who said, 'To the one who knows nothing, all is revealed.'

*

'What an insufferable prig,' said Tamsin as soon as Timothy Gershwin had left the room.

'He could be genuine.'

'As genuine as a £5 Rolex.'

'Time will tell.'

'Time's told me already. She came to an instant decision on this one.'

'That could have been someone else talking, someone other than time.'

'Don't you start. You'll be saying it's one of my many selves next.'

'Quite a frightened self, yes.'

'That man is a phoney.'

'And you may be right. It's a thin line between enlightenment and escapism – and where Timothy stands, for me at least, is not immediately clear.'

'And who on earth is this mystic Gokart – .'

'Eckhart.'

'Eckhart, yes.'

'Meister Eckhart. Haven't heard his name for a while.'

The Abbot looks wistful, like a man reminded of the love of his life.

'So who was he,' says Tamsin, 'apart from a purveyor of nonsense?'

# Thirty Eight

'N-N-Neville's been good to me,' said Boy.

It was Neville who'd brought him to the interview room, after he'd failed to arrive at his appointed time.

'Neville got me electricity.'

'For the caravan?' asked Peter.

'That's my home now,' said Boy. It would not have been everyone's pride and joy, but appeared to be his.

'You sleep in there?' Tamsin was trying to sound matter-of-fact; trying not to sound incredulous.

'Plenty of room for one.'

A fit 70-year-old, strong-armed with a ruddy face shiny from night cold down the years. He'd slept by fires, beneath the open sky, under arches in the rain, on the shingle in the summer ... on the edge of a world going home at night, home to front doors and heating, TV and toilets, hot baths and a front room, passing by, coins in a hat if he was lucky, but faces turned away, turned away in fear, there but for the grace of God, this is what they're thinking most of them, so don't look, don't notice and it might not happen to me.

'Some people are frightened of you,' said Tamsin.

She was frightened of him. He didn't fit in, didn't have a place here, which made him disturbing. He lived in an old green caravan, a small room on wheels, cold in the winter, claustrophobic in the summer, and what sort of a person lived like that? And his stutter was beginning to irritate her as well. People with stutters waste so much time.

'I c-c-can't imagine why anyone would be frightened of me.'

'So describe what you do here,' said the Abbot.

'I ring the bell each day at three o'clock.'

'Is the time significant?'

'The three o'clock, you m-m-mean?'

'It's not obviously helpful to anyone.'

'I wouldn't know.'

'It's not like the cock crowing in the morning.'

And when had a cock crowing ever been helpful, wondered Tamsin.

'It's the time when Jesus died,' said Boy. 'Th-th-thought you might know that, Abbot.'

'Well, I did know that, but – .'

'He hung on the cross for nine hours, from six in the morning until three in the afternoon.'

'I'm aware of the history … simply wondering how it helps Stormhaven?'

Tamsin was not concerned with this, and neither, it seemed, was Boy. Whether it was helpful for him to ring the bell at three, and how this helpfulness might be quantified in any meaningful sense – these were not things that kept him awake at night. There was a simplicity to Boy, a sense of a soul untouched by the world. He'd been told to ring the bell at three, the time when Jesus died, and that's what he did. His not to reason why.

'And is it hard work?' asked Peter.

'To ring a bell?'

'Yes.'

'A bell turns through 360 d-d-degrees.'

'So I hear.'

'And you have to maintain its momentum as it turns, manage the weight of the bell to create permutations, sometimes a quick pull, sometimes a slow one, sometimes just steady.'

No stutter.

'Quite a craft,' said Peter.

Boy nodded.

'And I look after the graveyard,' he said. 'A graveyard needs looking after.'

Tamsin nodded on a purely professional basis. The care of graveyards was not high on her list of significant jobs … it didn't make the list.

'And I c-c-clean the place, keep the place clean and tidy.'

'The theatre, you mean?'

'That's right … not that I keep it c-c-clean and tidy like N-N-Neville does his room.'

'His room is very clean,' said Peter.

'Neville's Niche, it's called!'

'But not such a clean niche this morning. In fact, it's a bit of a mess.'

'Oh, I heard all that, yes. Qu-qu-quite a b-b-banging around. But N-N-Neville does have a bit of a temper on him.'

139

'I'm sorry – what did you hear?'

'We all get angry.'

'Are you saying you heard his room being destroyed?'

'Couldn't not hear it! I was in the theatre cleaning. Watched them leave.'

'Watched who leave?'

'The young man left – .'

'Paul Bent?'

'That's right, yes, he's the writer and then Mr Neville – but the d-d-damage was done by then.'

'Did they see you?'

'No one sees me. No one's seen me for years.'

Again, no stutter.

'And what time was this?'

'After everyone's g-g-gone, that's when I like the place, I like it best when everything's quiet, after you police had gone, I d-d-don't keep a close eye on time, not at night, no need, the cold wakes me well enough, the c-c-cold's my alarm clock. But I'd say it was the witching hour … the n-n-noise, I mean.'

'The witching hour?'

What century is this, wondered Tamsin.

'Two a.m. perhaps?' said Peter.

'Something around then. It was a clear moon.'

They digested this information, the news of Paul and Neville being alone in the building after the police lock-down and not a vagrant in sight to attack Neville's office. Not that Boy was interested, more concerned with the cleaning, but then, as he said, there were different views about what was clean and what wasn't, and what was good and what wasn't, people had different views. Both Tamsin and the Abbot had drifted a little, it was easy not to see Boy, for so long at the edge of the world, easy not to hear him. But the Abbot tuned in just in time.

'Has there been good and bad here?' he asked.

Boy's face darkened.

'What's d-d-done is done.'

'What has been done?'

'But least I know now, at least I kn-kn-know … which gives us some time.'

'Meaning?' said Tamsin.

'My concern, lady.'

Lady?

'Not the concern of the police?' she asked.

'The police have n-n-never been interested before.'

'How do you mean?'

'All they've done is move me on.'

'We're not here to move you on.'

'It's what you might c-c-call a long-running d-d-domestic!'

'What is?' asked Tamsin. Speak some sense, for God's sake, sense without a stutter.

'I read the papers you know – I read about d-d-domestics.'

He was like a child with a new word, eager to try it out.

'Domestic incidents are usually violent in some way,' said Tamsin. 'Have you been violent?'

'Never violent.'

'And do you have a name?'

It was an important question.

'All there in my t-t-tin.'

'What's there in your tin – your name?'

'My writings.'

'And your name?'

'I've always been Boy.'

'You haven't always been Boy. You weren't called Boy at school. Do you remember school?'

'Always B-B-Boy.'

Tamsin decided to give up on the stuttering ramblings of this simpleton. It was all she could do not to intervene. 'Boy' had been particularly painful.

'You've been involved with this place a long time,' she said, with studied patience.

'I kn-kn-knew it when it was a church,' said a slowly nodding Boy. 'Well, the church was closing. And it was theatre and church for a while.'

Peter and Tamsin kept quiet.

'And then it became just a theatre, the church gone … the bells gone. Well, most of them.'

The 'th' of 'then' was a struggle, causing in Boy a quivering intake of breath.

'You were one of eight bell-ringers for the church?'

'I was the young'un! Older men, the others … St Augustine's Company of Bell-ringers, all older men than me, passed on down the years. Matthew, Walter the Conductor, Ezekiel, John, Tom, Frederick, Valentino, named after – .'

'So where were you when Hermione was killed?'

Tamsin felt the focus slipping again. A trip down memory lane was permissible if it had purpose, but a genealogy of the eight original bell-ringers? That was for documentary-makers and archivists – not the police.

'I wouldn't kill young Hermione,' said Boy.

'Did she treat you well?'

'She wouldn't talk to the likes of me now.'

He said this with stoic acceptance.

'So why wouldn't you kill her?'

'Because she was young.'

'How do you mean, she was young?'

'Younger than me.'

'You don't harm people who are younger than you?'

'And Nicholas was young, he didn't know.'

And he was going to say more, he'd like to have said more, because he liked the man in the habit, not the young girl, just the man in the habit. But he held back fearful, because you must be careful with truth, he'd learned that in the army, a lesson well learned, you learn to keep your head down in the army, rule number one, always keep your head down or it might come off! That's what the sergeant used to say: 'Keep your head down or it might come off!'

# Thirty Nine

While Boy was helping the police with their enquiries, he had a visitor – or rather, his caravan did.

Bill Cain was unfamiliar with accommodation like this. He'd lived in large-roomed houses for long enough now to expect space, to assume spare rooms, rooms in which not a great deal happened, rooms which were almost corridors, of no particular use, but in which things could be put, or in which things could happen, should the need arise, like a party of some sort or his wife sulking, that sort of thing … more of the latter than the former of late, ungrateful bitch.

But you couldn't hold a party here, not in this space, not unless you were a hermit; you could barely sip champagne, and quite where – or indeed how – Boy slept here, Cain was unsure, but also unconcerned, because that wasn't his issue, he wasn't a social worker, as he sat hunched in the green caravan in the graveyard, beneath the evergreen, seeking every paper item he could find. With Boy's interview just started, he had ten minutes, minimum – though he'd be out in five, no risks. But where to look? There was no filing system to wade through, no computer to open, no hard drive to explore – just clothes and plastic bags. If discovered, unlikely but you had to be prepared, Cain was checking out all the theatre property … new financial manager getting to grips with the task in hand; if not discovered, he was just making sure.

No one knew much about Boy, as he seemed to have spent most of his life either under Waterloo Bridge in London or sleeping the beaches and doorways of England's south coast, neither haunt a diamond staircase to fame. Cain had paid Karen, a young journalist on the *Sussex Silt,* to dig as best she could and she'd done well enough. There hadn't been a great deal, but what there was proved interesting, because Quasimodo hadn't always been homeless, this is what he'd discovered. In his teenage years, Cedric Mayfield – that was Boy's birth name – had been a pupil at Ardingly College,

143

in mid-Sussex, a minor public school, though charging major fees no doubt.

'You can see it from the viaduct, just before Haywards Heath on the London to Brighton line,' Karen told him, as if to confirm her investigative skills.

'You can see what?'

'Ardingly College.'

'Remind me to organise a day trip one day.'

Sarcasm, because Cain wasn't bothered if you could see it from the moon unless it related to the Bell Theatre, which he suspected it didn't. But Karen had also discovered that Boy had worked in London for a while. There was a record of him being a gardener for Westminster Council ... and then a possible spell in the army, almost certainly, after which it all went wrong, with some evidence, according to Karen, that it was triggered by an unhappy relationship.

'Nothing new there then,' grunted Cain, his third marriage probably about to end. 'A name?'

'Cedric Mayfield.'

'No, her name, you moron – the name of the woman!'

'No name, I'm afraid. And we don't know it was a woman.'

Cain made a face.

'Anything else?'

'Not really.'

'Not much bling for my buck, Karen.'

He was actually pretty pleased, he hadn't bunged her much, and she'd got more than he expected – but she didn't need to know that.

'We know he made his way to Stormhaven,' she said, 'joined the Company of Bell-ringers just before it became a theatre. After which – .'

'After which the others lost their bells and walked out in disgust, or walked out in disgust and lost their bells, whichever way round, leaving young Cedric to carry on with the one remaining gong, yes, I know.'

'It was part of the purchase contract – that the bell continues to be rung.'

'Any other contracts you've come across?'

These were the matters that most concerned Bill Cain. If it wasn't in a contract, it wasn't important.

'Not that I know of.'

'Well, let me know if there are, yes?'

'Of course.'

'I want to know of any other contractual arrangements between Cedric Mayfield and the Bell Theatre.' And because he'd seen a slight nervousness in her eyes, he'd moved to reassure her: 'He's had a hard life, Karen. I just want to make sure no one's fleecing him. You know what people are like.'

Bill Cain knew what people were like, especially when they wanted something, because he was like that too.

'It's a rarity, Karen, so make the most of it: Bill Cain, the knight in shining armour.'

'Oh, I see!' Karen was relieved. She may work for the *Silt,* but she didn't want to stay there, she had some principles. And Cain made people feel good about being bad.

# Forty

Peter and Tamsin had come outside into the graveyard to reflect on the interviews; an anonymous bench would suit them well, somewhere they wouldn't be disturbed and couldn't be heard. That was Peter's view, but for Tamsin, it wasn't a bench of choice.

'Do we have to sit here?'

'I rather like it.'

Peter disliked being trapped inside for too long; liked to feel the wind.

'I don't.'

'I find tombs strangely focusing – a call to go from this place and do something worthwhile before I join them.'

Tamsin looked a little uncomfortable.

'I should warn you that I don't have that long,' she said.

'What do you mean?'

Tamsin was not usually morbid.

'I'm just saying I don't have that long now.'

'What are you talking about? You're young – you won't be lying here for a good while yet … as long as you look both ways when crossing the road.'

'I mean, I have to be elsewhere.'

'Elsewhere?' Why would she have to be elsewhere when there were interviews to discuss?

'I need to be somewhere else. And please don't look like my parent.'

'Police business, is it?' He was fishing because normally she said where she was going, said what she was doing, but not today. Today, there was a sea of evasion so he went fishing.

'No, not police business.'

'Not police business.'

'Have you swallowed a parrot?'

'So it's not police business that takes you away from solving a murder.'

'No.'

'It must be very important.'

'And it's not your business either, so we're narrowing it down.'

'You've met someone.'

'My God, what century are you from?'

'I've been asked more difficult questions.'

'The idea that if a woman has a secret assignment it must be with a lover!'

'That was passionately put, but I note it wasn't a no.'

Pause.

'I am meeting someone. Or I'm thinking of meeting someone.'

'That wasn't so hard, was it?'

'But they're neither my lover nor companion – and nor will they ever be either of the above.'

'So why are you meeting?'

Pause.

'Only if you want to tell me, of course.'

'Shall we get on with the interviews?'

'If you have the time … I understand it's at something of a pre-mium.'

'I have some time, Abbot – but I have a cut-off point, that's all I'm saying.'

'A pressing, yet mysterious, assignment.'

'Yes it is – now, the interviews.'

Abbot Peter relented.

'So what did you think of young Paul Bent?' he asked.

'Actually, can we go back to Hermione's office? This place isn't doing me any good at all.'

A seagull approached them, inching forward step by cautious step, so tall in the flesh with that long-hooked beak, unblinking eyes fixed on theirs, off-piste in the graveyard grass, away from the barnacles and groynes, but still wondering about food and why not?

It's what humans were for.

# Forty One

❧

'And what are humans for?' asked the well-dined Fishwife in a rhetorical and flamboyant fashion, as the court case reached its climax. 'Just what are humans for, if not for the keeping and maintaining of external observances and devotions as the Church teaches?' There were murmurs of assent. 'Surely it is in such things that our almighty and most holy God is to be found?'

He used the Latin word 'nonne' which expects the answer 'yes', which implies, 'Surely this is so.' But apparently it wasn't.

'God is no more likely to be found in external observances than he is in sin,' replied Eckhart.

What?!

'Would the accused like to enlarge upon that?'

The court was in a state of some shock – no, much shock, even the Pope moving slightly, shifting uneasily on his throne, and when the Pope moves, you know you're in trouble. As Henricus always said, and he'd said it more than once to Eckhart, 'it's a bad idea to make those on thrones uneasy'. But Eckhart seemed not to notice, enlarging on the matter as he'd been encouraged by the Fishwife to do.

'I see people delighting in external observations – the singing of psalms, attendance at mass, the keeping of fasts – and these are people who have great status in the world.'

Everyone looked at the Pope, for no one had greater status than he. And then they looked at the Archbishop of Cologne who was only a few rungs down, one of the seven Imperial electors, able to choose the German king. There was a great deal of status in this court room.

'But such people only have great status in the world because they share its likeness,' said Eckhart, and Henricus knew what was coming next. 'These people are exactly like the world, no different at all! They have a high regard for observances, as if observances make them

148

*holy, but such things mean nothing! Such observances are external to us, things perceived by the outer senses, with no relationship with, or benefit to, the inner life of the soul.'*

*The Fishwife could not believe his luck.*

*'But, Eckhart,' he said, feigning pain, 'the Church has taught these things for fourteen hundred years, generation upon generation.'*

*'One ass is adored by another,' came the reply.*

*In the gallery, Henricus groaned. The court case was not going well for Eckhart, anyone could see that, but he was his own worst enemy, always had been. At this rate, he'd be lucky to be burned; his mouth was a dangerous tool. Eckhart had to help himself, this was the view of Henricus, and this had been his counsel to the man when they'd met in his cell before the trial: 'You must help yourself, Eckhart!' Eckhart must throw himself on their mercy, weep for any misunderstandings, cast himself adrift from any suspected heresy – particularly the Porete woman – and pledge his deep and undying loyalty to Mother Church and to the Pope ... the one in Avignon, obviously, not the one in Rome.*

*'It can be confusing,' said Eckhart, mildly.*

*'What can be confusing?'*

*'This surfeit of popes, each demanding allegiance.'*

*'It's the Pope in Avignon you need to honour.'*

*'He is more Christ-like?'*

*Henricus remained silent.*

*'Or with the backing of the French, does he simply have a bigger army?'*

*Eckhart could be so po-faced.*

*'Don't mention the Pope in Rome unless you're being rude about him.'*

*'You're a man of great vision, Henricus.'*

*The sarcasm was not hidden.*

*'I'm a man who wants to stay alive, Eckhart, who wants the Dominican order to flourish – and wants to see you avoid the flames.'*

*'Thank you.'*

*'So don't talk about God either.'*

*'What?'*

*'Don't talk about God.'*

*'I might find that hard. I talk about God all the time.'*

*'But you know how you get into trouble when you talk about God. So don't do it in court.'*

*But Eckhart did do it in court, he talked much about God, because the Fishwife asked him to, and it would have been impolite to refuse. Not that the question had been aggressive; indeed, it had almost been friendly, seeking a place of agreement.*

'Let us agree, Meister Eckhart!' declared the Archbishop. 'Let us at least agree to call God "good"!' And Henricus had not seen how anything amiss could arise from that conciliatory observation – but it did.

'God cannot be good for God is nameless,' said the errant Dominican.

'Nameless?'

'No one can either speak of him or know him.'

'Really? Is that so? Then we must all wonder what has the Church been doing these last fourteen hundred years, if not speaking of him – and giving him names?'

There was some mirth in the court, mixed with shock … shock and mirth, but Eckhart ignored it all.

'God is transcendent, so all words about him are nonsense.'

'So God is not good?'

'God is not good, no.'

'God is not good? Need the trial continue?'

'Let me expose the stupidity of this questioning,' said Eckhart, cutting across the hubbub. 'To say God is "good" – like one might say a dog is good or a juggler is good – is to suggest he can become "better", that God can become better! So who now is the blasphemer? You see, God is beyond our little words, which is why we best keep silence! As St Augustine said, "The finest thing we can say about God is to be silent concerning him."'

'So, let me understand, you, Meister Eckhart – the Church has nothing to say?'

'Silence is preferable to chatter, certainly.'

Chatter broke out instantly.

'We should not chatter about God, because by chattering about him, we tell lies and commit a sin. If you wish to be perfect and without sin, then do not prattle about God.'

Behind his necessary legal reserve – though legal reserve was not the Fishwife's forte – the Archbishop's blood vessels were bursting. To be accused of prattling by a monk from Cologne? He had never heard such a thing! Yet he was also ecstatic, indignant yet ecstatic, as any wise-thinking Franciscan would be: to see a Dominican making such a fool of himself, this could only bring delight in heaven. How could the Pope show any favour to the Dominicans now? How could he not favour the Franciscans and confirm their supremacy?

And yet there was more good news to come, as the Fishwife well knew. For he had one more question, a question that would be the final nail in Eckhart's coffin … or the torch for his funeral pyre.

There'd be no way back after this particular enquiry. And he decided to make it now.

# Forty Two

'The play will be opening again on Friday,' said Millicent.

'Rather soon after murder most foul,' said Janet, sniffing. 'Are you sure that's appropriate?'

'The performance will be in memory of Hermione.'

Janet smiled, but not happily.

'In memory of the theatre's bank account, more like,' she said. 'These people have no shame. Bill Cain was it, his idea?'

She still remembered his antics with Molly in the surgery.

'I'm just glad to get going again,' said Millicent. 'I don't like all this hanging around.'

Janet's grinding teeth indicated her disapproval. They were standing in the costumes room, as she made a few running repairs. It was the fight scene in the second act that usually did the damage.

'Isn't it best we all move on?' said Millicent.

'Someone has died, my darling.'

Janet used this endearment with Millicent sometimes, and Millicent liked it … it felt warm and motherly.

'I know. But everyone says we can expect much better audiences for the second half of the run. That's the good thing about a murder, I suppose. It might actually help the theatre.'

'So, that's all right then.'

'Well, you know – .'

'Never let it be said Hermione died in vain.'

'Life does go on, Janet.'

'Not hers.'

'And it's not as if you even liked her.'

'I wouldn't say that.'

'You said you hadn't spoken for years.'

'She had a rather blaming spirit which I took slight offence to.'

'Slight?'

'And how's Margery?' asked Janet, deflecting matters away from herself.

'Margery? She's a madwoman.'

'Still playing the professional to your amateur?'

Janet fed happily on negativity, and stirred it when necessary. She'd overheard their exchange earlier in the day, in the rehearsal room.

'It's a pastime for you,' Margery had said, during a break in rehearsals. 'But a profession for me.'

'Does that make you better?'

'Do the sums, Millicent. People are paying for me, the theatre's paying me a wage. They're taking you because you're cheap ... or for other reasons.'

Sadly, steps in the corridor had then forced Janet to move on.

'She thinks she's so high and mighty, she really does,' said Millicent. 'When the truth is, I can do anything she does, and do it better!'

'I have no doubt you can.'

'I can, believe me!'

Janet would reassure Millicent, whom she was fond of.

'I wouldn't worry about her,' she said. 'Margery's just a bitter old woman.'

It was slightly unfair. Margery wasn't old, similar to Janet in fact, early fifties probably. But she enjoyed passing a mantle given to her – 'bitter old woman' – onto the shoulders of another. And anyway, Janet wasn't bitter. What was the point of being bitter? If no one had ever looked after her, so what? Plenty of people had faced much worse – there were people starving in the world, so what about them? Plenty of people much worse off than Janet, so no stupid self-pity please!

It was just that no one had ever looked after her. They'd fed her but not looked after her, she did feel this, not in a complaining way, but that's the way it was, that's life, and it coloured things, so to speak. She hadn't moped, because there's no point in moping, she'd got on with things because she had to, and become known for getting on with things: 'Good old Janet, getting on with things!' But only because she'd been expected to get on with things, not because they brought her any joy. And so if there was a little devilry in her now, then wasn't it about time?

Millicent had dumped herself down on the couch, like the little girl she was, and Janet was stroking her hair.

'Timothy has been very helpful,' said Millicent.

'That's good' said Janet, not believing it was. She didn't take to Timothy, never had, quite apart from his rather obvious designs on the girl. He could do with taking down a notch or two, no question about that. And perhaps Janet was the one to do it.

'He talks about *shenpa*,' said Millicent.

'And what's *shenpa* when it's at home?'

'It's a Tibetan word.'

'Oh,' said Janet, feeling strangely nationalistic. What was a Tibetan word doing in Stormhaven? Wasn't English good enough? Janet would keep her thoughts to herself, but you had to wonder, didn't you?

'Somebody says a mean or spiteful word to you – say, like Margery did to me today.'

'And?'

'And then something in you tightens – that's the *shenpa*.'

'I see.'

'It's the reaction when a nasty word gets to you for some reason, that's what Timothy says. It, like, gets its hooks in you, because it touches a sore place – and the reaction, the feeling is *shenpa*.'

Where in Janet wasn't sore? *Shenpa* should be her middle name. But like a tortoise, her soft parts were well protected these days.

'And then the *shenpa* begins its work,' said Millicent. 'Timothy says it becomes low self-esteem.'

'Timothy says. New game everyone! Used to be "Simon Says". Now it's bloody "Timothy Says".'

'Or it becomes blame of the other person or anger towards them … or self-hate.'

Janet recognised all those. Clearly things were no better in Tibetan monasteries than they were here.

'And maybe, if you have an addiction, whatever that addiction is, you then go to it, to cover over the bad feelings inside you. That's what Timothy says.'

Well, bully for bloody Timothy! The girl is obviously in his thrall. But when he gets his next job in the US or wherever, with another pretty girl in the lead role, Janet doubted Millicent would be invited to join him. She was the guru's Stormhaven girl, nothing more.

'I try to remember these things when Margery gets aggressive, but it isn't easy.'

No, it's a complete waste of time, thinks Janet, and then Millicent changes direction.

'Janet, I'd like to tell you something,' she says. 'Can I tell you something in confidence?'

'Of course you can.'

'Because I don't know who else to tell – and you're like a mother to me.'

Janet let her hand rest on Millicent's head, they were such sweet words to hear, to hear the girl say that, to be here with her now, in

153

this way, after all these years. And then the door opened, no knock, and the figure of Bill Cain stood before them, taking in the scene.

'Lesbians in love?' he said. 'Kinky!'

And that was when Janet decided to break a confidence about the theatre's financial saviour, Mr William Cain ... as he was called in his doctor's records.

*

And unseen by anyone, as far as they could tell, a shrouded figure moved cautiously through the graveyard, at a little past 1.30 p.m., pausing at various stones to give the appearance of interest. If found, it would not be difficult to invent a story; and if not found, well, they would do what they had come for.

This couldn't go on.

He had to be stopped.

# Forty Three

'So question number one,' said Tamsin, 'have we just spoken with the murderer?'

Tamsin had won the day. They were back in Hermione's office, away from the tombs, and reflecting on the interviews.

'Are there other questions, while I consider that one?' said Peter, sinking into one of the two comfortable chairs.

'No. Probability out of ten?'

'Eight out of ten probability that we've spoken with the murderer.'

'And the favourite so far?'

'As in "most cherished" or "most dangerous"?'

'Paul's an unpleasant little shit, isn't he?'

Cards on the table. Peter at least pretended neutrality.

'The boy's still leaving home,' he said. 'So all sorts of insecurities around identity. It must be hard for a bishop's son to escape the perceptions and judgements of others.'

'"I am not my father!"'

'He has to get away.'

'And yet also determined to be the outsider at the Bell,' said Tamsin. 'No one's good enough for him to have a relationship with – though he's happy for them to want his play. I can see him as a scissors-in-the-neck man.'

'But perhaps not the head jerk?'

'Why not?'

'And his trousers.'

His trousers?

'What about them?' asked Tamsin.

'I was surprised at the number of holes.'

'Is this relevant?'

'Hard to say at the moment.'

Tamsin accepts the challenge.

'It's distressed denim.'

'I'm sorry to hear that.'

'No, that's what it's called, what he was wearing: distressed denim.'

'I see,' said Peter. 'Though I think we used to call them "seconds".'

'No, seconds are different, those were not seconds – distressed denim is expensive.'

'You pay extra for the holes?'

'It's a fashion statement.'

The Abbot looked blank.

'I do miss the desert sometimes,' he said.

Tamsin sighed.

'Don't pretend the desert was any less mad than the rest of the world.'

The Abbot was irritating her.

'It was a madness I could understand,' he said. 'We had distressed monks but not distressed habits – just habits with holes, habits that needed mending.'

'Shall we leave Paul's trousers now?'

'Are they distressing you?'

'Very funny.'

'Janet.'

'Janet, yes.'

'She hates it here, of course,' said Peter.

'She's hardly the theatrical type.'

'A determinedly good little girl, and she hates it here – but still carries on for some reason … and frightened of blame. I see her caught between a commitment to light and darkness. Can you feel that? An angel on one shoulder, a demon on the other, each putting their case.'

Tamsin raised her eyebrows. Talk of angels and demons was not a serious contribution to police work.

'The sensitivity to blame was pretty obvious,' she said.

'Yes, and fighting for a new identity in the world, to cover up those primal fears. You will have noted that she was never so happy as when you made her a woman of mystery, a keeper of secrets … that was a status she aches for.'

'But you haven't answered my question.'

'What is she doing here?'

'Yes.'

'Sometimes I can't answer the question.'

'You can try!'

'No, I just note that it's a good question and hold it gently – because the same question could be asked of Bill Cain: what's he doing here?'

Tamsin waited for his answer.

'"The brute in the suit" as Hermione called him – but, like Janet, why is he hanging around a theatre whose inhabitants he dislikes and whose reason for being he questions?'

'The man who solves things,' she said.

'Indeed. So what did the death of Hermione solve for him?'

'His next property deal?'

'Possible,' said Peter.

'And it's property deals that remind him he's alive. I know his sort.'

'Killing another to remind yourself you're alive?'

# Forty Four

'And then there's Margery,' said Tamsin, looking at her watch; and Peter saw her looking. She'd said she must go soon, though she couldn't say where, and the atmosphere was strained.

'You must go when you must go,' said Peter.

'Margery?'

'An actress on the way down, obviously.'

'And with an old score to settle with Hermione.'

'Maybe. Though that feels more like a headline than the truth. There isn't an actor on earth who hasn't been passed over for someone else. If it always led to murder, there'd be no theatre at all.'

'Every cloud has a silver lining.'

'Margery is a survivor, battle-hardened – but a murderer?'

'She seemed threatened by Millicent.'

'Because Millicent's attractive and perceived by her to have had it easy.'

'And also appears to be in a relationship with the director.'

'Salt in the wound.'

'I liked Millicent,' said Tamsin.

'An innocent in a nest of vipers?'

'Something like that.'

'But an innocent who so upset Hermione during the interval that the theatre director slapped her.' The Abbot pondered his words. 'That's angry, especially for Hermione, because while she could be cold, she was not physically violent, it wasn't her way.'

'And then five minutes later, she was dead. Millicent doesn't look that innocent, I grant you.'

'If Paul is telling the truth.'

'Why would he lie?'

'I don't know,' said Peter. 'But he hasn't been transparent about his activities in the building on the night of the murder. It does now appear that Neville may have trashed his own office. He certainly knows it wasn't a vagrant, so he's deflecting us from the truth, for one reason or another.'

'And if he wasn't protecting himself, who was he protecting?'

'The obvious answer is Paul. He was here in the building with him.'

'According to Boy.'

'And I'm inclined to believe him.'

'Why? Because someone who stutters must be telling the truth; because the disabled never lie?'

Peter breathed deeply, wondered when enough was enough, and then continued: 'So why were Neville and Paul in the building together, the night of the murder? We'll need to speak with them again.'

'And then there's Timothy Gershwin – "successful director".'

'Despite *Midsomer*.'

'We all have career lows.'

'When was yours?' asked Peter.

'Mine?'

'You said "we".'

'Ask me in twenty years.'

'I'll probably be dead.'

'I'll report to your tomb.'

'I may have lost interest by then.'

'We'd got to Timothy.'

'Yes.'

'A man who exchanged better-paid, and undoubtedly more glamorous work, for a summer of pro-am theatre in the backwater of Stormhaven. Why?'

'An old debt paid off. Hermione took his comedy show when no one else would. And of course a passionate commitment to community theatre … that's what he said.'

'That may have been for our benefit,' said Peter.

'Who's the cynic now?'

'We do like to paint ourselves in the best light possible, even Buddhists.'

'And any thoughts on his commitment to nothingness?' said Tamsin.

'My mind's gone blank.'

'Very funny.'

'He's certainly not shy about his spirituality.'

'Not shy? He may as well be wearing a neon jacket, with the words "Have you noticed how spiritual I am?" on his back.'

'You don't hear many speak of nothingness.'

'People in Stormhaven speak of little else.'

'It's a Buddhist concept, of course,' said Peter. 'The call to become nothing, to become no thing, unattached.'

'Sounds like a singles night.'

Peter was ignoring Tamsin for the moment.

'When you can walk into the river and cause no ripples, then you are nothing and at one with eternity. Nirvana.'

'But I like causing ripples,' said Tamsin. 'What would life be if there were no ripples?'

She could quickly sound like a child, and when she did, he forgave her everything.

'And you do and you do it well,' he said.

'And I don't want to be nothing! That's no ambition!'

'No.'

'I want to be something!'

This was suddenly about Tamsin.

'And not just ripples, no – waves!' She was talking to herself now, in a manner never witnessed by the Abbot: 'I want to make waves, large waves, crashing tsunami waves to smash through the camp, the outbuildings, the dormitories, take out the commandant, everything.'

Peter allowed the pause.

'I don't want to be nothing,' she said, quietening. 'I've been nothing already, I was nothing in the camp, I didn't like it.'

Peter remained still, holding the moment.

'Do you want to go, Tamsin?'

'No.'

'Leave for wherever you're going. You could do that.'

'No.'

'So what do you want to do?'

She looked at him, like a wild child in headlights, caught in the beam.

'I want to finish reflecting on the interviews, I want to do my job, the job I'm paid for.'

'Okay.'

'Well?'

'We were thinking about Timothy.'

'I know.'

'So is he for real?' said Peter.

'No.'

'Spiritual fraud or enlightened human?'

'The former. You agree?'

'I don't know.'

'Surprise, surprise.'

160

'And as Timothy reminded us, quoting Meister Eckhart, "To the one who knows nothing, all is revealed".'

'You say it as though it means something,' said Tamsin.

'Which brings us to Boy, who revealed almost nothing.'

'Who doesn't even know his name.'

'I think he does know his name.'

'He's a simpleton.'

'No, he's simple – it's different.'

'But he didn't kill Hermione,' said Tamsin. 'Unless he irritated her to death with his stutter.'

'I don't think he killed Hermione either.'

Pause.

'So was Paul right?' asked the Abbot.

'How do you mean?'

'About the concentration camp?'

'What are you talking about?'

'You haven't quite recovered from that observation. I've never seen you so unsettled.'

Tamsin was up out of her chair.

'I have to go.'

'I think you do.'

She picked up her coat and her bag and turned to Peter, who was half up out of his seat.

'This isn't working.'

'That's what you feel?'

'We both know it isn't working. It's obvious, isn't it?'

'So, what – you're dissolving our partnership?'

'It's not about you, Abbot – I just need professional help on this one.'

He felt dismissed, a difficult feeling, shock, self-pity … fury.

She left in haste and he sat alone for a while.

Was this the end of the case for the Abbot?

# Forty Five

'You *will* give me the cracker, Mr Potswallop!'

'No, you will give *me* the cracker, Mr Lickspittle!'

'But it's mine, Mr Potswallop!'

'No, it's mine, Mr Lickspittle!'

'Mr Potswallop!'

'Mr Lickspittle!'

Abbot Peter had been drawn in by the noise, hollering and hooting, screaming children watching two colourful clowns pulling madly at opposite ends of a large cracker and the children loving it, calling out as each of the clowns demanded loyalty from their fans.

'Shout for me – Mr Potswallop is best!'

'Come on, Mr Potswallop!' they shouted.

'No, shout for me – Mr Lickspittle is best!

'Come on, Mr Lickspittle!'

'Boo Mr Lickspittle!'

Boo!

'Boo Mr Potswallop!'

Boo!

'Your boo was louder!'

'No, your boo was louder.'

'Your boo could be heard in Australia which is halfway across the world!'

'And yours could be heard on the moon – which is halfway across space!'

'But Uranus is further!'

'Mr Potswallop!'

And then a loud bang from the sound effects department, and a cloth saying 'BANG!' came out of the cracker as the clowns both fell backwards to much hilarity.

And it was only when the children were gone – leaving the theatre with an excitement untouched by their harassed teachers – and the clowns had removed their masks, that Peter realised the performers were none other than Neville Brownslie, theatre administrator, and Janet Lines, theatre costumier.

'That was quite a performance,' he said, admiringly. 'I haven't seen clowns for a long time.'

He wasn't sure when he'd last seen clowns. Perhaps he'd never seen them, not live. He remembered a circus had once come to a nearby park. But when his mother mentioned it, his adopted mother, as they walked past the gates on some dull afternoon in South London, his father, also adopted, had said, 'I hardly think the boy will be interested in that!' And for some reason, Peter had imagined it to be a compliment. They seemed like words of baptism, a rite of passage into adult life, where hilarity and foolishness must be left behind: young Peter was beyond the infantile happiness of the circus now. He was a man at last! Or so he had thought at the time ...

But with breathlessness now calming, Neville and Janet were ready to speak.

'Hidden talents,' said Peter. 'Both clearly actors yourselves.'

'Well, one does one's best,' said Neville, with suitable self-deprecation. 'Income for the theatre and all that. And Janet's wasted in that costume cupboard.'

Janet looked bashful and pleased.

'So you liked the show, Abbot?' she said, even fluttering her eye lashes a little ... or was Peter mistaken there?

'I thought it was excellent. And those who can entertain children can entertain anyone. Is this something you often do?'

'Hermione organised their visit,' said Neville.

'Oh.'

'But I'm quite sure she'd not have wanted the little ones let down. She loved children.'

Neville was firm on the matter and Janet nodded, as Peter pondered again how useful it is to have the corpse in full agreement: 'It's what they would have wanted.' And clearly it was, because the dead never disagreed.

'I agree,' said Peter, 'And I'm glad the police did too.'

'They did seem to understand.'

'Well, there's no reason why murder should hurt a day out for the children and SOCO are long gone.'

'We don't mean to be disrespectful,' said Janet.

That seemed important to her.

'And Messrs Potswallop and Lickspittle should definitely be on TV,' said Peter.

'Any more applause and we may struggle to get our heads out the door, Abbot!' said Janet. 'Praise is rather intoxicating.'

'Well, I'm all for praise,' said Peter. 'So you can struggle with your head all you like as far as I'm concerned. And your office is back in good order, I hope?'

He was now looking at Neville.

'My office?'

'After the break-in.'

'Ah, yes, we're getting there, Abbot, minimal damage really, looked worse than it was.'

'But they were angry, weren't they?'

'Who?'

'Well, whoever the vandal was.'

'Who knows – perhaps they had good reason to be.'

'Perhaps so.'

'Life is not always the kindest of companions,' said Neville, as he removed his clown shoes.

'So the vagrant is being forgiven?'

'Well, perhaps I'm looking at things differently – after the initial shock.'

'Very gracious, Neville – and in the meantime, we await the verdict of the fingerprints.'

'I must be off,' said Janet. 'It's not good to be late for surgery. And I need a little shopping first.'

'Dutiful to the last!'

'Oh, I'm not a good girl all the time, Abbot.'

'Really?'

'Not at all.'

Yet another aspiring bad girl … the demon on her shoulder whispering exhilarating schemes in her ear.

'Well, in between your dark deeds, Janet, you're a very good clown.'

And in character, a clown who sounded remarkably like a man.

# Forty Six

'I know who you are.'

He said the words with such trepidation. Had he ever made a more important announcement? And no stutter.

'I know you do,' came the reply.

'I know who you both are – if you know what I mean. I got a visit today – .'

Dare he risk this frankness?

'I'm glad it's all over.'

'You are?' said Boy. 'Then we're both glad it's over … too glad for words.'

'It's time it was, really it is.'

'I could hardly believe it,' said Boy. 'I only discovered this morning! I mean, I'd suspected – .'

'I could hardly believe it myself. The greatest discovery, you might call it, and amid such tragedy.'

Boy nodded, the murder of course, a great tragedy. But the truth was, he could only think of the future now and could only be happy.

'So you don't mind?' he said.

He had this fear, it was natural enough, that, well – he wasn't good enough.

'Mind? How could I mind?'

Boy could think of a thousand reasons.

'It can never be the same again,' said his companion, 'for either of us.'

Tears came to the old man's eyes, breaking the hard banks and running down his cheeks. He wasn't given to tears, tears die after a while, the ducts close, you toughen up, lock it down and do what you must do. But hot tears now, coming from somewhere, they'd been waiting in a reservoir, stored up in waiting, waiting for now, for this … for this impossible moment. And it was true what he said, things would never be the same again, how could they be? There was a different sun in the sky, a warmer sun, a kinder sun,

165

that's how it felt. You wait for years and years, so many years …
and then receive it in a moment.

'So much to discover.'

'We have time,' said Boy. 'I have some stories to tell!'

'And we must start with the bell!'

'The bell?'

A surprise.

'Well, you are its keeper, aren't you – and those muscled arms
call it into play every day.'

'I do love the bell,' said Boy.

'I know you do. And I've never seen it.'

'You haven't? Really?'

Whatever he'd expected, it wasn't this, as they stood together
in the ringing chamber, where once he'd gathered in a circle with
his friends, the St Augustine's Company of Bell-ringers. But really,
there was no reason why he couldn't give a guided tour. Indeed,
nothing would give him more pleasure.

'If that's what you'd like.'

'It is what I'd like. I'd like it very much.'

And so without more ado, and leading the way, Boy started up
the ladder, climbing to the first floor.

'This is the bell chamber,' he said. 'It's the sound chamber that
houses the clock mechanism, as you can see.'

Still no stutter. Why would he stutter?

'Fascinating. The back side of a clock is a surprising joy.'

'And, in a way, time started again today – a new day, a new era.'

That's how it felt, his old body made young, the hands of time
turned back.

'And the bell itself?'

'You're eager!'

'You could say that.'

'We'll need to climb again.'

'Then let us climb.'

And so they did, up the next and final ladder, dusty … thick dust.

'No light up here, I'm afraid.'

'We'll survive.'

Boy hadn't been in the belfry for a good while, couldn't remember the last time, but now he climbed as if in a dream, not quite
believing, not quite touching the ladder's rungs, intoxicated with
wonder, that after all these years …

'Amazing!'

And really, what else was there to say on the first sighting of
Stormhaven's tenor bell, in the half-light of this small-windowed
space?

'Yes, this is the holy of holies in a way,' he said. 'The bell chamber – or belfry, as it's commonly called. Most call it the belfry.'

Boy felt so proud.

'And the frame holds the bell?'

'It does, yes.'

'I haven't seen one close up before.'

He'd never given a guided tour like this, never been up here with anyone. He moved towards the sleeping giant, this curved monster of sound, sitting quiet for now. 'And here is the thickest part of the bell, known as the sound bow – it's this part that the ball strikes during the rotation.'

Boy lovingly ran his fingers across the curved metal form, for so long his friend – his 'partner in chime', as they used to say! They did laugh, the St Augustine's Company of Bell-ringers. They worked of course, you had to work, but always time for a laugh, especially Ezekiel, God rest his soul. Boy found himself stroking the bell, stroking it like a dog, a faithful friend, for this it had been down the years.

It was an unknowing goodbye.

# Forty Seven

'Millicent!'

'Ah, hello,' she said, a little flustered.

Since Tamsin had left for her mystery assignment, Peter's life had not been dull. He'd been dismissed from the case, yet felt compelled to carry on; felt he had to continue, an overwhelming sense of purpose, like some missionary in the jungle, as if the dismissal meant nothing. And since then he'd met two extraordinary clowns, Neville and Janet as he'd never seen them before, and now Millicent ... emerging from Boy's caravan.

'What brings you here?'

He had to ask.

'Oh, I was just wondering if Boy wanted some food.'

'I didn't realise he employed a chef.'

'No, I'm just cooking some pizza in the oven – the theatre does have a pretty decent kitchen, and I was going to bring him over a slice.'

That all felt a little contrived, a little rehearsed, you might say. Or had he just been wandering round a theatre for too long and now everything sounded like a script? Once contrivance is in the mind, it can rather take over; he'd need to be careful of that. Someone here may not be acting; they might actually be telling the truth.

'You like to look after him.'

'I suppose so. I like him. And we talk sometimes.'

They fell in step as they strolled through the graves towards the theatre.

At that moment, Neville moved past them, with a walk to suggest he was gliding on wheels.

'Bell duty today!' he called out, without turning towards them.

'Does Neville ring the bell as well?' asked Peter. 'Not half an hour ago he was being a clown.'

'I'm told he's a very good clown.'

'But a bell-ringer as well?'

'I think he does it when Boy can't. He's not as good obviously.'

'So Boy's busy today?'

'He had to go somewhere this morning.'

'It must have been important.'

The Abbot is wondering where.

'Oh yes – he loves that bell, he told me that. He calls it his "faithful friend".'

'We all need those.'

'Do you have friends, Abbot?'

A rather sharp question, and quite out of the blue.

'Oh yes, well – they're very important,' said Peter, hearing only formulaic words leaving his mouth. He didn't have friends, not in the way she meant. When he spoke of the importance of friends, he was making it up.

'And in the meantime, Neville is the cheerful stand-in?' he said.

'He needs cheering up … he's been very down recently.'

'Has he?'

'He gets a little bitchy when he's down. Neville can be quite unpleasant, you know.'

'He has a temper?'

'You do know he half-owns that weird shop, *Onslaught Games?*'

'Really?'

Peter plays the innocent, because that's the way to learn.

'All very odd, if you ask me,' said Millicent.

'It has a devoted following, I'm told.'

'My brother spends half his life there.'

'Really?'

'He can't boil an egg or wash his socks but at *Onslaught Games*, he's Master of the Universe.'

'It's good to hear we're in such safe hands.'

Millicent smiles reluctantly.

'And you've been rehearsing?'

Peter hoped it sounded a casual enquiry.

'Not really, no,' she said.

Not really? You're either rehearsing or you aren't. Peter left the pause.

'Just discussing, er, scripts, with Timothy,' she said.

'Script discussions.'

'Yes.'

Why tell the Abbot what she'd been doing? She wasn't obliged, she wasn't under caution or anything.

'Future projects?' he asked.

'That sort of thing, yes.'

She'd say nothing more. He was asking a lot of questions, but Millicent didn't have to answer.

'He must like what you do,' said Peter, 'if you're making plans.'

'I think he does, yes,' she said. 'It's nice when someone likes what you do, isn't it?'

'I can only imagine,' said Peter.

'When someone listens to you, believes in you.'

'I'm sure. Now, I don't want to keep you from the pizza.'

And, as Millicent disappeared into the theatre, the Abbot was left wondering why she imagined that Boy might want some pizza – when she already knew he was away somewhere, and unavailable for ringing.

# Forty Eight

With the first tug of the rope, Neville felt the difference. And with the first ring of the bell, a dull thud of a chime, the matter was confirmed – something was wrong. He tried again, tugged again, and then again, perhaps it was lodged. But no, this felt different. Sometimes one just knows.

'What on earth was that?' said Timothy, as he appeared in the doorway of the tower, a slice of pizza in his hand. He was wiping the grease from his mouth, as if it shouldn't be there ... but really, if you didn't want grease, thought Neville, you shouldn't eat pizza, darling, disgusting habit.

'I have no idea,' he said.

He didn't like being caught out like this.

'Are you a little rusty perhaps?'

'I most certainly am not!'

'Fine. I was just asking. It's a skill after all, and skills need looking after.'

'I rang last week and my bell-ringing fettle was in fine form then.'

'Then something's wrong.'

'I know something's wrong.'

Timothy was not being helpful, but then that was hardly a surprise.

'Is the bell cracked or something?'

Neville was relieved to hear the bell now taking the blame.

'It didn't feel right as soon as I started pulling,' he said, 'it felt off-balance, if that makes any sense, the momentum wasn't there.'

'Do you think we should go up?'

'You mean into the tower?' said Neville. 'That's Boy's job, really.'

'And where is he?'

'I don't know – he just asked me this morning if I'd ring today. I think he'd had some good news, he seemed very excited.'

'I wonder why.'

'Not an excitable man normally, bless him.'

'But he was today?'

'Rather too cheery for the day after a murder, in my humble opinion, but there we are. Perhaps he was the murderer and is just relieved it's all over.'

'You think so?'

'I have no idea and even less interest.'

'I think we should go up,' said Timothy.

'And what do you know about bells? Or are you just looking for new locations?'

*

Abbot Peter arrived on the scene, followed shortly after by Millicent. They had their own observations about the faltering chime.

'That was a complete joke, Neville,' said Millicent, glad to have a boot to kick him with. 'Can't you do better than that?'

He'd not make a cheap joke about her performances in return. He'd think it but not say it.

'Young lady, I have rung this bell often enough to know when something is wrong.'

'And is something wrong?' asked Peter.

'Believe me, Abbot, something is indubitably wrong – and the fault does not lie with moi!'

'Shall we go up?' said the Abbot, looking skywards.

'Just what I was saying,' said Timothy.

'Try once more, Neville,' said Peter, taking charge as he once had in the desert, but never since arriving on these cold shores. He took charge well and Neville pulled, pulled down hard, allowing the rope through his hands, and then pulling again, a medium pull this time to be rewarded with a dull clunk, and then a double clunk, out of pattern and some way from health.

'We go up,' said Abbot Peter. 'I'll go first. It's this ladder, I presume?'

Timothy nodded, while Neville just looked shocked.

'Do follow,' said Abbot Peter, 'but don't touch anything.' He feared the worst, though which particular worst, he wasn't sure.

With Peter leading the way, the climb began, up into the belfry of the Bell Theatre. The Abbot arrived first in the sound chamber, looking around, but nothing here to catch the eye. His sight was adjusting to the enclosed gloom, but all seemed at peace behind the loud and deliberate ticking of the clock. As the head of Timothy appeared through the trap door, Abbot Peter started up towards the next floor, towards the bell … twelve simple rungs of the ladder,

172

but a sense of foreboding in Peter, almost a desire not to arrive, not to reach the next floor, not to reach the ailing bell.

And now Peter was standing in the belfry, a half-lit scene, daylight apparent only through the cracks. The bell sat quietly in its frame, with no apparent damage, but something was wrong. The sweet smell of Turkish delight, too sweet; and then Peter saw it, heart thumping against his chest. The axe once stored in a glass case on the wall, there for emergency, had been removed and swung ... and now lay sated on the floor, sticky with blood. And as he advanced in the haze, the slipping squelch of red beneath his feet.

'I want you to stay where you are,' said the Abbot as Timothy set out to join him from the room below.

'Is everything all right?'

'No, everything is not all right.'

'I'm coming up.'

'No, you're not coming up.'

'And you're in charge, are you?'

'Yes, I am.'

'If you're sure,' said Timothy.

'I'm sure.'

'Just wanted to help.'

'We're past help here.'

Peter wished to be alone in this syrupy darkness. In the absence of Tamsin – and where on earth was she? – he approached the metal silhouette. Here before him was the bell that had rung out across Stormhaven for over a century but seemed poorly today. No apparent faults, no cracks, no broken ropes or fractured frame. Blood all around but the bell seemed well; indeed all seemed well, until he took a look underneath, under the curved rim from where Boy gazed back at him, wide-eyed in shock, but without response, without life, his severed head in a clear plastic bag, taped to the hammer.

And then as Peter staggered backwards in the half-light, behind the bell, an apparition facing him from the shadows, half-human, half-gorgon, it was satanic, and such terror in Peter, his breathing lurched, his stumbling body seeking support, and reality now, a clearer seeing – a headless human body, Boy's decapitated torso, wedged up against the wall and held beneath one of the four gargoyles on the wall.

'Do not ask for whom the bell tolls, it tolls for thee,' said Peter without thinking. 'So what happened here, Cedric?'

It seemed right that the name given to him at birth, should be given back to him in death.

# Act Four

*The good die young but not always. The wicked prevail but not consistently. I am confused by life and I feel safe within the confines of the theatre.*

**Helen Hayes**

# Forty Nine

✤

*The bells of Avignon had just chimed three, the court wearying a little in the heat of the afternoon. Too much wine at luncheon, even papal wine, can render the best of saints short on concentration.*

*But the Archbishop of Cologne was wide awake, he'd only had one glass, not more than two, he'd have a great deal more later. But in the meantime, abstinence and self-discipline were the order of the day because the Fishwife had a question to ask, a trap to set, and then he would be done ... and so would Eckhart.*

*'We must all be grateful to our parents, Eckhart,' he said, cheerfully. 'Grateful to those who gave us life!'*

*The Archbishop was being disingenuous. He was grateful for neither of his parents, who would hopefully have a hard time of it in purgatory. He'd certainly not waste his money on the purchase of indulgences, which might have bought them some respite. His mother had been a weak woman and cold, distant as the edge of the world, while he knew his father only in punishment and snide remark. If the brute had done anything else in his time on earth, young Henry had missed it.*

*But such home truths were hardly the point right now; no, this afternoon, he was the delighted and grateful son. He'd been hunting down Meister Eckhart – 'Meister' so-called – for twenty years, and now he had him ... had him before the Pope, with the sharp point of his theological sword very close to the monk's defenceless neck.*

*Eckhart received the eulogy to parenthood, but heard the falsehood behind. The Fishwife did not speak for himself here – that at least was clear. Good parents do not create liars. Why lie if you are happy?*

*'The Archbishop', said Eckhart, 'uses the borrowed language of tradition rather than the fresh language of truth.'*

The Archbishop feigned surprise. He was beginning to enjoy the play-acting of the court.

'Oh, so the accused separates truth and tradition?'

'And like countless fools before you, you muddle the order of creation.'

'Is that so?'

'It is so, yes – for simply put, you had being before your parents conceived you.'

The court was suddenly awake, or a number at least, and temporarily sober.

'Nature makes a man and a woman from a child,' continued Eckhart, 'and a chicken from an egg.'

'Quite so.'

What was the monk talking about?

'But God is different, for God makes the man or the woman before the child and the chicken before the egg.'

And now the Archbishop was playfully frustrated.

'You're becoming incoherent, Eckhart! And while that might be a blessing in disguise, for you do seem most full of the perversities of Satan – we do so want to understand. So please, explain a little!'

In fact, explain as much as you like, thought the Archbishop, the floor is yours, you fool, for every clever word condemns you as the heretic you are, as the heretic you've always been.

Eckhart breathed deeply and continued.

'Nature first makes the wood warm and then hot. Yes? That is the way of things?'

'It is in my palace fire!'

Reassuring laughter.

'And only then, when the wood is warm, does she generate fire in your palace grate. But God is different, God is nothing like your palace: God first gives creatures being, and only later, through birth and all that follows, does he give them all that belongs to being. So you see, we were being before we were creatures – and that is still how God perceives us.'

And so to the final cut of the knife:

'And the fourth commandment, Meister Eckhart? The call to honour our parents?'

'We had our being before them, Archbishop, as I say. Before the joyous union of your parents, you already were.'

There'd been no joyous union between Henry's parents – it would have been assault on a reluctant victim.

'So your parents did not make you,' continued Eckhart, caught up in the beauty of this revelation. 'They merely made a creature of you, for good ... or for ill.' Some repressed mirth in the court. 'So does that *call for honour? On occasion perhaps, there is much kindness in the world. But there are also sick creatures in the world, the controlling and the cold, hurting children with their so-called love. Perhaps you knew two such people, Archbishop? So indiscriminate honour seems a little inappropriate.'*

*Sharp intake of alcoholic breath.*

*'So let me understand this, Eckhart: you are now saying we have only nine commandments left from the original ten?'*

*Eckhart stands silent.*

*'I have said what I have said.'*

*'And we are grateful, of course, Good Meister, though I'm fearful of how many other commandments we might lose before vespers!'*

*The killer blow amid much laughter. The only figure not laughing – apart from Eckhart, who stood unmoved, and the Pope, whose bowed face was hard to read, was Henricus. With his head in his hands, no one could see the expression he pulled. But it will have been a face etched with pessimism for himself, for his Order … and for the reprobate on trial, whom he could no longer help.*

*It was now simply a matter of awaiting the verdict.*

*And then lighting the fire.*

# Fifty

It was dark and Tamsin wished it so.

Four p.m. on a sunny August day, but Tamsin had drawn the curtains and now lay on her bed staring into nothing ... the nothing she so feared, so hated, so kicked against. She had no language for this paralysis, for this deep pessimism, like a heavy cloud inside her, yet always kept at bay, always managed ... until now. A frightening sense – and was this the worst thing? – the sense that she could no longer help herself and was therefore beyond help, for beyond herself who was there?

She'd driven home to her tidy flat, renting for now, unsure where to settle. She'd thought of making a phone call, taking the plunge, but had driven home instead, ignored the post on entering, couldn't remember entering, couldn't remember ignoring the post, couldn't remember driving. She'd been at the Bell Theatre but left, left the Abbot, she'd had to leave, an overwhelming feeling, and had then walked straight to her bedroom, closed the curtains and collapsed on her bed. She had had to come here, there'd been no choice, it was like an appointment, but how strange it felt – like a secret assignation she knew she must keep, a call from a stranger to be here, but without purpose, there was no purpose to this, just the white noise of a psyche closing down, of paralysis of mind and the despair of inaction; of not being able to act, of no activity to ward off the darkness.

It was as though Paul Bent had seen right through her, just for a moment, unpleasant little man, he really was, which only made it worse ... but the pinprick of truth breaking her skin, needling inside and curdling the blood, good blood curdled, her blood was good until now, this ridiculous sequence, bringing her down.

No feeling, she didn't feel anything, but then she'd never felt anything. It was the loss of action that made this different, the inability to function. These were the things that had brought her to her bed on a sunny day in August, when she should be working.

She decided on a phone call.
She'd take the plunge.

# Fifty One

It had been an irritating question at the time. Which question hadn't been, in his ridiculous interview with the police? But Paul now found it strangely compelling as he sat in his flat, listening to Pink Floyd's 'Wish You Were Here'.

'Do you know anyone who might have wished to kill Hermione?' Abbot Peter had asked.

He'd responded with scorn, but it's strange how things grow after the event, how things dismissed then find a place; how the stupid can acquire interest. He was even wondering whether there was a play in this. Not some dull Agatha Christie whodunnit, God save us from those. But how about an exploration of the human need to kill – the need to kill others, physically, emotionally, spiritually?

You could start with those caught up in the murders at the Bell. Who might have wished Hermione dead? He sat down with a blank piece of paper and his favourite pen.

Bill Cain was the murderer because, well, Hermione threatened his bank account, an extension of his penis, so a place of both vulnerability and power. Her presence came to feel like his own castration.

Or Janet Lines was the murderer because, in the end, she fell out with everybody, and when her sense of duty collapsed, all that was left was a blazing fire of knife-wielding resentment.

Or Margery Tatters was the murderer because history lodged in her body – you could see it, like water in a sponge – and cried for justice the loudest when her career was on the slide and self-hate on the rise. Remember Drury Lane!

Or Millicent Pym was the murderer because … Paul paused. Why would Millicent murder? She'd murder out of entitlement, her little-girl sense that she should have something which wasn't given and should have been given. Hermione was holding out on something. She'd break vertebrae for that.

Or Boy was the murderer, a figure from the past returning for vengeance, choosing the thirtieth anniversary for execution, but now dead himself, avenged by Hermione's guardian angel.

Or Neville Brownslie was the murderer because, in the end, his dark fantasies had to be more than games, his need to control, to stifle and suppress all things – and the woman had it coming, she made him feel like a failure.

Or Timothy Gershwin was the murderer, by-passing his raging ambition with spiritual sayings of calm; suppressing the need to succeed with second-hand mantras of acceptance. He wanted to be theatre director, anyone could see that. Denial is not a river in Egypt.

Or he was the murderer, Paul Bent, and why that might be so – well, hardly the need to go into that here. But if he was forced, the engulfing sense of abandonment simply has to destroy everything close.

Eight little demons, hungry for the kill.

# Fifty Two

'"THE MURDER OF QUASIMODO" … Ring any bells?!'

Chief Inspector Wonder was holding the *Sussex Silt's* evening edition.

'I had the same joke from the desk sergeant,' said Tamsin.

'It doesn't matter whose joke it is.'

It did matter whose joke it was and Wonder had hoped it would be his.

'The comedy seems a little borrowed round here,' said Tamsin, 'but then what's new?'

She'd come here straight from her dark room, and come unwillingly.

'I'd be very careful, Detective Inspector,' said Wonder, who didn't go with his name, not in any way at all. Wonder was clubbable rather than gifted, a triumph of rank above substance … but he'd be shown some respect, he'd damn well be shown some respect! He could make life pretty difficult for DI Shah, if he so wished, absolutely no question, and she forgot that sometimes, too attractive for her own good – but that was another story. Bloody attractive woman, DI Shah, but she needed to know her place.

'A murder under your nose, Shah. You were both there at the theatre, you and that monk fellow. And now there's a second murder in twenty-four hours!'

'We can't sit with everyone reading them stories. It's not a nursery.'

'No, it's a bloody abattoir!'

Now Wonder was being ridiculous.

'We're doing what we can there.'

'Only you weren't there! You were at home, not answering your phone.'

So much irritation to exorcise and Tamsin would have to be careful. Her disdain levels were high.

'There was a gas explosion in the next-door flat. My neighbour rang me.'

Tamsin had not lost her capacity to lie, which was reassuring; and anyway, as she said things, she began to believe them; speaking made them true, so they weren't lies, they were fact, that is what had happened. There'd been a gas explosion next door. That's why she was at home for the murder of Boy.

'You weren't in bed with Martin Channing, were you?'

'I beg your pardon?'

'Just wondering how the *Sussex Silt* got the story before the police did.'

Tamsin felt utter contempt for the man in front of her.

'Mr Monk's been handling it,' continued Wonder.

'Mr Monk?'

'The monk bloke.'

'Abbot Peter. He has a name.'

Wonder still found it difficult to refer to him as 'Abbot', to acknowledge an Abbot working with police on a case; in the twelfth century maybe, but in the twenty-first? That was a joke.

'But how well he's been handling it, God only knows. Forensics are there now of course, but the *Silt* is pretty up to speed – even if the same can't be said for the DI heading the case.'

'It was a gas explosion. What do you expect me to do?'

'Your job would be nice?'

He'd have been home if there was a gas explosion next door, of course he would, and pretty sharpish; but he preferred this surge of power, the dark pleasure of the moral high ground he so rarely had.

'Still, so long as I have the *Silt* to keep me informed of developments – they only rang me for a quote on the murder! They rang me for a quote on a murder I, the Chief Inspector, knew nothing about! No one here knew anything about it! Oh, they loved that at the *Silt*! I felt the smirk down the phone.'

'I'll go there now.'

'Where?'

'The theatre.'

'Only if it's not too much trouble.'

'It was a gas explosion.'

She must act again, be active. She dreaded returning to the Bell Theatre, but she must un-dread, she could do it. The floor had collapsed but she must walk normally through the wreckage, as though the floor was in place and all quite well. She must do things by memory, until life was restored.

Right now, anything was better than this idiot of a boss. Why didn't the murderer pick on him?

Tamsin was keen to assist.

# Fifty Three

'So who actually found the body?'

'I did,' said Peter.

'You did?'

'Is that a problem?'

'But what were you doing up here?'

The Abbot and Tamsin sat in the Belfry of the Bell Theatre, away from the dark puddle of sticky blood. Outside, the light of the day was fading, summer twilight and a fine array of stars emerging from a clear night sky on this coastal evening in August. Inside, a lone light bulb, brought by SOCO, hung from the ceiling, bleak illumination for the horror room, the bagged head of Cedric Mayfield removed for further tests along with the axe and his torso. Peter had spoken of his morning experiences, the performing clowns and Millicent's pizza lies.

'Once the body was discovered, I asked Neville to lock all access points in and out of the theatre.'

'From which we learned?'

'Not a great deal.'

'That's encouraging.'

'The murderer could have left before the locking.'

'Chronicles of wasted time then.'

'Of our suspects, now reduced from eight to seven, Millicent, Neville, Timothy and Margery present. Paul, Bill and Janet absent.'

'Where were they?'

'Paul taking a walk, Janet shopping, Bill working at home.'

'Witnesses?'

'None at the moment.'

'So that's all meaningless.'

'Have you come to help or destroy?'

Destroy. Because that's how she was feeling.

'It's called realism, Abbot. We're getting nowhere and it's a bloody embarrassment.'

'That sounds like your Chief Inspector speaking.'

'Well, *you* tell me where we are, if it isn't east of nowhere?'

'You talked about bringing in professional help.'

Had she said that? If she had, he'd misunderstood.

'What else do I need to know?' she said. Why put him out of his misery?

'There was one surprising discovery in the rehearsal room.'

'A murderer's confession?'

'The Bishop.'

'The Bishop?'

'The Bishop was there – claiming he was looking for his son. So to that extent, our seven suspects are now eight again.'

Tamsin wasn't enjoying being behind with the news, being the one catching up … she wanted to assert some authority, she wanted to prick his balloon: 'He could have been looking for his son.'

'A phone call would have told him he wasn't here.'

'Sometimes people don't answer their phones.'

'That's true.'

People like Tamsin, for instance.

'And perhaps they have their reasons,' she added, defensive.

The elephant in the room – Tamsin's unexplained absence from the crime scene at a crucial moment in the case – was noted at this point, but unremarked upon. For her part, she'd briefly considered a repeat of the gas explosion story, but didn't imagine the Abbot would believe it. It was difficult to get nonsense past him. As for Peter, there would be a time to know, as there was a time for everything, but this wasn't it. Tonight in the belfry was about catching up, calming her down and charting tomorrow's course.

But one thing was plain: his niece was a diminished existence at present. He'd seen her buckle in the interview with Paul Bent, an insightful young man despite his holey trousers. And while she needed to be held in her pain, this would not be at the expense of finding and facing the killer. Until she was well, he would go it alone – and after his meeting with Satan in the belfry, he feared nothing now. That had been terror.

Though as it turned out, only a rehearsal for more.

# Fifty Four

## Wednesday 4 August

It was 5.00 a.m. and Abbot Peter was taking an early morning walk through the streets of Stormhaven. It wasn't busy, no company except a fresh sea wind, a south-westerly, full in his face.

Six days of the week he ran at first light, but 'no one should run seven days on the trot, no pun intended', said an osteopath he'd spoken to recently. 'The body needs recovery time.' So, like God, on the seventh day, Peter rested, a walk replaced a run, the walk he now enjoyed around the quiet pavements of this seaside town before the daily footfall of anxiety and fear. People looked more peaceful in death than in life, this was Peter's experience.

An early excursion wasn't new, of course. He'd done the same in the desert but was always back in the cloistered shadows before King Sun rose over the mountains ... you didn't argue with the king in that land. But Stormhaven was another land, a different government; a land where the sun held less sway, no longer king but a mere courtier in these seagull skies – so changeable and various that rulers changed by the minute.

And today, on this August morning, a grey dawn haze was giving way to blue and the promise of a warm summer's day on England's south coast. Perhaps there'd even be swimmers in the shingle sea, enjoying the white-crested waves? They'd mainly be children but possibly others, reckless others, for while the water here was never warm – warmer than Whitby, but then so was the Arctic – it was sometimes less cold; and that was enough for the English.

And now Peter was smiling, remembering the *Stormhaven Stiffs*, an unfortunate name, but true to their madness, for at 6.00 a.m., they would take the plunge, every day of the year and whatever the

189

weather. Peter watched them from his front window and felt only admiration. He even gave them tea on occasion, if the wind was particularly cruel. And then suddenly, gate-crashing his thoughts, a tense figure on collision course, a cyclist accelerating towards him on the pavement, wordlessly insisting he move out of the way or be hit. It was tempting to move, tempting to scarper, with the cyclist speeding towards him, head down and hard. And perhaps other pedestrians did so as this helmeted tornado approached ... but not Peter. Instead, he walked straight towards the cyclist, and when the thwarted rider took evasive last-minute action and began to swerve to avoid collision, Peter invited it, indeed insisted, by swerving a little himself, following the cyclist by drifting gently to his left, and leaving his left shoulder unavoidably in the path of the speed merchant who was soon flying into the hedge. Peter turned round to check he was okay. He didn't wish the cyclist harm; he just wished them off the pavement, which they now were.

'What the hell are you doing?' screamed the cyclist, disentangling their lycra body from their bike.

'Thanks to the Romans, there are roads for cyclists,' said the Abbot.

The rider moved towards him. Without moving, Peter added: 'The roads are the wide tarmac paths, with white lines on.'

He indicated with his hands.

'I'll be reporting you,' said the cyclist.

Abbot Peter smiled at the desperation of the ridiculous.

'I think you'd be reporting yourself.'

'Call yourself a Christian?'

'Very rarely,' said Peter. 'In fact, I can't remember the last time.' He was angry now. 'But if Christians kow-tow to small-town pavement bullies, then consider me an atheist.'

He turned and walked on, making his way back towards the seafront and then on home. He'd made an enemy, because sometimes you do. Action brings enemies, this was all right. But perhaps more significantly, and more intriguingly, he'd recognised the voice ... fairly certain at least.

The hasty attempt at disguise had come too late.

# Fifty Five

'Do you really think I'd kill Hermione just to buy this shit-hole?'

'Your description not mine, Mr Cain.'

Tamsin felt confident with the cards she held.

'Whatever you bloody call it, my question still stands.'

'I have no inside track on your business brain, Mr Cain. But we do know it's a shit-hole you want to buy.'

'And how do you know?'

'We just do.'

'You're bluffing.'

Tamsin raised her eyebrows.

'So what if it is?' he said.

'You're admitting it.'

'I'm not admitting to anything.'

'Sounded like you were.'

'"Hypothesising" is the word. Good, eh? For a boy who left school at fifteen.'

'Still sounding like an admission.'

'And shit-holes can be cleaned up, because contrary to popular belief, you *can* polish a turd – otherwise where would business be?'

'Did you learn to speak in a sewer?'

'It's called real life, Detective Inspector.'

'So was that your plan?'

'Was what my plan?'

'A change of direction for the Bell Theatre? A bingo hall, perhaps? A car show room?'

The businessman brooded for a moment.

'Don't know how you bloody know.'

Cain was running through the possible sources in his mind. Who could have told Old Bill about the purchase? And why? He'd kept it pretty quiet, his plans to buy the place. Only a small circle were aware, all of whom he thought he could trust. But then a secret is something you only tell one other person, everyone knows that; and what if that one other person was the police?

'Obviously we can't reveal our sources,' said Tamsin.

But who cares, thought Bill, it wasn't sensitive information. It's not as if anyone else wanted the theatre.

'I trust this can stay under the radar for a while?' he said. 'I like to stay ahead of the opposition.'

'As long as it didn't make a murderer of you.'

'So who told you?'

'I said, I can't say.'

'Don't worry, I can find out these things for myself.'

And almost instantly, he knew – knew the stupid little gossip who'd spilled the beans, and knew how they must have found out. Well, he'd stuff their goose.

'As long as everything is above board and legal,' said Tamsin.

'Oh, the worst crimes are always legal.'

And even as he said that, a punishment came to mind, an appropriate humiliation.

'But you're wasting your time here,' he added.

'There's no such thing,' said Peter.

'No such thing as what?'

'Wasted time. Every moment is bringing something to the surface, something previously hidden.' Peter spoke in an eirenic fashion. 'And it was hidden, wasn't it – your desire to purchase the Bell? You decided, for whatever reason, to hide it from us?'

Cain smiled.

'I've bought fourteen companies in my time, Abbot – how many have you bought?'

'Fewer than you, possibly.'

'And do you know what? I've done it without murdering anyone, have you noticed that? Fourteen companies bought and no one murdered – not physically at least.'

'Such restraint.'

'My interest in this place was no great secret.'

'Though you're behaving as if it was, threatening revenge on the whistle-blower.'

'I don't like tell-tales, never have … tell-tale tits play a dangerous game in my world.'

'And of course this was different, wasn't it?' said Tamsin.

'How do you mean?'

'Well, it was hardly a normal business you wanted to buy – it was an affair of the heart, for Hermione at least. '

'You think so?'

'I do, yes. And perhaps affairs of the heart are a little more expensive to purchase? You wouldn't just be buying the premises; you'd be buying thirty years of her life, perhaps her happiest and most fulfilling years.'

Bill Cain looked at them with some amusement.

'Everything's a business, Shah.'

'Detective Inspector.'

'Whether it's Exxon Oil or some spastic's society – because nothing runs on fresh air.'

'I think you've made your point.'

'And here's another one. If the Bell Theatre was an affair of the heart for anyone, it was Nicholas Bysshe-Urquhart, not Hermione.'

'Her husband.'

'Her husband of blessed memory and all that, yes. Now there was a saint, mark my words. He's the one who should have had the MBE.'

There was a silence in the room as this news was assimilated.

'What made him such a saint?' asked Peter, interested in Bill Cain's version of sanctity.

'Only a saint takes on damaged goods,' he said.

'Would you like to expand on that a little?'

'Not really. I think that's what you're paid for, to investigate.'

'Maybe. But I'm a great believer in the help of volunteers.'

'I call them suckers.'

Peter smiled.

'But maybe I can help you, Abbot.'

'Really – how?'

'D'you want to know who your little letter-writer is?'

'How do you know about that?'

'I can tell you, you see. Give you a name.'

'Well, I'd certainly be interested.'

'There, you see. Change of tune now! It may not look like it, but Bill Cain is looking after the plods!'

He got up to leave.

'It doesn't mean we won't come for you,' said Tamsin.

193

# Fifty Six

'What "little letter writer" is he talking about?'

With Bill Cain gone, Tamsin wanted details.

He hadn't given them the name in the end; he'd merely teased them with his knowledge – his mysterious knowledge of Peter's recent post. He'd made the most of it, boasting that he appeared some way ahead of them in this half-cock investigation. Abbot Peter had said it wasn't a competition but both Cain and Tamsin knew better; they were keen contestants, both insisting on winning – with Tamsin insisting the most. It was a game for Cain, but life for Tamsin and she would win. She'd never needed to win anything more than this.

'I have had one or two letters,' said Peter.

'What sort of letters?'

'Letters suggesting I engage with the sender, er, more directly.'

Tamsin laughed at the Abbot's phrasing.

'What?'

'Obsessional letters.'

'And your guess at the identity of the sender?'

'I don't know – but they seem to see a lot of me. And feel ignored.'

'And Cain thinks *he* knows who it is?'

'So it appears; perhaps it's him, I've no idea how. I assumed it was someone in the supermarket.'

'Why the supermarket – do you have a fan club there?'

'No. I just don't go anywhere else. Apart from the church.'

'More likely, I think.'

'The church?'

'Where better for the socially inept to loiter and manipulate?'

'Maybe – but it's not Bill Cain's natural habitat.'

'Do you have the letters?'

'I have today's letter. It arrived just as I was leaving.'

'Give it to me.'

194

Tamsin was taking over and Peter meekly dug deep into the large pockets of his habit and, amid the debris, found the unopened envelope with a typed address, which he pulled out and handed over. Tamsin contemplated it, drew a pair of rubber gloves from her bag and opened carefully.

'The first letter suggested I lacked the courage of my convictions and should declare my intentions more openly.'

But Tamsin was already reading the typed note:

*'Peter darling, I did wonder if seeing you close up on a more regular basis, in and out of my kitchen almost – you know what I mean! – would be enjoyable or irritating, and I suppose it's a bit of both. But you know where to find me when finally you decide to follow your desires – as opposed to loping along behind that unpleasant police-woman, like a dog on a lead. Really, where's your self-respect? Your eyes were all over me when we spoke!'*

'Is this a man or a woman?'

'They haven't thought to enclose a photo,' said Peter.

'Underwear?'

'Underwear? No, I think I'd have noticed that. They did say in the first letter that there was some local discussion over "which way I swung".'

Tamsin's eyebrows rose.

'I believe it's something to do with my sexual identity,' he explained. 'So the woman in the library told me.'

'You've been in the library as well? You do get about.'

'She said, "It's about being hetero or gay, Abbot."'

'I believe it is, yes.'

'I have no idea why my sexuality is up for discussion.'

'I can't imagine either, what with you a single man – and an Abbot.'

This was a different world from the desert.

'And did they reach a conclusion?'

'Who?'

'Your stalker.'

'My what?'

'Your *stalker*.'

'What sort of a word is that?'

'It's the word that describes the person writing you these letters.'

'Stalker? When I left for the desert, it described a prowler or poacher … good sixteenth-century vintage. Has something changed?'

195

'Apart from the industrial revolution, the vote for women, the discovery of DNA, the rise of fundamentalism, the silicone chip and globalisation – very little.'

Abbot Peter smiles and applauds with gentle hands.

'I'm impressed.'

'Which is worrying. Do you not read the papers?'

'I'm topical until the fourth century.'

'So what were the headlines then?'

'The discovery of the seven deadly sins, and really, every headline since has been an echo of those.'

Tamsin wasn't interested in the seven deadly sins. But she was concerned about the stalker, who could be impacting on the case, could even be the murderer.

'A stalker, the twenty-first-century version, is someone who harasses or pesters others – usually celebrities.'

'I see,' said Peter.

'But obviously not in this instance,' she added, just in case the Abbot was getting delusions of grandeur.

'And what does a twenty-first-century stalker actually *do* – if they don't shoot deer on the lord's estate after dark?'

'It's a constellation of behaviours, really.'

'A constellation?'

Peter preferred a constellation of stars to behaviours.

'A series of repeated unwanted intrusions on another person's life – following, writing, phoning. Have they phoned?'

'I don't think so.'

'You'd know if they had.'

'Someone hung up yesterday, without speaking.'

'Could have been them.'

'But hardly a crime in itself.'

'No single act is a crime, that's the thing about stalking. It's not one act, but a series of acts, one little invasion after another – no act terrible in itself, or indeed a crime in itself … but cumulatively upsetting, and sometimes terrifying.'

'So when does it become illegal?'

'In this country, it becomes illegal when the cumulative actions breach the legal definition of harassment.'

She spoke as one who had recently passed the Inspectors' exams with the best results in the South of England. She liked to be best. Stalking had come up in the interview and she'd wiped the floor with them on the subject.

She continued: 'So an action such as sending an email is not illegal – but becomes illegal when frequently repeated to an unwilling recipient.'

'I'm always an unwilling recipient of emails.'

'That's because you're an unsociable hermit. But the good news for hermits, in the UK at least, is that the incident need only happen twice – after that, the stalker should be made aware that their behaviour is unacceptable.'

This is all new to the Abbot.

'So that could be just two phone calls to a stranger?'

'Yes – or two gifts, or following the victim and then phoning them, that sort of thing.'

'An aggressive legal response.'

'Because there's a lot of it about. And while it's the celebrities who get the headlines, because that's what celebrities do, most stalking is committed against those without much power to fight back or defend themselves.'

'I can see it could be very unpleasant.'

Abbot Peter found people he *did* know an invasion; but someone he didn't know, some unknown figure projecting their needs onto him in an obsessive way … this was the unutterable horror.

'Oh, it breaks people,' said Tamsin. 'It's a form of mental assault.'

'With a variety of psychological causes, no doubt.'

'It can be some form of negative obsession – jealousy, dependency, blame. Sometimes it's an ex-partner who can't let go. We dealt with a particularly vindictive little man a few weeks ago.'

'Small?'

'No – pathetic. But usually the stalker has no hostile feelings towards the victim.'

'Simply a longing that cannot be fulfilled?'

'Precisely.'

'But longing and hatred are close.'

'So, does your stalker hate you? '

'I don't know.'

'Did they have a view on your sexuality?'

'They said they knew, yes.'

Pause.

'And I presume this person works at the Bell Theatre?' asked Tamsin.

'You're referring to the bit about seeing me close up on a more regular basis? I did wonder.'

'That's a relief.'

'I'm sorry?'

'Well, it does have "obvious" written all over it!'

Dressed as a joke, but it was a sour remark which Peter sat with for a moment.

'But then I realised', he said slowly, 'that I received the first letter before we took on the case.'

Peter allowed the pause before continuing, looking briefly out the window to a bigger beyond: 'Which would appear to make it unlikely that the stalker works at the theatre … or at least not as obvious as a hasty judgement might declare.'

It was a put-down, delivered quietly, deliberately – but Tamsin was quickly up and running, she had to be, because she was the best.

'So where else do you go – apart from the supermarket, the church and the library? We need to find this person … these things don't end well, Uncle.'

Peter noted the moment of concern but it was a brief affair.

'We need to interview everyone again,' said Tamsin.

'No,' he said, 'we need the goat's path.'

'The ghost path?'

'The goat's path.'

'What in God's name is the goat's path?'

'It's the path you can't see from the ground. You look up into the mountains, sheer and unforgiving, and there are goats at the top. How did they get there?'

'On my Greek holiday, I was lying on the beach.'

'The goat's path is the hidden path that takes them to that impossible place, the path that explains their unlikely arrival.'

Tamsin's frustration is obvious.

'I do need to get going again.'

'Another mystery encounter?'

'But we have to talk about police work, Abbot, if we're going to work together. Not goat paths.' Peter notes the threat, the abandonment of the partnership, the use of the distant 'Abbot', the retreat into procedure.

'Go wherever you must go, Tamsin,' he says quietly.

It is a dismissal, but he's the first to depart, furious. This is the second time in two days Tamsin has had to leave, with no reason given.

From here on, with regard to the Bell Theatre murders, he will travel alone.

# Fifty Seven

Sobbing.

Peter hadn't been sure of the noise or its source, but when he pushed open the rehearsal room door, Timothy was in tears.

'Are you all right?' asked Peter.

It was a stupid and unnecessary question. You don't sob if you're happy, but at least a conversation is started … even if the response is a sharp 'Just leave me alone!'

But Timothy didn't want to be left alone; he wanted to talk as he wiped wretched tears from his face.

'He understands origins, doesn't he?'

'Who?'

'The old Meister – Meister Eckhart!'

The Abbot noticed the book in Timothy's hands, an unusual choice: the collected sermons of the fourteenth-century Dominican. Not that Eckhart had collected the sermons himself, he hadn't had the chance. As Peter well knew – he'd long felt an affiliation with the man – Eckhart had been bundled off to Avignon to be tried before the papal court, never to return home. So the careful collecting of his words, away from the persecuting gaze of the Church, had been the task of followers like Henry Suso, John Tauler and the brave nuns of the south Rhineland, grateful for his pastoral support; and of course his own friars in Cologne, they mucked in as well, all of them copying out his sermons from memory, lest the fire of his thought be extinguished completely. So while the Church declared him a pariah and the Inquisition snarled at his memory, there were determined souls who wouldn't be bowed, who thought him worth the ultimate risk. Not everyone had abandoned Eckhart after his demise in Avignon; and because of them, Timothy now cried.

'He does, yes,' said Peter. 'Eckhart understood origins very well – which is one reason the Church found him so threatening. He threatened their teaching on the family.'

They sat in companionable silence for a while, as the tears dried.

'He's the only writer who has ever given me hope,' said Timothy. 'Can you believe that?'

'I can believe that.'

Timothy watched Peter as he picked up the open book and read a little. He watched the Abbot's concentration, his interest; he almost felt as though he was watching the Abbot's enlightenment ... and he was.

'He interests you?' said Timothy.

'No, he changes me,' said Peter. 'Interest is overrated.'

Timothy the director smiled: 'You must entertain before you can teach,' he said.

'Oh, he does entertain – and then he kills you, if you know what I mean.'

The Abbot was engrossed again, he hadn't read these things for years.

'Perhaps he reveals things you hadn't previously seen?' said Timothy.

And now it was Peter's turn to look up and smile.

'Always,' he said. 'As you reminded us, "To the one who knows nothing, all is revealed". And so it has been.'

'So are there places that scare you, Abbot?'

He no longer wept, but Timothy's face was troubled.

'How do you mean?'

'Places where you'd be overcome by fear?'

'All the usual ones,' said Abbot Peter.

'What are the usual ones?'

Were Buddhists past such fears?

'Heights,' said Peter. 'I'm not good at the edge of cliffs.'

'Even the white cliffs of Stormhaven?'

'Particularly the white cliffs of Stormhaven. The view is fine but not the fall, believe me.'

On more than one occasion, he'd been called to bless a body dismembered on the rocks.

'Any other fears, Abbot? You strike me as such a resolved man; I cannot imagine fear in you.'

Peter remembered a visit to the Valley of the Kings at Luxor. The one thing worse than the crowds had been the sense of entrapment as they descended the underground corridors, down into those remarkable tombs, fatally enclosed.

'Being closed in,' he said. 'Sealed in. I wouldn't want to be a Pharaoh.'

'Ah, good old claustrophobia!'

'Yes, I like to know I have an escape route … particularly during sermons.'

Timothy laughed.

'You joke, Abbot.'

'You obviously haven't heard our vicar.'

The new vicar at St Michael's was a good man, but not someone who should ever be allowed in a pulpit.

'And your fears?' asked Peter. 'What do your fears look like?'

If someone enquired of another's fear, it was usually because they wished to speak of their own. Timothy looked at the Abbot, an assessing look, a look which wondered if this man could handle the truth. It appeared he could.

'The thought that no part of me is good,' said Timothy. 'That is my fear.'

Peter saw emptiness in the man's eyes … and then the emptiness curdled into something else, something like hatred.

# Fifty Eight

Tamsin looked over the cliff edge.

Behind her, a half-lived life, successful in its way; but the words of Paul Bent – casual words about a concentration camp – had left her paralysed and Tamsin was never paralysed. She was always action, achieving action … until now.

'I don't think it's my concentration camp you need worry about,' he'd said, and really, it was just another dig from a suspect, par for the course, the harassed suspect lashing out, trying to score a point or two for the sake of self-respect. Only this had been different … different because it was true and she'd never quite recovered. She'd struggled on but never recovered, put her uncle through hell, which is why she now stood at the edge, between life and death, on the edge of the cliff, the cusp of death, the edge of oblivion … for this is how it seemed, to be stepping off into who knows what?

There was the fall, easy enough, no threat in itself. But what lay beyond the fall?

The decision was made.

She rang the doorbell.

# Fifty Nine

Peter walked in the graveyard as the light began to fade. He was a lone figure, a monkish silhouette, glancing down at the leaning ranks of headstones, with chiselled grief: too dearly loved to be forgotten, or sadly missed, forever in our hearts, good night, grand-dad. Some tragically taken, some safe in God's keeping, my darling boy, just five years old, a small grave for a small body, watched over by stone angels, though slightly distant in their concern. More stories here than there'd ever be time to tell.

A netherworld of sanctity, grief and virtue. From the inscriptions, you might imagine everyone here a saint; for the chiselled words spoke of heroes, fine souls, noble and kind, devoted husbands, so many devoted husbands and each much missed, joined thirty years later by their wives, aged ninety-two, now reunited, bliss restored for eternity ... though in life, such relationships are more difficult to find. As Peter had once said, 'It's not that we become liars when people die, we simply change our tune.'

Peter paused by a recent stone and wondered: did the family of Reginald Reardon – 'Reggie' – really imagine him to be 'with the angels now, and making them laugh'? Was this bold belief in a future life, a glorious shout for life beyond the grave? Or simply sentimental thanks for the jokes he'd told; for all the times he'd made them giggle over tea? It seemed unlikely to the Abbot there was comedy in heaven. He wouldn't be telling Reggie's family this, but how could there be? Most jokes arise out of sadness, anger, self-importance or the misfortune of another – this is the stuff of comedy, yet not the stuff of paradise. He'd recently been given a box-set of *Fawlty Towers*, a popular series he'd been told, popular while he was otherwise engaged in the rocky wastes of Middle Egypt. And on viewing, he had found it funny, but only as funny as pain can be, for his dominant feeling as each episode closed had been sadness – sadness at the human agony played out before his eyes. This was more tragedy than comedy ... but then that's what comedy was. If there was no conceit, no ignorance, no absurdity, no frustration, no pomposity, no laughing at another's pain – where would the comic writer be? And so where will the comedy be in heaven?

Peter remembered where he was, remembered Reggie as the sunlight played on his stone, blessed his memory and sat down on the bench. As he looked up, he rested his eyes on a small pair of head stones, slightly away from the others, and they surprised him in a number of ways. There were, for instance, no dates on either and dates mattered on headstones. When was this person born and when did they die? How long had they lived? Were they taken 'tragically early' as a nearby stone lamented. And the other surprise, apart from the lack of dates, was the lack of any names.

LOST SO YOUNG, TOO PERFECT TO BE MISSED.
LOST SO YOUNG, TOO WONDERFUL TO BE WEPT FOR.

Why was Peter now thinking of Eckhart? He was thinking of Eckhart. He was looking at these tombs and thinking of the fourteenth-century monk … and looking at the caravan, Boy's green caravan, and remembering the tin. 'It's all recorded in the tin,' he'd said – so what was there to record? Whatever it was, it had been too dangerous for one individual. Boy had possessed dangerous knowledge about someone in this theatre. But where was the tin now? Had someone beaten him to it? He hadn't believed Millicent's story about the pizza, that hadn't been the reason for her snooping. But now Peter wondered if she'd been looking for the tin? He needed to look, because suddenly Eckhart and the two stones made a terrible sense, and explained that look in the eyes so recently seen. A curtain was opening; something hidden becoming visible … the goat's path now emerging from the mist.

This was all about origins – but he needed to find the tin.

He walked slowly through the graves to the single-berth home, scratched plastic windows and dark inside. And for the first time, he noticed the name of the caravan, painted over, but still pushing through: 'LUCKY'. He pondered the fading light and felt the chill of the shadows, here beneath evergreen and bell tower, a darkening presence now. No lights came from the theatre, all was quiet, everyone home and hosed; and he too looked forward to bed. He'd speak with Tamsin later, or maybe in the morning – perhaps allow her a good night's rest. He reached the caravan and opened the door, stooped low and stepped up inside. He switched on the light, a single hanging bulb, sensed Boy and smelt him, his clothes in various piles, old shoes, some trainers with holes, a sleeping bag rough from shop doorways; his life was here, the gathering of his few possessions. It would not take long to clear.

The first tin he saw was a biscuit tin, on the shelf to his right, above the kettle, and perhaps too close to the chemical toilet. He reached up, took the tin from the shelf, opened it, and there inside was what he came for – wrapped in a plastic bag, a battered book, that like its owner had lived the extremes. He sat down on the board sofa along one side and began to read.

And then a noise outside; a sound too heavy for a fox. It was a human step, crunching a stick and then tripping on a vase, a vase for flowers, falling on stone, and then silence. Peter got up, turned out the light and peered out through the window. There was nothing to see but a dark night and a silent graveyard. He glanced up at the photo, just visible, an older woman, perhaps Boy's mother. Oh yes, definitely his mother, and unsettling, somehow … Peter must be gone. He held onto the book, waited a short while, listening, felt himself alone again and stepped from the caravan out into the last embers of the evening light.

Then something hard, from nowhere; a crack on the back of the head, his buckling knees … and then nothing.

# Sixty

Prior to the attack on Abbot Peter – an assault which rendered him unconscious – various conversations and incidents had occurred in the vicinity of the Bell Theatre in Stormhaven. One involved two people who some assumed to be lovers, though gossip assumes most people are lovers, or at least having sex. People don't 'walk out together' these days.

'You need to calm down, Millicent.'

'And what if I can't calm down?'

'We can always calm down.'

'And what if you saying that just makes it worse?'

'Remember your breathing,' said Timothy.

'Sod the breathing.'

She wasn't in the mood for any of Timothy's bloody breathing exercises. All she knew was fear, screaming fear. It's all she'd ever known.

'Whatever you think you've done, Milly – and I don't want to know what it is – but whatever it is, it doesn't matter now.'

'It doesn't matter?'

'No, it doesn't matter.'

'But you don't know what it is.'

'Forgive them, Father, they know not what they do.'

'What the hell are you talking about?'

'So you're going to keep calm,' said Timothy, 'and you're going to keep quiet. Do you understand?' Pause. 'Do you understand?!'

Milly was calming.

'There's nothing to be gained by speaking of this,' he said. 'It will destroy us, you know that.'

She did know that, or it had crossed her mind.

'And Boy?'

She'd loved Boy in a way, a sweet man, the father she'd never had.

206

'I don't know, Milly, really I don't. It's terrible, but what can we do? What can anyone do?'

'So why send me to his hut to look through his books?'

It's the question she'd wanted to ask, and she asked it sharply now. But it brought from Timothy only a smile of regret: 'That was a matter between me and him – not even a very important matter, and nothing to do with what has occurred. You'll just have to believe me.'

Millicent wanted to believe him, didn't want to lose him now, wanted to be Milly, wanted to believe they were for ever, but she was struggling.

Trust did not come easily to Millicent; and she did think Timothy was lying.

*

Janet did not do regret; it was a banned substance in her psyche, and for very good reasons. To admit regret, of any sort, would be to admit she might have done things differently in her life, and that was impossible to accept. If she allowed regret, even for a moment – a sad look over her shoulder or the thought she might have chosen a better way – this might suggest she could have done things differently, and then the terror and the nightmares, for there was blame in the air, self-blame. You should have chosen differently – bad girl! So no regrets, for Janet, no looking back, no self-indulgent 'if onlys'. *Je ne regrette rien!*

But if not open to blame, she was perhaps open to wondering if the game should now end, for that's all it had been, all it had ever been, a naughty excursion, nothing more; even if it had gone slightly further than she'd imagined.

And while she could not undo her harmless fun, she could destroy the evidence. And then who could blame Janet?

*

'I was simply wondering, Margery, if there's anything you wish to say.'

Neville had invited Margery into his office, recently cleaned after violent assault. It was pristine again, order resumed, surfaces clear.

'Were you thinking of anything in particular, Neville?'

'We go back a long way.'

Neville sat back in his Chiro Plus office chair, a rather expensive purchase, given the funds available, but what price health? Or what price his health at least, he deserved it, deserved everything. He'd enjoyed the years of budgetary freedom afforded him by Hermione and made full use of them. He couldn't be doing with all this accountability nonsense, and neither could she, until the silly girl panicked and brought in the odious Bill Cain, and then, well … the writing was on the wall, dear chap, Neville's last stand.

'Our paths have crossed a few times,' said Margery. 'I'm not sure that's the same as "going back a long way".'

She wasn't giving him encouragement. If he wanted to reminisce with rose-tinted glasses and revisionist memory, then he'd have to lead the way and be prepared to travel alone.

'And I've followed your career avidly, of course,' added Neville.

Avidly? Slight over-statement … and overstate your case and the whole case collapses. As if anyone follows anyone's career avidly? As if anyone cares about anyone else that much.

'I'm sure you have, Neville.'

'So I was just wondering – and how does one put this? I was wondering whether there was any matter you might like to raise with me, remove from your chest, so to speak.' Had he been clear enough? 'With one who will understand, and is quite the soul of discretion.'

Margery to Neville, looking him in the eye: 'I don't know what you're talking about.'

'No?'

'Was there anything else?'

'It's just that I did overhear a certain conversation recently.'

Now we were getting to the bones of the matter.

'Glass at the door was it?' said Margery. 'Eye to the keyhole? People always say you like to know what's going on.'

Now Neville felt powerful. He'd allow the fish to tire itself thrashing about in the depths … and then slowly draw her in.

'It was between your good self and Hermione,' he said.

Margery felt disgust rise in her again as she remembered – Julie Dicks losing it, Julie Dicks closing the show … and now Julie Dicks dispatched. It still made her feel good.

'If I killed every little shit who crossed my path in theatreland, I'd be a crime legend by now.'

'At least you'd *be* a legend, Marge – because your acting hasn't done it for you.'

Neville could be a bitch, everyone knew this.

'Whereas you've made such a success of your life, Neville – king in your office and a joke everywhere else. Unfortunate business with that young man at *Onslaught Games*, of course, who proved such a tell-tale tit.'

'Boring.'

'But your word against his, and I'm sure you've got a new young man now … painting your bits. '

Neville rose and stood by his desk.

'As long as you feel secure in your story, Margery, that's my only concern … just in case the police seek my wisdom on the matter.'

Margery got up and picked up her bag without comment.

'Things to do, Margery, tracks to cover?'

As she reached the door, she turned: 'Before you offer the police any wisdom, Neville – a conversation which shouldn't detain them long – consider your grubby pursuit of pretty boy Paul. And what occurred the night he finally told you where to go.'

'It's hardly murder, Margery,' said Neville with a dismissive smile.

'It never is at the start, Neville. You see it in drama a lot. How things begin is not always how they end.'

\*

'How many times do I have to say it, Mr Channing – I don't know where my father is!'

The editor was making him angry.

'But you're our stringer in this story, Paul.'

And he'd done very well. The *Sussex Silt* had found Quasimodo's body before the police, which for Channing was obscenely pleasurable.

'I'm not your stringer.'

'I was trying to be kind, Paul … "stringer" is a polite word for "rat", for someone who rats on others from the inside … for payment.'

'I've simply given you relevant information.'

'So give us some more about your father.'

'I can't tell you anything.'

'But if you can't tell us – or is it won't tell us? – then what are we going to print? We'll have to print something.'

'Why do you have to print something?'

'Our readers are a demanding bunch, Paul. It would be dishonourable to let them down.

'I don't wish to continue our arrangement.' Paul had had enough.

'Oh, Paul, you don't mean that!'

'I do mean it.'

'Paul, tomorrow morning, my secretary will be sending out letters to every West End impresario I know – which is all of them, I believe; and the letter will be commending your work. And suddenly you want to call the whole thing off!'

'I'll just have to make my own way, won't I?'

'The pauper's path to oblivion, you mean?'

'I'm not giving you anything.'

'I mean, I suppose a little press conjecture is possible and it would be rather good copy: "Following a double murder at the Bell Theatre, the local bishop goes missing after being seen on the premises." But it would be nice to have a quote from "an insider".'

'You think I care about my father's reputation?'

'It would be a cruel son who didn't.'

Paul didn't care and he did care, which wasn't an answer, but was the truth; childhood is not so easily left. He too wanted to know where his father was, especially as he'd been seen at the theatre shortly before the murder of Boy. It couldn't possibly have been him, not his dad, that would be a step too far. He was a Grade One Pharisee, consumed by rules and appearances – but Pharisees didn't murder people, did they?

But where was he? Paul wanted to know, perhaps even more than the repulsive Martin Channing.

*

And then another letter dropped through Abbot Peter's front door.

# Sixty One

The therapist was a kind woman, as kind as a snooper can be; kind for a jackal feeding on the unhappiness of others. And she'd welcomed Tamsin with polite efficiency at the door and made her feel at home. Though how at home can you feel when jumping off a cliff?

'My name's Anita,' she said. 'We spoke on the phone.'

'DI Tamsin Shah,' she replied, before realising she wasn't here on an investigation. Well, she was, but it was self-investigation, the most terrifying of all. She'd prefer to have been chasing the Ripper.

'Would you like to come through?'

'Thank you.'

'And perhaps leave your job title by the door. You can collect it as you leave.'

Tamsin smiled nervously. She didn't know the rules of this game.

On entering the room – not the front room, this was smaller, obviously for clients – everything around her was normal. But then what did she expect? There was a plain brown sofa and matching chair, a large book case, photos, the red silk curtains, utter normality, yet everything strange, another planet, an alien zone, where Tamsin had come to talk about herself ... and she could still hardly believe it.

She'd driven to the ancient town of Lewes: a quick twenty minutes by car from Stormhaven, but unrelated in every other way. All the therapists were in Lewes. You couldn't find people like this in Stormhaven, and you couldn't find homes like this, the sense of deep reading, the sense of – well – money, really. Sometimes you walk into a house and feel, 'These people don't have a financial care in the world,' and so it was here: the ticking clock, the expensive carpet, the mahogany and pine. Did the therapist have a rich husband, working somewhere in the city? Or was he a property developer in Brighton? Tamsin didn't see him working in the local supermarket, that was for sure. Her eyes searched for photos, for clues.

'Looking for clues?' asked Anita.

'No, just – er – so how does this work?'

'Well, you can sit on the couch if you like and not see me. Some people like that. Or we can sit opposite each other in chairs, and glance at each other occasionally, the choice is yours.'

This was not a decision Tamsin had ever had to make, and she hesitated. The couch sounded crazy, did she want to lie down and gaze at a wall? The chairs were more normal, but did she want to see anyone? Why pretend this was normal when it wasn't?

'Is this your first time?' asked Mrs Morgan.

Anita Morgan was in her late forties, attractive face, keen eyes, hair just beginning to grey, and she had a husband, it was possible, the man in a photograph on the mantlepiece, could be a husband, but it could have been a brother … or possibly her father.

'So is that your husband?' asked Tamsin.

'I don't think we're here to talk about me.'

It was like a slamming door.

'No,' said Tamsin. 'Well, I think I'll sit on the couch.'

She didn't fancy looking at Anita Morgan.

'That's fine.'

'And do I call you Anita or Mrs Morgan?'

'You don't need to call me anything, really – this isn't a friend-ship.'

'No.'

'It's a relationship but not a friendship, a relationship for your health.'

They seemed cold words, but purifying … and something of a relief. It cleared the space of small talk and Tamsin hated small talk. But then with small talk gone, what did it leave? It left a space that Tamsin feared as she settled herself on the couch, not hurrying. Mrs Morgan was behind her somewhere, she thought she'd heard her pulling up a chair while Tamsin looked at the wall, a picture of a wood, a path through a wood, that would be nice, a path to somewhere, somewhere other than where she was; or if she turned her head slightly, she could see outside through the lace curtains, out onto the street she'd walked down, and a safer place than this.

'So how is today for you?' asked Mrs Morgan.

'Today? It's just another day, a murder investigation.'

Silence. What else did she want to know? Again the question, 'How does this work?'

'And are you handling it well?'

'Pretty well, yes, I'd say so. Yes, it's all going well. Closing in.'

It's what she always said, but now the words seemed empty, Mrs Morgan wasn't helping her and Tamsin was beginning to panic. Why had she come? This was a ridiculous idea, sitting here in someone else's house, someone she didn't know from Adam, on a couch – you couldn't make it up! There was a moment when she started to leave, in her mind, she could feel the instruction forming, the instruction to herself to get down off the couch, say 'Thank you very much but on reflection I think this is a bad idea.' She could be out of the door in three minutes, safe on the street once again. But instead, she asked a question.

'Have you ever visited a concentration camp?'

'I've visited Buchenwald,' said Anita. 'Why do you ask?'

Silence.

# Sixty Two

His attacker could certainly deliver a line, and now spoke the rhyme with some venom:

'Tell-tale tit!

Your tongue shall be split,

And all the dogs in the town

Shall have a little bit!

They don't write children's rhymes like that anymore, do they Abbot? All a bit more politically correct now.'

Peter lay with his hands and ankles tied in the body bag. This is what he had woken to, on recovering consciousness. He was held in by cold earth either side, he could smell it, smell the clay, though he could not see. His captor had told him he lay in a freshly dug grave, and called him the graveyard's 'new boy'. But now they returned to the rhyme, it was a woman, which surprised him, though not a voice he recognised.

'You can feel the playground savagery, can't you? Tell-tale tit, your tongue shall be split! Real hatred towards the one who tells tales and gets other children into trouble. We all hate that sort, don't we … all hate the tell-tale? And that's what you were going to do, Abbot … become a little tell-tale tit, I did notice.'

Peter couldn't move and had no desire to speak. He needed to think.

'And I'm the one more at risk here. As Albert Camus said, remember him? "Every murderer, when he kills, runs the risk of the most dreadful of deaths – whereas those who kill him, risk nothing except promotion."'

Silence.

'Perhaps not promotion in your case, those days are long gone for you. But you know what I mean – adulation, praise, enhanced standing.'

Peter listened to his breathing. There was limited value in conversing with the insane, whose defining characteristic is their

214

stuck-on certainty ... certainty stuck over terror, like a poorly applied plaster. And really, what is there to be said to anyone who clings to certainty? There are defences impossible to breach.

Yes, Peter understood how things were. He was dealing with a sociopath, this was clear, a sociopath rather than a psychopath. Psychopaths are all about power, sociopaths about people ... and this was the Abbot's companion now. Psychopaths are simple really, pretty straightforward in their view of others: the only issue is how you affect their power. If they believe you enhance their power in some way, they're friendly to you, charming even. But if you don't enhance their power, then you're threatening and you'll need to be eliminated; and since psychopaths are always paranoid, it won't take much for you to threaten them.

But the Abbot's present host was different, she was a sociopath, with a more relational outlook, asking only: how can you please me? This woman wanted a conversation, contact, relationship, as long as she remained in control. In the office, if a sociopath boss likes you, they'll bring you under their complete control and all will be well. But if you don't allow them to control you, there will be trouble; they'll dislike you and actually enjoy harming you. And that was another difference: psychopaths get no pleasure from the harm, but sociopaths do. In fact they enjoy it so much, they may even risk their own power interests to pleasure themselves over your downfall.

And so it was with the Abbot's soil-shovelling socio now; it was for them an entirely enjoyable experience, and one she wanted him to be part of. Normally, on meeting such a crackpot, you'd just take your leave, choose to be somewhere else, but this was not possible tonight. Peter could move a little in his confinement, but he couldn't catch the bus.

'And of course I now have the book,' continued Socio, eager for connection. 'The book you kindly found for me, full of an old man's ramblings – yet strangely precious. He didn't stutter when he wrote, did he, which is something of a relief! And he could have had it cured, obviously. God knows what images of victimhood made him keep it. I have no doubt she found it endearing. We'd probably at least agree about that.'

Peter thought that was probably true. Hermione did like to save people.

'It won't exist in a short while, obviously, the book I mean – and then the matter will be closed and I'll be on my way. I like happy endings, I like to make endings happy, they must be happy – otherwise what hope is there? But not for the tell-tale tit, obviously. No happy ending there, that wouldn't be right.'

# Sixty Three

The Bishop had seen enough, more than enough, it was quite terrible, truly, and he left the flat as soon as he could. He needed to get away, needed to think – no, he needed to get drunk.

Paul hadn't been there – so where was he? His flatmate, or whoever it was, you never knew with Paul, had allowed him in, 'father dropping-by' stuff: 'So sorry to have missed him, could I leave a present? I want it to be a surprise!' And so he'd been allowed into Paul's bedroom, and how strange to stand there, an alien room, a bedroom away from home for the boy he'd watched grow. And then he saw the shirt, saw the blood and staggered out of the house.

It had been bad enough to discover his son was gay, a problem that neither he nor Margaret had wished for; what parent would? Of course they'd hoped it was a phase. Paul had never talked about it though – never; he hadn't seen fit to discuss these things with his father, somehow imagining it was of no one's concern but his own. Oh really!? Wake up and smell the coffee, Sunshine! So they'd been left to speculate and deduce, to draw their own conclusions, as they waited in vain for him to bring a girl home. But the creepy man at the theatre – Neville someone, and rather affected, in the Bishop's opinion – seemed very clear that it wasn't a phase. 'I hardly think it's a phase, Bishop!' he'd said, adding that Paul wouldn't be bringing any girl home soon, and that he was 'extremely active' in the gay community.

The Bishop was a man of the world and knew exactly what that meant … and it made him feel ill, frankly. But that was as nothing compared to the blood-red shirt. He pulled off his dog collar, undid the top button of his purple shirt, rammed the collar in his coat pocket and went into the small supermarket for a special purchase.

He had to do this sometimes.

216

# Sixty Four

'Is it difficult to begin?' said Anita.

'It's difficult to be here.'

'Why is it difficult?'

'Because when I see the word therapist …'

Silence.

'How does it feel when you see the word therapist?'

'I see the rapist.'

Pause.

'That's a strong reaction.'

'I suppose.'

'And why do you think that might be?'

'I don't know, I never really thought about it.'

Pause.

'Because they invade,' said Tamsin.

'You feel that therapists invade you … that's what you fear.'

Silence.

'And yet you're here,' said Anita.

'At the moment.'

There was much in her demanding she leave, much in her screaming she should be gone; and only a thread for hanging in. This was going nowhere, a mistake, advancing nothing.

'Have you had a bad experience of a therapist?' asked Mrs Morgan.

'No.'

'So how are you feeling now you're here?'

How was she feeling? It was the worst question anyone could ask. It didn't mean anything, she didn't know what she was feeling, and didn't want to either.

'I don't know what I'm feeling. It's not important.'

'Do you ever know what you're feeling?'

'I know what others are feeling.'

'Really?'

217

'I think so. I can respond to their feelings ... get them to do what I want.'

A brief moment of pride, self-satisfaction.

'So you can respond to other's feelings, or at least use their feelings ... but you can't respond to your own. Is that fair?'

And then from the deep came a word, extracted with pain, like pulling at a splinter:

'Vulnerability.'

Tamsin breathed deeply, exhausted by that one-word extraction.

'Is that what you fear?'

Pause.

'It can be used against you,' she said.

Tamsin was sweating.

'Has your vulnerability ever been used against you?'

Silence.

'Relationships ask us to be vulnerable,' said Mrs Morgan after a while.

'Relationships aren't real. We all pretend.'

'You pretend. Is that what you're saying?'

'Everyone pretends.'

'How do you know everyone pretends?'

'Everyone's full of deceit, they're no different to me!'

Silence.

'It must be hard to feel deceitful.'

That was enough.

'You're invading me.'

She could feel herself locking up, seizing up like a crippled knee joint. The silence continued for a while, though it felt noisy to Tamsin, too much disturbance below, unwanted disturbance, like neighbours downstairs who won't shut up, their endless bloody racket coming through the floor. Then Mrs Morgan spoke again:

'Do you think inmates felt invaded in the concentration camps?'

'I suppose.'

'Some felt so invaded by the experience that after the war, they did a strange thing. When it was all over, and after many years had passed, they had to go back there, back to the site.'

'No.'

'They did.'

'Mad.'

'They felt they had to.'

'Why did they do that? Why would anybody do that?'

'Well, in one way, the camp had no power now ... they had husbands, wives, lovers, children, new lives. But somehow the camp still held power, still disturbed their dreams, still tortured their lives. So they went back, back to the place, to see for themselves that it was just rubble and ruin … that it was nothing any more, with no power to hurt. Would you have done that?'

Well, would she have done that? How could anyone do that?

'It must have been the hardest thing,' said Tamsin in a whisper, the whisper of a little girl, she had no voice.

More noisy silence for Tamsin: 'Shut the bloody neighbours up, too much noise down below!' And now she couldn't move, couldn't leave, even if she wanted to leave, paralysed and numb. And it was Lewes resident Jenny Jeffes, passing outside with two-year-old Michael, who heard the scream and did wonder for a moment, because you do, don't you? You can't help it. She heard the scream from the house, and it pulled her up and she thought of taking a look … before realising it came from Anita's place, from Anita Morgan's house, and Michael was miserably tired. If she hadn't had Michael with her, she would have done something, but all seemed quiet now, and she didn't want to appear nosy or a busybody and Mrs Morgan could be slightly scary.

'He used to touch me,' said Tamsin, exhausted but on the other side of the wall, the wall of fire, this is how it felt. Had she screamed? She may have screamed but the noisy neighbours downstairs were quieter now.

She'd finally got back to her father.

# Sixty Five

Peter was familiar with the process, as he lay in the body bag. A small gash had been made to allow breathing, for now at least, breathing for now ... breathing but constricted movement, feet tied, hands tied, but tied separately, allowing a little more scope.

'You will now know what it feels like to be buried alive,' was the promise of the sociopath, 'buried before your time.'

Peter listened but said nothing. He was closing down as the first soil was shovelled onto his feet.

'In other words,' says Socio, 'what it has felt like to be me all these years, to have a headstone of my own, while I still walk the earth; to be dead while still alive, declared dead at least, as if nothing I do means anything or can ever mean anything, someone of no substance – like Vincent Van Gogh.'

They pronounced it like the Dutch, which for some reason irritated Peter, 'Gogh' like a guttural 'Ho'. It was how the Dutch discovered Germans in the war.

'You do know about Van Gogh?'

Peter did, and knew what was coming ... it would make sense of this dysfunction, but really, so what?

'Did you know that the first Vincent Van Gogh, the real one so to speak, was born exactly a year before the painter – to the day?'

Peter did know this, as more earth was shovelled onto his knees.

'But he died – tragic of course, so tragic; and so when the Van Goghs' next child came along, on the birthday of the deceased by happy chance, they called him Vincent as well! Another Vincent! How lovely for the parents, a brand new Vincent, but less good news for the boy, who would for ever have to compete with the beautiful son they lost, who never grew up and never disappointed. It was a contest the second Vincent would never win, for ever second best to the original.'

Peter was waiting for the point, for this wasn't the point, the point was on its way.

'And he knew about graveyards, young Vincent,' continued his grave digger. 'As a child, he was taken every week to the tomb of his dead brother; Vincent taken to the tomb of Vincent, where he could contemplate his own name on the headstone, and feel his parent's sadness that he existed, rather than their firstborn. In short, he could visit his own tomb, like I can visit mine, here in Stormhaven, here at the Bell Theatre!

LOST SO YOUNG, TOO PERFECT TO BE MISSED.
LOST SO YOUNG, TOO WONDERFUL TO BE WEPT FOR.

Welcome to the "Buried Alive" club, Abbot.'

Peter shifted his position as best he could, constraints permitting, as soil now fell on his stomach, moving up. The living should never have to feel this, they shouldn't have to feel the burying soil … and now he was remembering Brother Elias and the hypothalamus, the remarkable body part found at the base of the brain and the size of your average pea – he'd always remembered the size. And it was a busy little pea, the hypothalamus, regulating body temperature, emotions, hunger, thirst and the autonomic nervous system. How it all came back to him, here as he was slowly buried alive … and who knows, it might help, might be an angel?

And Brother Elias must have been a good teacher, or perhaps Peter was just desperate, remembering things he didn't know he knew, dragging them up from somewhere, remembering that the autonomic nervous system has two branches: the sympathetic and the parasympathetic … was that right, Brother Elias? And if he re-membered correctly, these two worked in opposition, yes, that's right, like the break and accelerator in the car, to guide response, the response of involuntary, unconscious functions such as heart rate, respiration and blood vessel regulation.

He hadn't always been Brother Elias obviously. No one is born Brother Elias, they have another life first, and his other life had been as Frederick Balliol, respected professor at some distin-guished London hospital, eminent psychologist, before taking holy orders in the undistinguished monastery of St James-the-Less where Peter, for his sins, had been Abbot. And so he knew about the sympathetic and parasympathetic nervous systems from con-versations over the evening meal, which at weekends, high days and holidays was not silent but spilling with interesting conversa-tion … a slight exaggeration. There were many conversations Peter didn't remember quite so well.

His captor had left him for a while, Socio had some other busi-ness, some other plan to attend to, leaving Peter with only half his body covered; so he stayed with the air, air to breathe, precious stuff. She'd said she must first light a fire, and then disappeared, giving Peter time to remember – to remember that his sympathetic system was the flight, fright or fight mode, there for when action was necessary; while the parasympathetic system, this took over when withdrawal was required, relaxing the body, and calming.

He could hear him now, Brother Elias lecturing young doctors on the sympathetic and parasympathetic systems, in his cravat, which he declared to be his greatest loss on becoming a monk … he clearly hadn't enjoyed any strong relationships in his life. He'd possessed seventeen different cravats apparently, which was a lot, Peter didn't know there were seventeen in the world … and the letting go had been difficult. Someone claimed, a rather petty soul, that Brother Elias still wore one under his habit, but Peter didn't believe it, and he certainly wasn't carrying out an inspection, or declaring an amnesty on all secret items worn. God knows what that would have thrown up. And anyway, letting go is a process not an event, gradual rather than sudden. Perhaps he had brought a cravat to the desert, it was quite possible, there wasn't a body search … and perhaps he did wear it under his habit, a necessary security blanket until it was no longer necessary …

And it was his tiger illustration Peter remembered. The tiger! When jumped by a tiger who has escaped his cage, Brother Elias would say, your action response kicks in, initiating developments you know nothing about: your pupils dilate to let in more light, your heart beats faster and your blood pressure rises to give your organs extra oxygen. And then the blood vessels – that's right – the blood vessels would constrict to reduce bleeding in case of wounding, the sympathetic system thinks of everything, you see, even ensuring higher blood sugar levels to give more energy. Remarkable. It's our emergency mode, he'd say, when thinking is reduced, and action is the call and demand of the moment.

But then supposing on the same visit to the zoo, he'd say – strange how you can hear someone's voice so clearly, years ago now, different place, different days and a time when he could move, when he wasn't tied and bagged, laid in a grave and waiting to be buried alive – and on this visit to the zoo, said Brother Elias, you encounter not a tiger but a diamond-backed rattle snake, coiled and ready to strike. This is different, he'd say, and in your terror, instead of everything speeding up, everything slows down and the pressing question is this: what should I do? And this, of course, is the territory of the parasympathetic system, the system which seeks to conserve and withdraw. Your pupils constrict to lessen light, your heart rate and blood pressure slow to reduce oxygen use, while your muscles relax. Outward focus is reduced, inward focus paramount. In this state of withdrawal, the mind is able to think and reflect, as slowly, with tiny movements, you move away from the snake. Or as slowly, and with tiny movements, you consider how you might escape this living grave.

And then the roar! What was that? Not a tiger but a fire. Peter heard the explosive roar and crackle of a fire leaping into life, gulping in the air, a big fire, fuelled and eager, almost a 'whoosh', a conflagration released, young but ambitious, feeding hungrily on a surfeit of oxygen and old wood, the tower was burning, he knew it was the tower, the bell tower was alight … and, even at distance, Peter felt the heat, felt the firestorm through the earth, felt the burning on his uncovered face, the growing heat as the minutes passed, heard the beams enveloped and consumed and then the faint ring, an agonised chime, a bell-frame fracturing, an involuntary toll across Stormhaven, awkward and clumsy, the death throes of a tenor bell, no longer held, a great weight released from its holding, slowly but surely before the splintered letting go … and the moment is now, a tumbling tenor, through burning floors, a peel of destruction calling the faithful to panic, the awful crash of a bell falling through beams no longer there, decking devoured by fire, smashing its way downwards through the flames, shuddering impact, a spastic gong now helpless in the embers, lifeless on the ground.

Would he now join it on destruction day?

*

'Killing is a surprisingly existential experience,' said his captor. 'In a moment of intense meaning, I return you to your original form. It feels like a quotation, but it's mine, really!'

The sociopath had returned excitedly from their arson, smelling of petrol but full of adrenaline and wonder … wonder at what they'd done, at what they'd achieved. The bell tower was in flames! They'd done it! And now they wanted the Abbot to be excited, to join them in the thrill, they wanted applause. But Peter wouldn't play, declining to be in their control. And then his captor was bending down, speaking into his ear, in a dramatic stage whisper:

'"Then the king's countenance was changed and his thoughts troubled him, so that the joints of his loins were loosed and his knees smote against each other!" Recognise those words, Abbot?'

Peter knew them well enough. They described events at Belshazzar's famous feast, recorded in the book of Daniel, when Belshazzar celebrates his father's defeat of the Israelites, drinking wine out of goblets stolen from the Temple in Jerusalem. Suddenly, amid the merriment, a ghostly hand appears and writes on the wall, words of God's anger, Nebuchadnezzar and his son Belshazzar have been judged, this is what the ghostly hand writes, they've been weighed in the scales and found wanting. The king is terrified, his countenance changed, his loins loosed and his knees knocking in terror.

'Are your loins a little loosed, Abbot?'

'The writing on the wall is for one of us,' said Peter.

'And I'm free to go – so it must be for you. Any famous last words?'

Silence.

'No? A man with nothing to say?' They were irritated. The Abbot wasn't playing the game. 'So let's get on with it, then. I mean, I slit your bag because I've always found you interesting – well, you know that. But now you've gone all silent and mysterious on me, so time to bring the curtain down. Not even the Sussex Fire Service can miss this blaze … and what a distraction it'll be, big fires always are, think of bonfire night!' Fifty yards away, something large crashed to the ground. 'While Peter in his tomb will be a barely remembered thing. People, people everywhere – nor any help at hand!'

They were shovelling quicker now, earth upon earth, piled high in their hurry, for they must be gone, they'd wasted time with their talking, with their gloating, as socios do; they love to hurt, but now they must rush, and prepare in time to merge into the wailing crowd, mourning the destruction of the Bell Theatre.

*

Though, there was another tell-tale tit in Stormhaven that warm August evening, tell-tale tits abounding. For at the very moment, at the precise moment when the bell fell crashing through the burning rafters of the tower, the murderer of Hermione Bysshe-Urquhart was turning themselves in at Stormhaven police station.

# Sixty Six

The firemen left the Bell Theatre at 3.30 a.m., with the flames extinguished and the extent of the damage clear. The bell tower was largely destroyed, a gutted shell, the bell itself buried beneath burnt timber and ash. The main building had sustained some damage, but surprisingly little given the intensity of the flames in the tower. It seemed the wind had been kind. So the outer walls of Sussex stone had survived, and inside, though few rooms had entirely escaped the charring fire, only the theatre itself, closest to the tower, was blackened by smoke and heat, along with Hermione's office, where the photos had not survived, its pictured history gone.

'Did they find any bodies?' asked Wonder.

He'd been a late arrival on the scene after Tamsin rang him at midnight.

'No,' said Tamsin.

'But you think he might be in there?'

The whereabouts of Abbot Peter was a cause for growing concern.

'I don't know where else he is.'

'Not at home?'

'Not at home, no.'

What a bloody stupid question – of course he wasn't at home! Wasn't his home the first place she'd have looked? Sandy View was empty.

'Never got to meet the bloke,' said Wonder carelessly. 'You talked about him, of course, seemed to find something there to value – but I never got to meet him.'

'You don't need to speak like he's dead.'

'Funnily enough, though – and life's like this, isn't it? – the wife heard him last week. Some W.I. event in Stormhaven, she likes that sort of thing, and he was there in his funny clothes, talking about the ancient Egyptians and how they spent all their time thinking about death … which sounds like a wet weekend in Cleethorpes, I know, but wasn't entirely without interest, apparently.'

Pause.

'It may of course have been a premonition.'

'What are you talking about?' said Tamsin.

'His talk – on death.'

Why had she left Peter? What insanity had driven her to leave a murder scene, leave the Abbot at a murder scene … leave her uncle at a murder scene?

'Got to face up to that possibility, my dear.'

'No, I don't, and I'm not – because he's alive.'

'It's good to hope – but not always wise, not always. Just saying.'

No harm in a bit of straight talking.

'He's indestructible,' said Tamsin.

'If you say so.'

And this was unlike her, all this emotional stuff, very unlike her, she wasn't the emotional type, DI Shah – she'd always been a differ-ent sort of woman, she frightened colleagues, as a rule … but now she was being ridiculous. Indestructible?

'And we have Millicent Pym at the station,' she said.

'Millicent Pym?'

'One of the actors.'

'Why?'

'She turned herself in.'

'She what?'

'Claims she killed Hermione.'

'And you believe her?'

At that moment, a man appeared alongside them, hesitant in the dark smoky air.

'Excuse me, but are you Detective Inspector Tamsin Shah?'

'And if I am?'

Inappropriate. Get back in role, Tamsin.

'I just felt we had to speak,' he said.

He spoke gently.

'And you are?'

'My name's Colin Gibbs.'

'And you have some information for us.'

'I don't know. And I'm sure you have other things on your mind. This is terrible.'

He indicated the holey tower, full of stark holes, like a tooth with no filling, empty inside for the first light of dawn.

'So who or what does your information concern?'

'Until three weeks ago, I was Neville Brownslie's boyfriend.'

'Until three weeks ago.'

'Yes.'

'So the relationship ended?'

'Yes, I ended it.'

'And how did Neville take that?'

'Well, he wasn't pleased … I mean, he was devastated. Very angry, very – well – turbulent.'

'Shall we find a quieter spot?'

# Sixty Seven

He must keep calm, this was the first task: breathe into the nightmare or the nightmare will breathe into you. And it was a nightmare, so name it as such, this was a nightmare, acknowledge it. He was trapped underground and running out of air, the most terrible nightmare, but you have to keep calm if you cannot escape ... this was okay, this was the snake not the tiger, the parasympathetic system, lowering the heartbeat, reducing oxygen use, conserving and withdrawing, thought not flight, there was no flight, tied hands and feet, no running away, so calm the fear, accept the nightmare of the earth pressing down on the body bag, but some oxygen held, tied hands making a tent, holding air but not for long, as the time went by ... feet tied but some movement allowed, how much soil above? Kicking up might disturb things, sound the alarm but exertion would use air, and if no one saw, wasted air. Worth the risk? Who might be watching? No one would be watching, they'd be watching the fire as Socio had said; and then his hands, he was considering his hands, constrained but movement allowed – but what movement and to what end?

He needed air, he felt himself faint, and then overwhelming terror, like water crashing through a dam ... and he was back in the unit, in his memory, overwhelmed by panic, after university, the months he never spoke of, never really acknowledged, the psychiatric unit, North London, the lost months, locked doors and trying to calm his being, panic used up air, it wasn't good, calming the terror, this was what the nurse did, there in the unit, North London, Highgate Hill, she soothed him, calmed him, said there was air enough for living, enough air to carry on, a good nurse, Rosemary, that was her name, saved his life, she'd lived in Enfield, and he loved her, didn't know her but he did love her, he'd loved Rosemary then and never loved again ... watching now the flood pass through, the terror flood passing, but would he be alive when it had? No Rosemary now, long gone, no Rosemary to calm ... and so stupid to go it alone, he'd been stupid, self-recrimination, a waste of time, he needed air, there was no air in recrimination so let it pass, focus on the air, the need for air, moving his hands within the body bag, one way and then another, gently, no exertion, he could reach his pockets but what good was that, though everything counted, the deep pockets of the habit, everything noted, no sound from above, sealed from the world by Stormhaven clay, no noise underground, the dead lay in silence, Peter lay in silence, the living among the dead, the only sound his breathing ... but for how long, Lord? For the Lord is my shepherd, old words made new, the Lord is my shepherd, I shall not want, yea, though I walk in the valley of the shadow of death, I will fear no evil, for thou art with me finding air, getting air into my lungs in the valley of death, fresh air instead of the fading life in the body bag.

All Peter wanted in life was some air.

# Sixty Eight

The air was fresh, cooling after a hot August day, and across the other side of Stormhaven, at around 1.30 a.m., there was a break-in at the Wellbeing Medical Centre in Cressley Road.

It wasn't a traditional break-in, for the intruder had a key, a key to the black front door. But instead of a traditional entry, they chose instead to smash a pane of glass, cloth wrapped round the hand, and enter through the back door, not a security door at all. They then switched off the alarm, they knew the alarm code, no problem there, and entered the dim reception area. It was quiet – and of course, it was quiet. It was 1.30 a.m.. Eyes slowly adjusting, they moved behind the reception desk left clean and tidy, so unlike the day, all quiet and calm, no phone a-ringing, no faces a-waiting, no patients a-fuming.

The intruder now felt for some cables and removed them, after which the office computer was lifted from the desk and taken from the premises. The computer was nothing in itself, a dinosaur with no value. But then this technology wasn't destined for ebay; its future less certain, rather bleaker, for in the hands of the burglar was the awkward witness to everything, a silent whistle-blower, a teller of virtual tales about what went on in this place; and a witness who wouldn't forget and couldn't be bought. But also one who could be removed and destroyed … removed and dumped, and the burglar had somewhere in mind, somewhere damp like the River Ouse, where its clever memory would be worth nothing.

Let it sit with the silt, the fish scales and the weeds. Computers should know their place.

*

Neville Brownslie gazed at the ceiling, unable to sleep.

Administrator and front of house at the Bell Theatre … but so what? It was an empire in its way, he'd made it an empire, with his own lackeys to order about. But it was a small empire, rather contained, and over these past weeks he'd sensed it would soon get smaller still. He did sometimes wonder if he should have stayed with the acting, stayed in the performance game; and perhaps that was his frustration, the feeling that he could have succeeded, had he stayed with it, that he could have been quite as good – no, better – than those he now looked after, found rehearsal space for, found audiences for, had the toilets cleaned for – he drew the line at wiping their noses. Because he would have enjoyed the applause, the curtain calls and the bows ... the wonderful buzz of recognition and appreciation well worth the emptiness that followed, and emptiness did follow, of course it did, the emptiness after the show, when you returned to being yourself, a rather more difficult role. And my God, it had been difficult of late, playing the part of Neville Brownslie – mainly due to Paul, who had torn him in two somewhat.

And then a surprise encounter with the Bishop yesterday, and a measure of revenge exacted, definitely a measure. God knows what the cleric was doing in the theatre, he didn't want to know, he really didn't, past caring – Neville was quite beyond that, darling. But he'd taken the opportunity to fill old mitre man in on a few home truths, which were clearly news to him. The Bishop had looked as though he'd seen a ghost, he really did. So Neville's day had not been entirely without pleasure.

What the Bishop now did with those truths was nothing to do with him: don't shoot the messenger and all that. And then the phone call from Janet, timed at 3.04 a.m., informing him that the bell tower was burning down. What could he do but go and merge with the wailing crowd?

# Sixty Nine

## *Thursday, 5 August*

It was 7.03 a.m., and opposite Millicent Pym sat Tamsin Shah, with a cup of strong coffee and a desire to be elsewhere. She wished to be at the Bell, the Bell Theatre as was – no bell now and not much theatre; just a smouldering ruin, where the search for bodies continued … mainly the search for a particular body, the body of Abbot Peter. Returning to the scene at first light, further exploration had again found no hidden flesh and bones, no charred remains for identification.

So where was Peter?

She'd asked to be informed of any developments, no matter what she was doing.

'Should the interview be interrupted if we hear anything, Ma'am?' asked Baines.

'Yes it should,' said Tamsin.

But in the meantime, with Baines still silent, she sat across the table from Millicent Pym.

'So you killed Hermione, Millicent?'

Why beat about the bush? This was a large waste of time and the sooner it was over the better.

'I did, yes.'

'And how did you do that?'

'It was a military move.'

'What was?'

'Disengaging the vertebrae.'

'So you were in the army?'

'I learned it from a military man.'

Millicent seemed strangely disengaged.

'You put your hand at the top of the back,' she explained, acting it out, 'and push forward, while yanking the head back, broken vertebrae. Though I stabbed her with some scissors as well.'

'And why did you do that?'

'Why?'

'I mean, it seems a bit unnecessary. She was already dead.'

'I did it because I was angry with her. I just wanted her to know.'

'I think she may have guessed that already.'

'I wanted to stab her as well.'

'You were angry, weren't you?'

'I suppose.'

'And what did you then do with the scissors?'

'Janet has them.'

'She's keeping them for you?'

'She doesn't know she has them.'

Tamsin was struggling. She didn't feel for one moment that she was talking to the killer of Hermione Bysshe-Urquhart; but even more worrying, she wasn't even bothered. She was thinking of her previous interview, the conversation with Colin Gibbs in the graveyard.

'Millicent,' she said, 'this may sound strange, but I want you to return to your cell and consider the charge of wasting police time.'

Horror on Millicent's face.

'I'm not wasting police time!'

'Who knows why you're doing this – I'm sure you have your reasons, but your life is ahead of you. So let's speak again when you've had time to reflect.'

Tamsin was surprised by the kindness in her voice.

'I did kill Hermione,' said Millicent.

'I don't know why you're so determined. Interview terminated at 7.08 a.m.'

And after Millicent's shocked and complaining exit, Tamsin stayed seated, sipping her coffee and returning to her conversation with Neville's ex, Colin Gibbs, as the tower burned. They'd sat in the graveyard, by that newly dug grave, and he'd spoken of his fears for Neville:

'Neville does stupid things when he's angry.'

'Has he threatened you?'

'No, it won't be me he turns on, not normally; it'll be others.'

'What others are there?'

Colin paused.

'I know he's very smitten by the young boy who wrote the play.'

'Paul Bent?'

'That's him, yes.'

Colin had found this admission difficult, found even the name hard to hear, hard to stomach. Perhaps Paul was the reason they broke up, this was Tamsin's sense, Colin the gooseberry.

'He destroyed his own office the night Paul rejected him.'

'That was Neville?'

'There'd been nothing in it, the boy was never interested. Paul isn't gay. And so Neville turned to drink.'

She'd remembered the scene in his office, remembered Peter remarking on the smell of alcohol ... and how she wished the Abbot was with her now.

'When he's drunk, there's a terrible rage, and then he can do anything.'

'He did tell us that if he ever let out his anger, he'd pull down the whole world,' said Tamsin.

'That's Neville – there's no way I could help him.'

'Might that include pulling down a bell tower?'

'I don't know, I find that hard to believe.'

'Okay.'

'He's such a kind man.'

Tamsin's eyebrows are raised.

'Don't get all maudlin, Colin. Why call someone kind when they're not?'

'But he is kind, there's such a good heart there!'

It wasn't hard to read: Colin was feeling bad for being truthful about his ex, guilty about his honesty, so what does he do? He starts backtracking, he layers honesty with dishonesty, covers truth with sentimental cliché, and suddenly Neville the mad rhino is a sensitive soul in search of love and daffodils.

'I'm sure,' said Tamsin.

'But when I heard what was happening here, well – I had to speak.'

'And you were right to speak, Colin.'

She'd liked him as they'd talked in the graveyard. He could have come forward earlier, that might have been helpful, but she understood these things were not always clear-cut. Mrs Morgan had listened ... listened with no attempt to control, a different sort of listening, and Tamsin would try and do the same, pass the listening on to Colin as they watched the dawn among the tombs, both the old and the new – the *new*? When was that new grave dug? Colin had commented on it, and she'd ignored him, intent on his story, she'd stopped listening – .

She needed to get back to the graveyard.

And she was feeling sick.

# Seventy

He had to keep awake.

He had to keep the brain busy, no loss of conscious thought, that would be the end, remember something, anything, the talk to the Stormhaven W.I., the one last week, Egyptian attitudes to death, hadn't realised it would be so topical at the time, hadn't realised he'd be a Pharaoh quite so soon. But could he remember? The opening line, just get going, Peter, standing in the church hall, sparse attendance, twenty-two, he'd counted twenty-two, he always counted, so how about the talk – ah yes, the opening line: 'To the ancient Egyptians, life was just a dress rehearsal.' A good opening line, Peter, but what then? He harried himself in this way, because there was more to the talk than that, what came next? 'To the Egyptians, life was just a dress rehearsal. To an Egyptian, death was the most important moment of their life, the beginning of the much more significant journey into the next world.' Imagine you're giving the talk again, Peter, just give it: 'Death was merely the beginning of a much more important journey, the journey into the next world. If you'd prepared for it, you were entering a much better place. If you hadn't … well, we'll get to that.'

Death was Egypt's greatest interest, his talk was flowing again, he could see their faces, he could even see his notes, here among good people doing good things in the world, and they'd come to listen, before tea and cakes, excellent cakes, and he was saying that in twenty-first-century England, supermarkets are the biggest employers, but in ancient Egypt, death was the largest employer, and by some way, because preparing for your end was everything and time-consuming, it took a lifetime to get ready for death, Peter remembered that phrase, a lifetime to get ready for death, so remember more, keep remembering, keep the conscious thoughts, and how it wasn't just the Pharaohs but ordinary Egyptians as well. Everyone was obsessed with death as they walked along the Nile.

The Book of the Dead, he'd spoken about that, the book that offered various incantations to facilitate the journey into the next life. People even made their own books, an early example of self-publishing, some knowing laughs, the W.I. did laugh, but it was also possible to get them off the shelf, books offering good spells to deal with any monsters you met in the afterlife … and because success in death isn't about what you know, but who you know, you paid attention to the appropriate gods. Osiris and Anubis were the gods of the dead, so it was wise to keep them onside, starting with as much worship as possible. Like humans, gods do like a bit of unquestioning worship …

And then what? Yes, stuff about building your tomb in the rock, a time-consuming business, much harder than putting up a shed in the garden, and something you started when young … you started building your tomb when young. After all, life was fragile and you didn't know when you'd need it – and still true today, thought Peter, but don't lose the flow, keep going, and your neighbours helped you with your tomb, just as you helped them, perhaps they had 'tomb parties', when they'd share some beer, roast duck and dates – and then hack at the rock until it was time to go home.

And here was another difference from customs today: you'd include all your possessions in the tomb, everything would go with you, so often children got nothing in Ancient Egypt. The reading of the will could be a brief affair, even for the offspring of the rich, as there was nothing to share out … which saved poisonous family disputes over furniture, obviously, because it was all there in the tomb – chairs, tables, death mask, vases, bed, statuettes and coffin. So no gains in death for the survivors; indeed, there'd probably be considerable loss, because there was the large funeral bill to consider. Some say funerals are expensive today – yes, there were some nodding heads in front of him – but they're nothing like the Egyptian funeral of old, with their professional mourners – it would not be a proper funeral without the professional mourners. They'd cry according to the rates of pay: the louder they cried, the more they charged. Quiet wailing and you'd be accused of being a cheapskate.

And then there were the last-minute extras to be placed inside the tomb, extras on top of the furniture and jewellery. These would be adornments like flowers, incense, expensive food offerings, often an entire banquet – onions, garlic and bread, which were the staple diet, but also roast duck, grapes, dates, vegetables and beer. There were special spells to ensure an eternal supply of beer, the beer would regenerate itself … though sadly these spells only worked in death.

And then of course there was the body, and Peter was aware of his own right now, trapped and sealed. The process of mummification, and he could identify with that, took seventy days, starting with the removal of internal organs, the brain extracted through the nose. A rather ignominious end to this magnificent organ, but there we are ... though as new techniques were developed, organs could be left in. Traditionally the drying out of the body took forty days, using dry salt piled on the corpse to draw out body fluids. But they soon discovered this could also be done by putting the corpse in a concentrated salt solution, effectively pickling it. This had advantages: the organs could now remain in the body with no decay, but was pricey, which meant that only the brains of the wealthy, often the smallest – more laughter, though not from the wealthy – could remain in the skull cavity.

And then there was the question: what shall I wear? We usually ask this when going out for the evening, or perhaps to an interview, but the Egyptians asked it most eagerly when embarking on their journey into the next world. It was important, you see, to look your best when entering the afterlife, which would certainly include the wearing of jewellery, so there was no chance of the family getting that. Egyptian women were often dressed, dare I say it, rather sexily for the next life, and while I'm not an expert in such matters, I'm told it was like someone today being dressed for death in their negligee. He remembered the happy murmurs in the room, negligee memories. And when did someone last speak of those at the W.I? Perhaps they speak of them all the time ...

And the Egyptians wrote letters to the dead, keeping in touch, just as today people visit the gravestones of loved ones and speak with them there. Did he really say that just last week? He could do with someone speaking with him now, please someone speak! But whether they ever got a reply we don't know, and the truth is, the Egyptian dead may have been more concerned with their journey into the underworld than with emailing the living, for there were perils to encounter and problems to face – and in particular, the great Hall of Judgement, where the heart was weighed in the balance. This was the moment: the weighing of the heart! If the heart was light, lighter than a feather, free of sin, then you breathed a large sigh of relief, for you were considered to be good and you would continue as a living soul. If your heart was too heavy, however, heavy with sin, you would not have time to breathe, for it was fed to a terrifying creature, half-lion, half-crocodile and you were no more, your identity gone, dead for ever.

Your identity gone, dead for ever, thought Abbot Peter, drifting a little, dead for ever, he mustn't drift, and so thirsty, thirsty for air, thirsty for water, think of the questions afterwards, at the W.I., what were the questions, they weren't all asleep, there'd been questions, before tea and cake, nice cake, and then he heard noise above him, faint like distant thunder, earth shifting, earth moving, and he was choking again, when he mustn't choke … was his captor back?

Had the sociopath returned?

# Seventy One

'But what about Millicent?' said Wonder.

'Forget about Millicent.'

'But she's confessed.'

'She didn't kill Hermione,' said Tamsin, wearily. 'She was in custody when the tower was burned down.'

'That's supposing – .'

'Yes, it's supposing the same killer was at work, a not unreasonable supposition. How many killers can a small theatre produce?'

Tamsin was bending the driver's ear as they drove – no, raced – to Stormhaven, siren blaring, emphasising the need for speed, constantly in his ear – 'we need to get past that car' – while dealing with Wonder, who shared the back seat and was getting on her nerves.

'Timothy was the last person to see Peter yesterday. He says they talked in the afternoon and Peter left him about 4.00 p.m.'

'And you believe him?' said Wonder.

'No reason not to.'

'Last one to see the victim and all that.'

'Possibly. But Timothy met Millicent later, we have verification.'

'Perhaps they've worked together, two ill-fated lovers.'

'And perhaps neither of them has anything to do with it at all,' said Tamsin.

Tamsin didn't need this conversation as their car travelled from Lewes along a busy A27, where it was clear they were in a hurry, clear they weren't going shopping, so why didn't the other cars just get out of the way? She just wanted as many police as possible in the graveyard, with shovels – and Wonder had opted in. It was necessary to bring in the suspects again, they'd need to do that, to find the whereabouts of Janet Lines, Neville Brownslie, Paul Bent, Bill Cain and Margery Tatters during the hours in question … oh, and the Bishop. Where the hell was the Bishop? Last seen in the theatre before the murder of Boy, but not seen since? Where do bishops hide?

'You don't seriously think it's the Bishop?' said Wonder.

'He was there in the theatre shortly before the death of Cedric Mayfield and hasn't been seen since.'

'It's never the Bishop, believe me.'

'Don't sound so disappointed.'

She didn't think it was the Bishop, but then who did she think it was? So many people she didn't think it could be and all the time, the murderer staring her in the face, shovelling soil on her uncle. Had they really done that?

'He's a sherry drinker, anyway,' said Wonder as the car entered Stormhaven, passing down-at-heel, edge-of-town shops, dog-grooming, electrical repairs, pound store, et al.

'I'm sorry?'

'The Bishop. Drinks sherry mainly, so it's hardly likely – .' His reasoning petered out.

Tamsin sat back in dismay. It was comments like that, comments about nothing at all, comments which brought only eye-rolling contempt, spoken or silent, it was these sort of comments which ensured for Wonder such low levels of respect. But hang the lot of them, this was his take on the matter; for the Chief Inspector had his own concerns this summer morning, and he'd have to raise the matter, or rather return to the matter, because he'd already touched on it, feeling fatherly perhaps, if that was allowed these days.

'You do know, Tamsin' – and he just held back from putting his hand on her leg – 'that if he was buried last night, and that's pure supposition on your part, and I have to say pretty unlikely – and I know you don't want to hear this, but it has to be said – .'

Tamsin looked at him blankly as Wonder continued:

'If the Abbot fellow was buried last night, as you're suggesting … well, there's no way he can now be alive.'

It did have to be said and Tamsin didn't hear it.

'Of course he can be alive. He's indestructible. I told you.'

They sat in silence until the car pulled up at the Bell Theatre, which unusually for a show venue, also possessed a working grave-yard, a place of burial.

# Seventy Two

'Then look in the caravan!' shouted Tamsin.

There'd been no police shovels to hand, shovelling was generally sub-contracted to council men in neon yellow, a civilian contract; so they'd need to adapt. The caravan, 'Baines, look in there!' It's where the gardener lived, he lived in the caravan, it wasn't rocket science, it was common bloody sense, so why was she having to tell them? Wasn't this what men were good at, there had to be something, tool cupboards – they liked those, didn't they?

'It's locked,' called out Wheatley, Baines' colleague.

'Break in!'

'Break in,' said Baines, by way of confirmation. It wasn't locked, as it turned out, just a little stiff as Baines discovered, one hearty pull and it was open, what was it with Wheatley? But they called it breaking-in, because he wasn't bothering the DI again, didn't want any more of her tongue, and she was busy anyway, digging with her hands, quite a sight, the DI digging at the new-born grave, when suddenly a voice behind her said, 'Wait!'

Tamsin looked up. It was Bill Cain, now kneeling beside her.

'What are you doing?' she asked.

Shock.

'You want to be very careful. Look.'

Tamsin paused and followed Cain's pointing finger.

'That's a straw.'

It was a straw, poking out from the loose grave soil.

'If that's what I think it is – .'

But now Tamsin was feeling sick, sick with hope and fear … and sick with the knowledge that she'd sat here last night with Colin, sat here last night with Colin Gibbs, talking. Had Peter been alive then? He could have been alive then, almost certainly alive – but now? Wheatley arrived with a shovel.

'Out the way, miss,' he said eagerly.

'Go away,' said Tamsin, who now had other ideas.

241

Cain was gently working the soil around the straw, so as not to disturb the fragile pink and white plastic tube; while Tamsin, filthy hands and arms, burrowed in the lower half of the grave where the legs must be … and then she felt plastic, what was that, a body bag? Shit! She carried on scraping, more of the black bag appearing through the chalky soil.

'Well, help me, Baines!' she said.

Baines and Wheatley now put down their shovels – the unwanted shovels, found in the caravan, at the end, by the window – because the DI was doing it with her hands like a mad woman, never seen her like this before, and so they got down on their knees, while Wonder rang for an ambulance. He couldn't believe they hadn't rung for one already, too obsessed with shovels and Tamsin as manic as he'd seen her, not enough sleep; they'd need an ambulance whatever they found, and there was one on its way.

'And tell it to hurry!' he added.

Tamsin left the bottom half of the body with Baines and Wheatley; she felt they could manage, while she watched Cain at work at the top end, but could she trust him? She had to trust him, sometimes you do, sometimes you have to jump off a cliff and talk to someone, speak of things to a Mrs Morgan or whoever, you just had to trust, and the skill was keeping the thin tube standing while removing soil around it, until the moment when all the earth could be swept away, and the straw unnecessary for breathing, unnecessary at last, if there was still breathing, there didn't seem to be breathing, no sign of it in the morning air – how could there be breathing beneath this heap of mud? And the hope and the fear again, the body-bag figure apparent, soil cleared, a slit in the upper part, eyes covered by plastic, and Tamsin in the grave, pulling back the bag, away from the face, pale and cold, Wonder telling her to get out, Tamsin unzipping the body and pumping the chest, keep pumping.

'Uncle, Uncle!' she kept saying. 'Uncle!'

'Is he her uncle?' said Wheatley to Baines.

And then Abbot Peter started to choke.

# *The Final Act*

*Choosing to be in the theatre was a way to put my roots down somewhere with other people. It was a way to choose a new family.*

**Juliette Binoche**

# Seventy Three

The police had received the tip-off from Eric Wright, who was an employee at Newhaven Fort. He believed the man in question had slept there overnight, though he was unsure where; somewhere on the premises, which afforded many hideaways for vagrants – as well as being 'the best family day out in Sussex', according to the publicity, which was clearly untrue but doing its best, as publicity must. The lone figure had been seen on the ramparts of the fort but had moved quickly away when challenged and had last been seen heading down towards Newhaven beach.

Mr Wright, night security, had thought twice about making the call. He'd rung the police before and knew what to expect. They didn't even pretend to care these days, let alone respond, and they could be rude, because, as one officer had explained to him, 'If nothing's been stolen, Mr Wright, what are we going to do but give a vagrant a room of his own and three hot meals a day? Which, if you think about it, is just encouraging them.'

They had a point, and no one wants to encourage vagrancy, they needed stamping out, not a helping hand. But Eric had been told to report everything, an exercise in box ticking; and it didn't matter if nothing was done, that wasn't the point, it was at least on record: an intruder spotted and reported, backs well covered and all that, just in case he turned out to be something awful and Newhaven Fort was for ever tarnished with being a hideout for paedophiles or whatever. And perhaps they were, because today the police were very interested. They were round in no time.

And Eric did feel something for this place, it was more than a job, he was the guardian of history after all. A fort had been here since the Bronze Age, set high on the cliffs with its panoramic views, and the Romans had built here too. Hardly surprising: the squabbling siblings of Stormhaven and Newhaven had always offered an easy landing to invaders, though as Eric's wife said, 'That wouldn't have been for the shopping.' She always went to Brighton for hers, a bit snobby like that.

Eric looked with satisfaction across his domain, a place to be proud of. Newhaven Fort today was made of red Victorian bricks, six million of them, all made from Newhaven clay, built in the 1860s, and the largest defence work in Sussex ... Eric had read it, and he remembered facts like that. It was a ten-acre site and as the brochure declared, 'had been a vital element in coastal defence through two world wars'. So why – and this, for Eric, was quite unbelievable – why had this historic site been so abused of late? No other word for it: abused! You should honour your history, especially your military history, stand proud, this fort shook its fist at Hitler, for God's sake! Yet after the war it was left to rot by the council – left to rot, before being sold to developers, the first of whom turned it into a holiday camp, and the second into a leisure centre! You couldn't make it up!

Newhaven Fort was like a girl passed round, a girl abused, that's how Eric viewed it, a bloody disgrace, excuse language ... until sanity returned and someone in Lewes Council said: 'No, let us honour this site.' And, helped by lottery funding, that's what they'd done, and God bless them all, not a religious man, Eric, but God bless them anyway, Newhaven Fort was restored, restored to former glory which was worth a pint of the local Harvey's ale. This fort had seen off the Spanish Armada who sailed close; it had seen off Hitler and his Nazi jackboots; but best of all, most cheering of all, it had seen off the developers and their bloody leisure centre! Made you proud to be British.

'Do you have a description?' asked the policeman on the phone.

'A description?'

'Of the man you think you saw.'

'Oh, I definitely saw him.'

'So what did he look like?'

Eric didn't have a description, apart from it being a man. Or he thought it was a man, couldn't be sure, may have been a woman, you don't know with vagrants because they're shapeless in the coats they wear, the sort of coats that don't have shape, or not any longer, the shape goes over the years. So he wasn't as specific as he could have been, man possibly woman; but then he hadn't expected questions. They never usually asked questions, apart from a bored 'Has anything been stolen?' And if it hadn't – if they'd just trespassed or loitered or urinated on the gift shop wall, it was 'Thank you and goodnight'.

But this morning it was different. Eric was told they'd be 'right round', which he didn't believe, but they were true to their word, two squad cars arriving within seven minutes of the call.

Three police officers emerged, and were guided by Eric towards the path the figure had been seen on, and that was that, with Eric putting the kettle on and returning to the *Daily Express*. And then ten minutes later, couldn't have been more, the police were seen returning to their cars with the suspect, with *a* suspect, who was loudly proclaiming both his innocence and his outrage. But then as Eric knew, a lot of vagrants were ex-public school boys these days who somehow still felt they had rights.

*

But it was not just Eric Wright who was busy this morning. Various other people were going about their work, with varying degrees of satisfaction. And at about the same time that Eric was dealing with the police, a determined figure was disposing of a computer, the one they'd removed from the doctor's surgery, throwing it over the bridge on the quiet country road winding its way through Barcombe Mills, flood capital of the world, no shortage of water here. The technology smashed and splashed in the foam, and then sank, swallowed whole, towards the silence of the river bed.

And then there was Colin Gibbs leaving another message on Neville's answer phone, asking him to get in contact and still feeling uncomfortable about contacting the police, you shouldn't do that with your ex, because if Neville found out, he'd go mad; maybe he had found out, which would be terrible.

While Paul Bent, playwright, sat in the kitchen of the Bishop's house, his former home, comforting his mother and telling her that everything would be all right, though how that could be so without the world starting again, he wasn't sure … but you say it, don't you?

And then back in Stormhaven, Timothy Gershwin was in the police station, demanding that he be allowed to see Millicent, insisting that the custody sergeant was acting illegally in holding her. And he was still there making his point when the same custody sergeant received a new guest, fresh cell fodder, the vagrant from Newhaven Fort, reeking of stale alcohol but wearing expensive shoes beneath the coating of mud.

And as the custody sergeant bagged up his belongings, it became apparent, while filling in the form, that the vagrant was Stephen Straight, the Bishop of Lewes.

'No, Bishop *for* Lewes,' he corrected. He wanted them to get that right.

'Bishop *for* Lewes,' wrote the custody sergeant, aware this was all quite unusual and wondering if he was also a bishop for murder?

# Seventy Four

'Just routine questions, Mr Gershwin,' said Tamsin. 'We simply need to establish where everyone was last night.'

'Terrible, terrible,' he said. 'The beautiful bell tower, I loved that tower. Loved it.'

'I'm sure we all did.'

She didn't.

Before her, across the table, was Timothy Gershwin who hadn't made it out of the police station before being invited, firmly, for interview.

'I thought we might as well start with you as you're here,' said Tamsin, cheerfully. 'Saves you a journey.'

'You've got this all wrong.'

'Here on important business?'

'I need to talk with Millicent.'

'With whom you have a relationship.'

'With whom I have a relationship, yes … an entirely professional one.'

'So that's cleared that one up.'

'Actor/director – such relationships are not unknown, it's how plays and films are made.'

'Purely professional?'

'And I don't know what she's said, but she's quite innocent, of course.'

'Well, there's time to sort that out and I'm sure we will. But last night, Mr Gershwin, where were you between 6.00 p.m. and 10.00 p.m.?'

'I was at home – well, my rented home, home for the season. I was looking at one or two TV scripts which have been sent to me.'

'Another *Midsomer Murders*? There do seem to be a lot of them.'

'I don't really believe in facetious policing.'

'What do you believe in?'

'I believe in the flower growing through the tarmac in the road.'

'Very poetic.'

'A flower like Millicent.'

Tamsin nodded reassuringly.

'And sometimes the tarmac's very thick, Inspector, and it's tough for the flower, almost murderous. I'm sure you know what I mean.'

The words hit her like a stomach punch, they winded her. Tamsin felt something inside her shift, tectonic plates move, tectonic plates for so long in place, holding everything down and everything in, but now a hole on the ocean floor, gaping and dark, and terrible currents of disturbance and she was fighting, fighting to steady her breath, to find rhythm, to find a deeper breath. She did know what he meant, like a bad dream, only she was awake and she knew about the tarmac, but she didn't want to know, not here and not now.

'Are you okay?' asked Timothy. 'Can I help? You suddenly look very pale.'

# Seventy Five

Neville remembered how it started, this briefest of brief affairs. It started with Paul's plan to burn down the tower.

It was hardly the beginning for Neville, of course – no, that had been months back, from the moment he'd met him in the foyer, little boy lost, when Paul had been looking for Timothy and didn't know where to go. And from that moment, nothing spoken, but he'd always found the young playwright a compelling sight, despite dear Colin – but you can't help how you feel. And a bishop's son, of course, which made him yet more delectable, forbidden fruit, so to speak, this creature from Eden, a ripe apple for the plucking. Not that the minx had encouraged him in those feelings, other than by being around, which was encouragement enough, constant fuel for the fire, and the boy was around a great deal – perhaps more than he had to be? This was Neville's feeling, which did make you wonder, it made Neville wonder, he wondered all the time, seeking hidden meanings; playing hard to get, the little tease.

And Neville may have made his feelings known, dropped comments into the pot now and again, harmless flirting, testing the water, there are ways, all quite mad on reflection, utter madness, the things we do. But they'd not been good days for Neville, this shouldn't be forgotten, not good days at the theatre, and yes, he'd needed the attention, the distraction, the intrigue ... my God – listen to yourself, Neville!

And then, quite out of the blue, at 5.00 p.m. on the day of Hermione's murder, on the day of the thirtieth anniversary celebrations, when he was about to greet the first volunteers for the evening, his office door opened and in walked Paul Bent.

'How about we burn the Bell Theatre down?' he said, standing by the door. 'We could do it, you know... and I don't think anyone would catch us.'

The confidence of youth!

# Seventy Six

Tamsin said she was quite all right, that she did not need Timothy's help or anyone else's for that matter, and moved to wrap up the interview.

'So there's nothing else about last night that you can help us with?' she said. 'You didn't see anything?'

'Sadly not, no. I left promptly after seeing Abbot Peter – a very helpful meeting, I should add. Interesting man. I'd like to speak with him some more.'

'I'm sure.'

'I do hope he's all right.'

'Why shouldn't he be?'

'I had heard – .'

'He's fine.'

Tamsin feels tearful and looks away; she needs to harden up.

'We spoke of Eckhart,' says Timothy, 'for whom we share a mutual passion.'

'Everyone should have a hobby.'

'I think he's a bit more than a hobby, Detective Inspector.'

'That's what the stamp collectors all say. Anyway, thank you very much, Mr Gershwin.'

Timothy is angry but also professional.

'Then we'll agree to disagree, and I do disagree, but if there's any way I can assist, really anything – I will. The Bell Theatre is very dear to my heart.'

'I'm sure.'

'And look after yourself. You really don't look well.'

Tamsin smiles distantly and there's a knock on the door. The constable in attendance moves towards it.

'Well, I'll be off,' says Timothy, getting up. 'It would be good if I could see Millicent before I – .'

But then he stops dead, like a man shot, further words drying on his lips. A ghost has just walked into the room … who turns out to be Abbot Peter.

*

Meanwhile, further down the corridor, the Bishop *for* Lewes – yes, the sergeant had taken note of that – was confirming that his son, Paul, had murdered Hermione Bysshe-Urquhart, and that her blood was on his shirt, if anyone cared to visit his flat, if the evidence hadn't been burned … adding only that he now wished to go home and sleep for a very long time.

# Seventy Seven

'But you recognised the voice?' said Wonder.

He was wedged, with Tamsin, into Abbot Peter's bedroom at Sandy View, and couldn't believe it; couldn't believe that the Abbot hadn't recognised the voice. Talk about amateur!

'It was a woman's voice.'

'A woman's voice?'

'I don't know, I think so.' He was still weak and had been hurried back after his brief visit to the police station. 'A woman, a sociopath … but something contrived, as if a part was being played.'

'Hardly a surprise in a theatre!' said Wonder.

'So you really don't know who buried you,' said Tamsin, with some blame attached.

Abbot Peter did and didn't know. He knew somewhere inside, could taste the truth, a fleeting aroma, but without recognition; because he had known, known for certain, until his certainty became unsettled and now he needed time and space, he needed to be left alone as soon as possible. It wasn't a large room, his bedroom, and his two visitors filled it with both their questions and their bodies – particularly as one of the bodies was the Chief Inspector's.

'He looks a bit different in his night gear!' he'd said to Tamsin in the kitchen. They'd arrived to find Abbot Peter asleep. 'You know, without his habit thing.'

'And your point is?'

'He looks less of a – well, you know – .'

'Less of an Abbot?'

'Well, yes … just a man, like the rest of us.'

The kettle boiled.

'And how do you look out of your uniform thing, Sir? '

'I'm just saying. He's not quite the big I AM in that get-up!'

He was jealous of the Abbot's relationship with Tamsin.

'I think most men struggle to look authoritative in their pyjamas, Sir. You should try it at the station one day.'

The Chief Inspector liked his uniform. Sometimes it was all he had to keep him together. When he knew nothing, or felt himself disappearing into a vortex of non-existence, his uniform was still there at the meeting, still there at the table, the silver pips on his shoulders, declaring him someone of value, insight and authority. It didn't help him at home, but that was another story.

For now however, sitting bedside, he was trying to get things straight about the whole Bell Theatre business – and finding a large number of curves. He didn't enjoy knowing less than an abbot at the best of times, and he hated the Church, always had. But the old fellow did seem to know his onions, in an amateurish sort of way, not proper police work obviously, but not without interest; and the doctor had said he'd be fine for a short conversation. The Abbot's neighbour, Annabelle Rusty, sat downstairs to oversee fair play. She was a nurse of thirty years standing, not that she'd done much of that, always on the move, Mrs Rusty. And she'd enjoy evicting the Chief Inspector should it prove necessary. The young woman with him might be more of a challenge.

'Like I said, it was all about origins,' said Peter, speaking weakly but clearly. He was a striking shade of pale, a translucent quality to his dark skin.

'You didn't say that to me,' said Wonder.

'No, I said it to Tamsin,' he replied. 'I thought she might have passed it on … but maybe that's not how you work.'

An awkward pause. Peter and Tamsin had not spoken since the Abbot's resurrection from the dead. The ambulance had arrived promptly at the graveyard, not a normal pick-up point. But the morning is a good time for a crisis in the Brighton area, there being no club-land inebriates vomiting themselves unconscious on the town's streets. And the paramedics, Charlie and Chris, had been first rate, if initially taken aback by their task.

'Never dealt with anyone in a grave before.'

'Raising the dead above your pay grade, is it?' said Tamsin.

'And he's been buried here for how long?'

'We think since about 6.00 p.m. yesterday evening.'

'That's over twelve hours!'

Charlie was still trying to get his head around it all.

'So how come he's – .'

'Alive?'

'Yes.'

'He was breathing through a straw,' said Tamsin, as though it was fairly routine for those buried in graves. 'Well, two straws in fact, dovetailed together and held together with sticky tape.'

She bent down and pointed to the exhibit ... an exhibit she'd seen somewhere before but couldn't quite place. And then Charlie had another question, because he was bright and could immediately see a problem.

'So how come the straw didn't fill with soil as he pushed it upwards? You'd think it would fill with soil.'

'Good question,' thought Tamsin.

'Because he was a very clever Abbot' said Bill Cain, intervening. 'His brain must have been working overtime. See this?'

Kneeling by the graveside, he held up something Tamsin had missed, a small sweet wrapping.

'He must have covered the end of the straw with it as he pushed it upwards. It acted like a little hat, keeping the passageway clear. Bloody clever, that.'

'Very clever,' said Charlie, nodding in appreciation, like one does when gazing on the work of a craftsman.

'Oh yes, he's quite a boy, your Abbot,' said Cain to Tamsin.

'Something like that,' said Tamsin who didn't know what to feel. But Charlie had another question, the graveside questions just kept on coming, while Chris sat with Peter on the grass, helping him to drink.

'And, er, how come he had straws, tape and sweet wrappings handy?' asked the paramedic who knew his girlfriend would just love all this. 'It's not the sort of thing – .'

'It isn't, no.'

And then Tamsin remembered, it all came back: the afternoon of the show, the afternoon before the murder during *Mother's Day*.

'Because he clears up after children's parties,' she said. 'And never empties his pockets.'

# Seventy Eight

Later that day, two interviews took place at Stormhaven police station on a day of comings and goings, both of people and perceptions. Dr Elsdon had reported a break-in at the surgery, but while you always take a doctor's complaint seriously, particularly if you're on his books, break-ins do play second fiddle to a double murder, this is the way of things.

'One of the practice computers has been stolen,' he said, calmly but firmly. He was used to being heard and he'd be heard by this police idiot.

'We'll send someone round as soon as we're able, doctor.'

Baines hoped that would be enough.

'Do you know the personal details which are stored on that computer, Constable?'

'Sergeant.'

'Whatever.'

That sounded a bit careless to Baines.

'Well?'

'Well what?'

'The personal details on that computer – have you the least idea what's there?'

'I don't, sir,'

'No, you don't.'

'But then I didn't steal it … I can imagine though.'

'Oh, you can imagine, can you?' said the doctor, very aware he was not being taken seriously. 'Well, that's reassuring, Sergeant, but the trouble is, someone won't have to imagine, that's just my point' – and he was beginning to lose it now – 'someone will have it all there in front of them, right now, as we speak, every prescription, every diagnosis, at the click of a button, while the police do nothing, every ailment dancing before their eyes on the screen, every condition of my three thousand patients!'

There was an obvious response to this, if you were bored of the prig at the other end of the line: 'Which makes it all the more unbelievable that security was so poor, Doctor. In the surgery, I mean ... if, as you say, the intruder needed to break only one pane of glass ... hardly worth locking the door, really.'

It was a knee to the groin from a copper irritated by this middle-class Nigel who somehow imagined everyone must stop what they're doing, everything must bow and make way for the good doctor, because some spotty teenager has removed his little office computer. So what if the world knew Mrs Phipps had chickenpox last year? So bloody what? Precisely which world empire would now come crashing to the ground? And in the meantime, there was the small matter of two murders, with the bishop fellow in earlier, smelling like a mop in a brewery and claiming it was his son what done it, saying he'd seen the blood on the shirt, and then Millicent Pym, in the holding cell, swearing blind it was her. Could all those claiming to have killed the theatre woman please form an orderly queue?

'I wish to speak to your superior,' said the doctor briskly.

'I'm afraid that's not possible at present.'

'And may I ask exactly why is that not possible?'

Layers of condescending patience.

'She's in the interview room, sir, speaking with a murder suspect. You may have read in *Sussex Silt* – .'

'I don't read that rag.'

'No, Sir.'

Might do you some good, mate, might land your plane in the real world.

'Well – as soon as she's free.'

'As soon as she's free, sir.'

'And I expect to hear back from her in the next hour.'

And perhaps he would, but before any assurance could be given, he'd rung off, he had a practice to run, as DI Shah sat down in the interview room with the abbot bloke, still a walking corpse, my God! Baines had seen him, pale as paper, though hardly a surprise – buried for fourteen hours with only a straw for company. Imagine that ... no, don't imagine that, you'll start having nightmares, and so Baines busied himself with form-filling, there was always a form, that was the good thing about the police, always a form and always a file, as Tamsin and the Abbot contemplated Millicent across the desk; and as Millicent gazed back, all elfin-eyes and defiance.

And Baines had a fiver on it not being her.

# Seventy Nine

'How are you feeling, Millicent?' asked Tamsin.

'How d'you expect me to be feeling?'

'I don't know.'

'I've not been believed. That's the worst feeling.'

This was her issue, not being believed when she said something.

'I suppose I was wondering if you'd changed your mind about Hermione's murder … but it doesn't appear that you have.'

'It's not the sort of thing you forget.'

She looked piercingly at them both and thought Abbot Peter looked awful. What on earth had happened to him?

'No. But it is the sort of thing people sometimes make up.'

'Why make it up?'

'I don't know, Millicent. In order to protect someone else, perhaps?'

'I'm not protecting anybody. Why would I protect anybody?'

'But you didn't kill Boy, did you?'

'Why?'

'What do you mean, "Why?"'

'Why do you ask me that?'

'Because it wasn't possible,' said Tamsin. 'You couldn't have killed Boy, you were with Abbot Peter at the time.'

Millicent looked at the Abbot who nodded in confirmation.

'That's a good alibi,' said Tamsin. 'You ought to be delighted.'

Millicent was now an actor doing mental calculus.

'No, I didn't kill Boy,' she said.

'So who did?'

'I don't know.'

'Really?'

'Really.'

'It's strange to have two different murderers in the same place, each unaware of the other, as they go about their business. Almost unbelievable.'

'Well, perhaps you better get used to the unbelievable; because it happened,' said Millicent, looking at them both, alert as a rabbit and demanding belief. She would make them believe.

'So why kill Hermione? Director of a theatre which had given you a break.'

Tamsin noted more calculus from the amateur actress, and couldn't decide if it was a good act, a bad act or no act at all.

'Because she didn't believe me.'

'She didn't believe you.'

'And I think she owed it to me, to hear what I said and to believe what I said.'

'Is this why she slapped you?'

'It is, yes.'

'So she did slap you five minutes before she died?'

'She did.'

'You previously said that was a lie.'

'It wasn't a lie.'

'Today it's the truth. What about tomorrow? A lie again?'

'It can all be proved.'

'Really?'

'But I didn't kill her because of the slap – I killed her because she didn't believe me, didn't hear me.'

'What didn't she believe or hear?'

'That she was the worst mother in the world.'

Silence.

'That's quite a judgement.'

'Perhaps it's just the truth.'

And Peter knew that it was, in that instant, as Millicent was back there now, back in the theatre that night, on the thirtieth anniversary, and the overwhelming feeling that she had to confront the woman, no more pussyfooting about, perhaps it was the script, the sheer force of *Mother's Day* constructed around abandonment, just as she, Millicent, had been abandoned and made out of disappointment; and so she'd go and speak with her, speak with Hermione, she had ten minutes, and when she found her in her study during the interval, thirty-four years spilled out:

'How do you feel on Mother's Day?'

'I beg your pardon?' said Hermione, looking up.

'Mother's Day. Do you miss the cards?'

'I – .'

'Regret the fact that you don't receive any?'

'Why would I receive cards on Mother's Day?'

'Most children send them.'

'I don't have any children, Millicent – now shouldn't you – .'

260

'What about me?'

'What about you?'

'LOST SO YOUNG, TOO PERFECT TO BE MISSED.'

'LOST SO YOUNG, TOO WONDERFUL TO BE WEPT FOR.'

Millicent remembered the terror in the woman's eyes, craters of oval fear, hollowed by exposure and shame.

'It's the one thing you gave me, Mother – a headstone! Some mothers give love, you gave some chiselled marble, like I was dead to you, like I didn't exist any more!'

'You're talking nonsense.'

'So let's see then, shall we? Blood tests, let's see!'

'You selfish bitch!'

And the stinging slap, Hermione leaping up and reaching out, but not in love, in assault; and now Millicent shocked, stunned by the attack, and Hermione gathering herself and saying how they'd speak no more about this, there was nothing to be gained, and how she must go out on stage, how Neville had persuaded her, on this special night, to introduce the second half; and meek Millicent offering to go with her, and Hermione not caring whether she did or she didn't, it was time to move on, and no plan to kill, Millicent had planned nothing, just the longing to be heard, that's why she'd come, but standing behind her on stage, as Hermione composed herself, as Hermione Bysshe-Urquhart MBE composed herself for the limelight and applause, turning her back on Millicent once again, turning her back, always turning her back, that was it, that was the trigger and from somewhere, memory of Boy's army stories, unarmed combat, training in the military gym, such a simple move, the only one he remembered, and he'd told her of it in the caravan when once they'd talked.

And so it was, centre stage and first time lucky, grabbing her hair, jerking back the head, pushing the upper spine forward, maximum force, and the scissors, she didn't even realise she was holding those, she'd been cutting loose thread, they were Janet's scissors, but the assault on the neck felt right, turning her back on Millicent, years and years of it but never again, and then hasty exit, stage left, there'd be no more play tonight …

They sat in brief silence, broken gently by Peter:

'So why confess, Millicent, why turn yourself in?'

'Because I feel ashamed.' She sounded like a 6-year-old. 'I shouldn't have done it, should I? I should have loved her.'

'Did someone help you find your mother?'

'No,' said Millicent, older again. 'Why would they?'

Too hasty.

'You found her yourself.'

'It wasn't hard. I mean, it can be done.'

'And then you got lucky with the part here in *Mother's Day*?'

'I suppose.'

'And tell me, Millicent – did anyone help you find your father?'

The girl looked confused.

'I never found my father.'

'Oh?'

'There were no records. I would love to have found my father.'

She really would, thought Peter. So what to say now?

'You did find your father.'

Millicent looked blank.

'I don't know what you're saying. I think I'd know if I'd found my father!'

'How? How would you have known?'

Millicent didn't know how; she didn't know how you find your father unless someone gives you the paper trail, the address, the pub where he drinks, a photo, something like that.

'Boy was your father,' said the Abbot.

'What are you talking about?'

And then he remembered; he remembered the terrified look in the eyes, that afternoon in the rehearsal room, the moment of recognition. And of course, yes, the photo in the caravan, the photo of Boy's mother, their grandmother … and the unsettling likeness.

'What is your relationship with Timothy, Millicent?'

# Eighty

'He thought he was bringing me good news!' Timothy exclaimed. 'He really did – unbelievable!'

Timothy Gershwin, Interview Room No. 2, and across the table, DI Tamsin Shah and Abbot Peter.

'He was bringing himself good news,' said the Abbot. 'And imagined it would be shared by you.'

'Like that was going to happen!'

'You didn't want a father.'

'I didn't want that father, no. He was bringing me the worst bloody news, stupid little man!'

Timothy was feeling his Belfry fury again, the contorting rage that had left Cedric Mayfield beheaded and a bell-ringer in death.

'You hated your mother for leaving you,' said Peter, 'and you hated your father for finding you. A little inconsistent?'

'As I say, I didn't want *that* father ... as if anyone would, some homeless nobody!'

'Not so into calm now', thought Tamsin.

'And after all Millicent and I had been through!'

What experiences justify murder?, wondered Peter. Can a victim kill a bully, a householder kill a burglar? Appropriate force in self-defence? But then what is 'appropriate force' when someone has destroyed your life before you knew you had one?

'Abandoned by a mother who threw me away.'

'She had you adopted,' said Tamsin.

'No, thrown away, believe me, declared inconvenient and passed on, never mind who to ... and she didn't, she didn't mind, too eager to be with her saviour Nicholas ... and then the idea of a gravestone, just to show she cared, just to help her sleep ... given my very own grave, to remind me just how dead I was to her. Alive but dead!'

Tamsin was churning again but Timothy wasn't done.

263

'And then thirty-six years later, a vagrant turns up, an oddball with a stutter, a no-mark with nothing but the smell of the shop doorway, and says he's my dad and isn't that great! Well, I wanted something a little better than that! I wanted to stop being ashamed!'

He was sweating with rage, hiding nothing, exploding frustration.

'Your mother had a relationship with Cedric Mayfield in London,' said Peter.

'So it has transpired.'

'You read his book?'

Timothy paused.

'What book?' he asked.

'It doesn't matter.'

It had been worth a try.

'But you weren't aware he was your father – until yesterday?'

'No, I didn't know.'

Calmer now.

'You didn't come here to kill him.'

'We didn't come to kill anyone.'

'But you hired Millicent. That was hardly chance.'

'Of course it wasn't chance.'

'You came here as brother and sister?'

'We were separated when toddlers, different families, she was in Somerset, but we found each other a long time ago, it's not that difficult, not if you both want it.'

'And?'

'And I just thought it would be interesting for us to come back and see our mother, up close and personal. Are you all right, Abbot? You look a bit pale.'

'I'm fine, thank you. I had an encounter with a sociopath.'

'Hermione was a bitch,' continued Timothy.

'A bitch with an MBE and a fine local reputation.'

'Undeserved,' said Timothy. 'It was all Nicholas's work. I have no love for him but everything good here is the work of Nicholas – it's a dry shell of what it once was.'

'But her killing wasn't planned.'

'In no manner was it planned. We expected to do our thing and then leave when autumn came.'

'Very poetic.'

'I don't know what got into Millicent … well, I do, she was overwhelmed, poor girl, flooded by thirty-four years of neglect, and went and told her who she was. I couldn't believe it.'

'She has told us what happened.'

Timothy shook his head.

'Couldn't help herself, she told me.'

'A military move which Boy had shown her, being a military man himself, of course.'

'Briefly.' Timothy said it with contempt. 'Before the vagrancy.'

'But Millicent liked him, she liked her father,' said Peter.

'I wouldn't use the word "like".'

'She did. She used it.'

'He was just an old man she felt sorry for … that's not the same as liking someone.'

'She liked her father, liked his company, liked to talk with him. There was connection.'

'He would have been an embarrassment – he was the last thing she needed, believe me.'

'I don't believe you.'

'More fool you.'

'And he did begin to wonder … wonder about the gravestones. But it was the Reverend Ainslie Meddle who confirmed your identities, at least confirmed the names of the two children, and then suddenly the picture of his mother made sense, it started to sing.'

'You've spoken to Meddle?'

'I've spoken with him, yes.'

'Someone else who deserves to die.'

'Really?'

'Willing participant in the gravestone charade.'

'You can't kill the whole world.'

'Just those responsible.'

The Abbot nodded.

'But your father wasn't responsible. Hermione had told him you were both dead.'

A pause.

'That was cruel, I grant you that. But what else did the loser deserve?'

'I think he deserved the truth, don't you? Just like you deserved the truth.'

'I wanted my origins to be finer,' said Timothy. 'Much finer.'

'Which was why Eckhart made you cry.'

'The tears were genuine, you know.'

'I believe you.'

'But longing and hatred sit very close; too close. That German monk spoke of such wonderful origins, such eternal origins.'

'He did.'

'What they made of him in his own day, I can't imagine.' Timothy almost smiled. 'But to me, he made parents quite secondary and I needed that, I needed another beginning, better origins … that matters when you've been abandoned.'

'But Cedric never abandoned you.'

'You don't understand.'

'He didn't know about you.'

'LISTEN TO ME!'

It was a roar, a primal scream, and Timothy was out of his seat, the attendant police officer moving towards him, a stand-off by the window, like a trainer with an angry lion, easy now, calming the power. The Abbot stayed seated and still; nothing much moved him at present … Timothy making gestures of peace with his hand, 'It's all right, I'm fine,' and returning to his chair. But then he wasn't used to sitting, he directed standing up, he shouted to crew and performers standing up, he couldn't abide read-throughs when everyone was sitting down, how could you express passion sitting down? No, you had to be standing up to let go, like he was in the belfry, as law and order buckled and he felt lava rage rising … and then he was losing it, swamped by it, drowned by it, overcome by the years, and he was pushing this man, pushing him and his stupid face back, smashing him hard against the wall, the shock in his eyes, his scream as the metal wall pin penetrated his lower back, skewered like meat and held there – 'How does that feel, loser!' – head pushed forward by the gargoyle above, almost like it was bowed, like a head on a block, then Timothy smashing the glass, freeing the axe and swinging, heavy metal swinging, the second strike severing the head, and the axe crashing through to the wall behind, leaving just the torso hanging, hanging on the wall like a jacket on a peg, and the gargoyle above, replacing his head – now that looked evil!

But the man was dead, his bloody head on the blood-soaked carpet, the last living symbol of everything that was wrong, who somehow thought it was good; somehow thought that here was a happy ending and just couldn't understand, like these people couldn't understand – so what was the point?

'He was just part of the shame,' said Timothy, seated again.

'The shame?'

Timothy paused before speaking.

'Do you know what I was called at home? I was called Meetoo! And do you know why I was called Meetoo? Because that's what I always said, apparently, when they forgot to include me. My brother and two sisters – my adopted brothers and sisters – they all had names, they'd all appear in the roll call when we were going somewhere or doing something together, but mine would be forgotten, so I'd add 'Me Too!' And that's what they started to call me, they all

266

called me that. They were all good enough, you see, but I wasn't ... little Meetoo was never good enough to be included. You ask about the shame. I always felt there was something wrong with me ...'

There was a silence in the room. Abbot Peter spoke, with sadness: 'You've made a success of life, Timothy, coped for so long.'

Timothy smiled. It was the first time Peter had seen his smile, which was warm and open.

'What happened to that person?'

'I don't know him any longer,' said Timothy. 'He's not someone I know.'

'So much good in you.'

'The good in me is dead.'

'Mislaid, perhaps.'

'Dead.'

Timothy Gershwin sank back in his chair, an exhausted figure and older, much older ... though younger in a way, thought Peter.

\*

'So who buried you?' asked Tamsin, as they passed the duty sergeant on their way out.

'A sociopath whose name I don't know.'

'Any clues.'

'Oh, I know their name, but it doesn't fit. We still have a curtain to open.'

# Eighty One

## Saturday 7 August

It was a strange meeting, in the rehearsal room of the Bell Theatre, where a fire had recently destroyed the tower. The theatre space was a blackened shell, but structurally secure, as was the rest of the building: charred in places, and the furniture reeking of smoke, but old pillars still standing, old walls unbowed. In the car on the way, Tamsin had insisted it was the Abbot's show, though he baulked at the word.

'It isn't a show, Tamsin.'

'It is a show, Uncle.'

'I suppose it's a show.'

It was a show.

'But an important one,' he added. 'Endings matter.'

'Convictions matter, that's ending enough for me. Two murderers nicked.'

'I was thinking of King Charles earlier.'

'I'm sorry?'

'Charles the First.'

'Still wondering what you're talking about.'

'There was a reason.'

'Which I'm sure you'll explain.'

'He was beheaded.'

'That was savage.'

'Charles?'

'No, Cedric. Charles probably deserved it.'

'Maybe. A rather stupid man, and yes, author of his own downfall, because no one sets out to kill a king, no one wants it … Charles was the first and last English king to irritate the nation to that

268

degree. But noble in death, this is what struck people, a bigger man in death than he had been in life. As the poet Marvell wrote, "Nothing in his life became him like the leaving of it."'

'Very nice.'

It wasn't a compliment; Tamsin had no time for history, because it was over, so what was the point?

'Death's approach can bring out the best in people; but Cedric's life was ripped from him.'

'At least he died happy.'

'Happy?'

'He'd found his son.'

'And his son looked him in the eye and killed him.'

'Because he was stupid – like Charles. He couldn't see beyond himself, I'm with Timothy on that one. We're nearly there,' she said. 'I hope you're ready.'

And the Abbot started to sing, a simple voice, untutored:

> 'There is no end I know
> Like the end of a show
> When the orchestra's packed up and gone.
> There is no peace that I find
> Like the one left behind
> When it's time to lock up and go
> Before the curtain's down
> One last look around
> There's no end like the end of a show.

Tamsin sat silent, hoping she didn't have to respond.

'We used to sing it in the desert,' he added.

'Where probably it should stay.'

'It's a song by Peter Skellern.'

'I refer you to my previous answer.'

It had been the Abbot's first public solo on earth and, given the reaction, would probably be his last.

'So come on then,' she said, 'let's bring down the curtain on the show.'

# Eighty Two

There were nine people present in the rehearsal room, including Abbot Peter and Tamsin Shah. The others in the chair circle were Janet Lines, Neville Brownslie, Paul Bent, Bill Cain, Margery Tatters, the Reverend Ainslie Meddle and Bishop Stephen Straight, who could not see why he was here – and had said so to the Abbot on arrival:

'I hardly think this has got anything to do with me.'

'It was something you couldn't cope with, Bishop; something which sent you spiralling – .'

'I just went for a walk, for God's sake!'

'I'm not sure God benefited hugely.'

'I like to get out sometimes, to reflect on my ministry. Jesus went to the desert, I go to the cliffs.'

'But Jesus didn't take a large bottle of brandy – so you may find a goodbye helpful. Bear with me, please.'

The Bishop briefly remembered professional concern.

'Very sorry, of course, to hear about your, er, ordeal underground. You've been in my prayers, of course.'

'Thank you,' said Peter briskly. 'Shall we go on in?'

It was two days since the fire; two days since Millicent Pym was charged with the murder of her mother, Hermione Bysshe-Urquhart, and Timothy Gershwin for the murder of his father, Cedric Mayfield, also known as Boy. It was now common knowledge that as a teenager Julie Dicks had had a brief relationship with soldier Cedric, 'older man syndrome' as they called it – a union, if that was the word, which produced two children, Timothy and Millicent. But when Nicholas Bysshe-Urquhart had begun to show interest in the bright young thing, Julie had felt it was time for a fresh start – a fresh start which included four becoming one. So Cedric was dumped and the two children fostered out and then adopted, while Julie Dicks became Hermione Bysshe-Urquhart and setout on a new adventure at the Bell Theatre on her path to an MBE.

'I wanted us to gather here,' said Peter, 'because this space has played an important part in all your lives in different ways. Mine as well.'

There was an edge to the anticipation in the room.

'Have you found out who buried you yet?' asked Bill Cain.

'No,' said Peter. 'Well, yes and no.'

'So that clears that one up.'

'But endings matter,' said Peter. 'Whatever the future holds – and for myself, I hope my burial rehearsals are over – endings matter, they help us proceed.'

'I'll never again complain about being buried in paperwork,' said Neville drily.

'The gift of perspective,' said Peter. 'But one we so quickly lose, I fear.'

'I'm sure we'd all like you to get to the point, Abbot,' said the Bishop, but Peter was already reflecting on the burning: 'We sit in ashes now,' he said, 'the ash of things no longer so, but these are ashes from which we'll rise.'

'Hear, hear,' said Cain, who liked rising.

'And that's why I wanted this gathering.'

'This show,' thinks Tamsin.

'Because you can't leave somewhere until you've arrived there.'

'It was a ruin long before the fire,' said Neville.

'Maybe that was so,' said Peter.

'Never the same since Nicholas died.'

'Nostalgia isn't what it used to be, eh?' said Cain.

Neville: 'You were part of the ruin.'

'But before we go any further,' said Peter, intervening like a UN peace-keeper, 'I would like to thank one of you for your recent correspondence.'

Surprise, combatants distracted. But what was he talking about?

'And more particularly – for the final letter which brought the correspondence to an end.'

Confusion in the circle.

'The recent break-in at the doctor's surgery, and the theft of the computer, is something of a mystery to the police, DI Shah tells me.' He looks at Tamsin, who nods theatrically. 'And as long as the correspondence remains closed, it will stay that way. It's a very unpleasant stunt, stalking – I learned a new word, you see – and not worthy of the civilised. But perhaps on this occasion it was foolish rather than criminal.'

'May I ask what you're talking about, Abbot?' said the Reverend Meddle. 'Is there something that I've missed?'

'There's someone here who knows,' said Peter, which caused everyone to look round the semi-circle, everyone but Janet, who looked firmly at the coffee table in front of her; it had just been a game. But Peter wasn't done.

'And of course another of our number, another of this little circle, needs to remember the Highway Code. Cyclists should always stick to the roads.'

'Couldn't agree more,' said Margery.

Further puzzled glances; though one face, beneath thick luxuriant hair, was more concerned than puzzled.

'Pavements are for pedestrians ... even when you've just delivered early morning hate mail to someone who doesn't share your feelings.'

Paul shot an accusatory stare towards Neville, who responded by looking at his polished shoes.

'*Onslaught Games* are best left as fantasy,' said Peter.

'Still struggling to see what we're doing here,' said the Bishop, in a chairman-like way. 'It seems little more so far than the private pursuit of some personal vendettas.'

'And of course others here,' continued the Abbot, 'no names, no pack drill, need to find a new way through life's challenges; a way which doesn't include alcoholic annihilation and trespass. Newhaven Fort is private property.'

'And wasting police time,' added Tamsin.

'Oh yes, wasting police time.'

'Is that where you were?' said Paul, looking incredulously at his father.

The Bishop looked straight ahead, rigid.

'Mother didn't know where you were. She was terrified.'

There was some fear in the gathering now; no one, it seemed, appeared safe.

'And a small reminder, of course,' continued Peter, 'that cherry juice on a white shirt can look like blood ... though the sober will usually discern the difference.'

'He thought I was the murderer,' says Paul to Janet, who's sitting next to him. Janet manages a nod of acknowledgement, but still feels queasy as the Abbot speaks again.

'Though it was unwise to joke about burning down the tower, Paul. Perhaps you really wanted Neville to do it; you were aware of his feelings.'

'A joke, nothing more.'

'And every joke a surreptitious truth, you should know that, being a writer. And so of course Neville told your father. You didn't help yourself, Paul.'

272

'I'm leaving,' says Paul, getting up from his seat.

'No, you're not,' says Peter, moving towards him. 'Don't abandon us, it won't help you. Stay until we're done. And you wrote a very good play, by the way, a brilliant play.'

Paul sits down.

'Mr Cain wants to say a few words. Mr Cain?'

'The Bell Theatre will be back,' he says enthusiastically, as if this will solve everything. 'It will be back, things in the pipeline.'

Some positive noises from people.

'And the bell tower?' asks Margery.

'The bell tower?'

'Will that be returning, with the old bell?' Margery is not asking for herself, but for her mother, who is already missing it. 'It is a Stormhaven tradition.'

'Watch this space,' says Cain enigmatically. If he can find a sponsor for the bell, then Stormhaven will certainly hear its chimes again; it was the brand, in a way. And after a few words of thanks and encouragement from Peter, the meeting broke up, conversation freed by the fact that this was goodbye, they wouldn't be together again, may not even see each other again ... and sometimes that makes things easier to say.

'Coming?' said Bishop Stephen, as he prepared to leave.

'I'm staying,' said Paul. He wasn't ready to go.

'Just a series of unfortunate misunderstandings,' said the Bishop, but more to himself than anyone else.

Paul didn't answer, he didn't know what to say, so no goodbye to his father apart from the faintest nod; and as the Bishop left, Margery came up and thanked him for his play, just as Peter had.

'I hope it goes further,' she said. 'It deserves to.'

This was a surprise.

'Thank you.'

Paul wanted to cry. He'd wanted to run away, but now he wished only to stay and cry.

'See you then,' she said. 'Theatre folk never say goodbye.'

'No.'

And then she turned.

'How about writing me a one-woman show for Edinburgh ... for the Edinburgh Fringe?'

'You'd be interested?'

Paul was interested.

'Let's meet and talk,' said Margery.

She gave him her card, he said he'd be in contact, definitely, he had an idea already; and Margery smiled and then wandered off towards the burnt-out theatre, needing to be alone, but needing to be here, this was the thing, here in the ruin where she climbed up onto the charcoal stage and sat down on the ashen chair, Hermione's last rest.

*

While back in the rehearsal room, Neville spoke with Cain about future plans, man's chat about building projects, planning permission, finance, that sort of thing.

'You probably won't want the likes of me here,' said Neville.

'Probably not.'

'No.'

'But then who knows? What are you worth to me, Neville?'

Bill knew about worth, he could put a figure on anyone.

'I'm worth a great deal,' said Neville, making his pitch.

'You've got lazy.'

'I got bored.'

'Too much time at *Onslaught Games*, I'm told. Lacking focus.'

'I'm selling my stake to Simon and Jamie.'

'It would have to run at a profit.'

'It would have to get back to being a theatre.'

'But plays people wanted to see.'

'Quality shows. Cole Porter.'

'Who's he?'

'And then a clown school as well.'

'For the kiddies?'

'They love clowns.'

'We need to get them in, certainly.'

'I can think of two clowns ready to go.'

'As long as they're not in charge of the finances.'

And a few feet away, Janet risked a cheeky smile in Abbot Peter's direction, and asked him how he knew.

'It was the theft of the computer from the surgery,' he said, 'it jogged my memory. I remembered where I was the day the letters began – in the surgery queue. No one would want an old doctor's computer unless it stored awkward information. So when the final letter arrived and the computer disappeared, everything made sense – or as much sense as anything does. And of course it was all confirmed by Bill Cain yesterday.'

'Bill Cain?'

'You'd made an enemy there, Janet.'

'Really?'

She looked uncomfortable.

'As you know, he'd had a confidential chat with Dr Elsdon about his plans to buy the theatre, the doctor saw fit to tell you, and you saw fit to make sure everyone else knew … seems he wanted to get his own back.'

'I didn't mean them, of course.'

'The letters?'

'It was just a game.'

'There's a lot of playfulness you missed as a child, Janet. But I will expect preferential treatment in future, when trying to make an appointment.'

'I never give preferential treatment to anyone.'

'Not even if you like them?'

'Who said I like you?'

'Fair point.'

Awkward pause.

'There's another thing, Abbot. Could we sit down a moment?'

'We could sit down.'

Janet had something on her mind.

'And I want to tell you a story about a church which burns down.'

'Very topical.'

'And all the people inside are killed.'

'I see.'

'But it's a mystery and here's the reason why: the people inside were warned.'

'Warned about the fire?'

'Yes, someone came to the door before the flames took hold and told everyone to leave; warned them of the danger and told them to get out.'

'But the mystery is that they didn't?'

'That's right, no one moved, they ignored the voice of warning and died where they stood. So why didn't they move?'

The challenge laid down.

'A mystery indeed, Janet.'

'Well?'

'As the one who tells me the story deals in costumes, I wonder if costumes are important here?'

Janet indicated this might or might not be the case.

'They didn't believe the messenger, so perhaps they wore a costume that encouraged disbelief … uniforms matter, they can encourage both belief and disbelief, so a costume that encouraged them to think – ah, yes! – that encouraged them to think he was joking, that he was joking about the fire. Was the messenger a clown?'

'Might have been.'

It was as good as he'd get from Janet.

'And of course you are a very good clown, Janet.'

'Me?'

'I've seen you, remember? Messrs Potswallop and Lickspittle.'

'The uniform gives me a different voice … a voice with which I can reach children.' She's wistful. 'And I love speaking with children, Abbot – but children won't give me a second glance if they meet me as Janet Lines.'

'Don't give up.'

'But I didn't tell the story to test you – or to fish for compliments.'

'So why did you tell it?'

'I hate costumes.'

'I'm aware of that … it always puzzled me.'

'I know their power. I was frightened of my soldier father, because of his costume … a weak man hiding behind his uniform.'

'But you've spent your life putting people into costumes.'

'Spent my life giving people, who have nothing to say, their moment in the sun. Father liked a uniform, you see.'

Peter allowed the moment.

Janet: 'And then you turn up in your habit, Abbot, and I hate you for that, because it's just another costume, just another lie, just another bid for attention, the last resort of the weak.'

Peter's habit seemed to burn on his body. What was coming next?

'But I think you're real, as it happens. As vain as the next man, all of whom disappoint, men do disappoint. But beneath the nonsense, beneath the costume, I don't think you're weak – I think you're real.'

And with that, she got up and walked away … at which point Neville called her over to meet Bill Cain, that would be interesting, and Peter watched her go, in a strange state of shock.

'Are you all right?' asked Tamsin.

'I'm fine,' said Peter. 'Janet just took me through the fires of judgement, but I may have survived.'

*

It took a while for people to leave; there was a spirit to linger in the ash of what had been. Margery was the last to go, stepping down from the silent stage when the Abbot and Tamsin appeared in the doorway.

'I auditioned for his first show here,' she said.

'Whose first show?'

'Timothy's.'

276

'*Life's a Drag*?' said Peter. '"A disreputable comedy", he called it.'

'That's right, but at least it was work – though obviously a waste of my time.'

'What was?'

'Auditioning. Or applying for the audition.'

'The parts had been taken.'

'That – and the fact that it was men only. It was a drag show.'

'Men in drag?' said Tamsin.

'Timothy did a very good woman in those days.'

'He still does,' said Peter.

The jigsaw was complete, the case put to bed.

'And he can do it with a shovel in his hands,' he added, in case anyone had missed the moment.

'He buried you?' said Tamsin.

'I knew he buried me, it had to be him; but I also knew he wasn't a woman and he was very good.'

And when Margery had gone, having wished them well, and they finally stood in the theatre alone, Tamsin asked:

'When did you know?'

'When did I know what?'

'The murderer? The burier?'

'Timothy told me himself.'

'He told you?'

'He didn't actually say it, but he might as well have done. I mean, it was the clearest confession I've ever witnessed.'

'In your long experience of police work.'

Sarcasm.

'I heard a few confessions before this all started. The police don't have a monopoly on them.'

'And when was this great confession?'

'The afternoon before the tower burned down.'

'You knew then?'

'We were talking, Timothy and I, in the rehearsal room about Eckhart, about origins.'

'As you do.'

'And I knew something of significance was occurring, I had that feeling: here was a man out of relationship with his past, desperate for another past, an alternative one, but I couldn't quite give it shape. And then he looked at me as I read Eckhart – and I saw that he knew that I knew.'

'But you didn't know.'

'Correct. He was too sharp for his own good, you see. A director looks at the eyes, and he saw mine, saw what they were *about* to

277

see, saw himself being found out – and his reaction told me what I didn't know, gave it sudden shape, clearly outlined.'

'I think I understand. His awareness gave birth to yours.'

'After that, it was all a bit of a rush – the headstones, the book in the caravan and of course the photo of Cedric's mother.'

'His mother?'

'Yes. Timothy and Millicent don't look alike.'

'No, they don't.'

'But they both resemble Cedric's mother. Her face brought them together and the puzzle was solved.'

'Waiting to be solved.'

'Yes, I didn't see their faces in hers then, and I was thrown by the voice. The missed clue was in the name of the show, of course.'

\*

They left the Bell Theatre, charred but standing, making their way through the graveyard, passing an empty tomb, recently dug up; and two head stones which said:

LOST SO YOUNG, TOO PERFECT TO BE MISSED.
LOST SO YOUNG, TOO WONDERFUL TO BE WEPT FOR.

278

# Eighty Three

## *Sunday, 8 August*

'So where did you go?' he asked.

'How do you mean?'

The Abbot and the detective, uncle and niece, the buried and the unburied, sat on the wall and looked out to sea, turbulent today in the misty August rain. Tamsin had suggested remaining in her car, but the Abbot wanted the wind and the wet, forces he never believed he'd feel again. Various figures dotted the undulating shingles, some swimming, a couple throwing a frisbee across the choppy waves; you had to keep moving and teeth chattered as they emerged to dry themselves, conquerors of the cold, towels wrapped around like fur in a Russian winter.

But most stayed dry, from the sea at least, safe behind windshields held firmly by the stones, they were good for that, with a thermos, sandwiches and the *Daily Mail,* a peculiarly British holiday; while Mr Whippy did business from his tuneful van, occasional business, a cornet here and there. But what do you expect from Stormhaven in the rain, as the hollering seagulls swoop, dive and scream?

It was Sunday, three days since Peter's pale emergence from the tomb, and Mrs Rusty, his vigilant nurse, had allowed him out. She hadn't been happy about the interviews with Millicent Pym or Timothy Gershwin, and yesterday's meeting at the Bell had also taken its toll. But how good to feel the elements, breathe in the air and drink tea from a plastic cup.

'And to think it's only a week since you invited me to the Bell Theatre for their thirtieth anniversary performance of *Mother's Day.*'

'It does seem longer somehow,' said Peter.

'Hermione's complimentary tickets.'

'Which I had to pay for.'

'Get over it.'

'I'll feel better when I'm running again. Running helps me to get over things.'

'Though a shame we never saw the second half.'

'That wasn't what you said at the time,' said Peter.

'Wasn't it?'

'You were very rude.'

'True. I'm forgetting how awful it was.'

'And the fact that I survived, the fact that I'm sitting here now, and enjoying the rain, is mainly due to Brother Elias – so here's to you, my friend, wherever you are!'

He raised his cup to toast the eminent psychologist – even if he had been hiding a cravat beneath his habit.

'Who's Brother Elias?'

'Another time. But now you do need to tell me.'

'I don't see why.'

'Because the guilt is killing you?'

'What guilt?'

She knew what guilt.

The grey horizon had entirely merged with the sea, but above them, even as they sat, patches of blue appearing, distant and small but growing in the grey, as wind harassed cloud.

'It shouldn't be killing you, of course, it's misplaced,' said the Abbot. 'But then guilt generally is.'

Tamsin hadn't forgiven herself for leaving her uncle to face what he'd faced alone; and so even now, four days on, she felt awkward in his presence, hostile towards others and to him because hostile to herself, the root of the discomfort. But to tell him why – to tell him why she left him, where she'd gone, why she'd had to lie in a room with the curtains closed, that was not easy. She must calm her breathing before releasing the words.

'I went to see a therapist.'

Abbot received her words with a nod.

'A good therapist?'

'I suppose so.'

Pause.

'That must have taken some doing.'

'It was like jumping off a cliff.'

Peter smiled and noticed the rain had stopped.

'Did you speak of the camp?' he asked.

'The camp?'

280

Peter stayed silent.

'I did, yes.'

'Then she must have been good.'

'Why do you say that?'

'You felt safe there.'

'Not really.'

Another pause.

'No, I don't think safe was the word,' said Tamsin vaguely.

Abbot Peter returned a bouncy ball to a little boy, whisked away from him by the wind.

'She said sometimes survivors of the camps had to go back there, back to the place.'

'They did. And that's what you were doing with her,' said Peter. 'Daring to go back.'

But would she return for another session? They'd spoken briefly on the phone, she and Mrs Morgan – she wasn't quite able to call her 'Anita'. She'd booked then cancelled, booked then cancelled, before feeling a conversation might be best; but not in her scary home. So she'd phoned from her bedroom, sitting on her own bed, and Mrs Morgan had asked her if she was running away, which seemed a bit forward, but Tamsin had said she probably was running away, and Mrs Morgan had said that sometimes it's good to run away.

'It's good to run away from a polar bear,' she'd said coolly.

'It would be, yes.'

'So running away is good if your life is threatened.'

'My life *is* threatened.'

'Which life?'

'"Which life"?'

It seemed a curious question.

'I only know of one,' said Tamsin.

'*A* life is threatened, or rather, a way of thinking and feeling is threatened; but perhaps it's one that needs threatening. Perhaps it's a liar.'

'Do you mind if I call you back?' said Tamsin. She'd suddenly felt the need to get off the phone.

'Not at all.'

'I'll be in touch, Mrs Morgan.'

She ended the call in a state of stress, all rather hasty, just needing to get away, ungoverned feelings arising; sitting on her bed unable to move, longing to escape her skin but in the meantime, drawn to the safety of the same, to the tried paths of the habitual, to battening down the hatches, to carrying on carrying on. Perhaps Mrs Morgan could wait …

'And so of course you will allow all feelings of guilt to dissolve,' said the Abbot.

'I'm sorry?'

Her mind had wandered from the big horizon and the incoming tide.

'You're allowing all feelings of guilt to dissolve.'

'Who said anything about guilt?'

'I did … in the absence of you mentioning it.'

'Are you absolving me or something, Abbot?'

Incredulous.

'Not in my power, sadly. You can only absolve yourself; and when you have, you'll know you're well.'

But as a boy and his dad argued over a kite that wouldn't fly, a kite that kept nose diving into the stones, Tamsin had a question of her own.

'Why did you enter the darkness with no back-up?'

'Me?'

'You don't like being questioned, do you?'

'Not particularly.'

'Not at all.'

'Maybe.'

'So?'

Abbot Peter paused. He didn't know why he'd gone to the grave-yard alone that evening, and entered the caravan alone.

'What do you want me to say?'

'How about an answer?'

Slowly he lowered the bucket deep into the well and drew up an answer:

'I suppose – well, I've always faced darkness alone.'

'Yes, but why?'

'I don't know why, Tamsin, I don't know why. There are reasons, no doubt, but they are lost to me, those "unrememberable but un-forgettable" things. Perhaps I always did, perhaps that's what I always had to do … I had to work it out alone.'

'And it nearly killed you.'

'It was close.'

Peter gazed at the horizon, a long line of straight, and above the line, a changing sky. Sun was breaking through the clouds, light beginning to play.

'Have you seen Stanley Spencer's painting *The Scorpion*?' he asked.

'No.'

Peter said nothing.

'Should I have?' said Tamsin.

He seemed to need prompting.

'Christ gently holds a scorpion in his hand.'

'More fool him.'

'The cost of encountering the world's darkness.'

'So he holds that which could kill him, and I'm meant to applaud?'

'You're not meant to do anything.'

Straight-talking needed:

'But for Hermione asking you to clear up after the children's party; and your insistence on putting rubbish in your pockets, instead of the bin – .'

The moral of the story was clear.

'It's a big "but",' said Peter.

'No, it's a tiny "but".'

'Big enough for me. Here I am, breathing, and it feels very good.'

'No one else knows, by the way.'

'About my pockets?'

'About Mrs Morgan.'

'Why do they need to? Going back?'

'I don't know.'

And now a rainbow ark above them, as sunlight strengthened. A small cheer from the beach, blue sky to the west, and though dark above, the west was on the way and for now, a double ark of strong colours, linking distant horizons.

'I must get home,' said Peter.

'A lift?'

'No, I'll walk. I'll enjoy the walk.'

'I'll be in contact.'

Peter smiled. He'd heard that before.

'A nice thought, Tamsin … if a little unbelievable. But I hope I'm not completely closed to miracle. Do we hug?'

They attempted a hug, uncomfortable smiles and then she watched him as he turned and walked away; as he walked without turning along the sea wall towards the cliffs in faint sun and misty rain.

'Til next time!' she shouted, though she wasn't sure if he heard. He probably thought she was a seagull.

# Eighty Four

❖

*The soldiers paid little attention to the vagrant by the side of the road, though the vagrant watched them, and even blessed them as they passed, with the sign of the cross.*

*'Forgive me, father, for I have sinned!' they shouted. 'And greatly enjoyed it!'*

*The vagrant needed a shave, his head in particular, he felt hair growing, grey hair, and his clothes could be a better fit. But maybe this was what clothes felt like, normal clothes, clothes other than a monk's habit. And the sun was shining, sunshine after the rain, so fresh scent in the air, and if he didn't know where he would sleep that night, he knew he was free from imprisonment. Though how strange it was to walk without the habit, the clothes he'd worn since the age of fifteen … some fifty years ago. How unsettling this new cloth felt on his legs and how disturbing on his soul! How defining clothes can be …*

*There were things he didn't know, and probably never would. In particular, the identity of the figure who'd come to his holding cell in Avignon at two in the morning. Who had he been and why was he sent? Had the Pope wished him away or were these the instructions of his own Order? He was an embarrassment to both, he knew that. Or was it a private supporter with the means to arrange his escape? Money can arrange anything, regardless of God.*

*Whoever it was, and why ever it was, they'd brought a change of clothes from his worn Dominican habit, placed coins in his pocket, good coins, coins with value, led him through the quiet cloisters and out into the dark streets. They'd finally said goodbye to him, brusque but kind, at the south gate of the city, where money was exchanged with the gate-keeper to allow him on his way. After all, this was not the hour when the good men travelled.*

*And whether he was glad of this freedom, he didn't know. Part of him had wished to remain in his cell, remain true to his life's calling, for this was what he knew, and how could a life's calling end? He felt the unease now, as if every step along the road was a crime, a sin, something less good than before, something unreal. But he still walked, for he'd seen the document, or at least been told of its content. After the accusations of heretical teaching, twenty-one in all, and his careful rebuttals of each, the Pope had made his decision: Eckhart was accused of being 'evil-sounding, rash and suspect of heresy'. Fairly plain, really. He'd been censured for misleading 'the uneducated crowd by his teaching and preaching'. He was not formally declared a heretic, despite the exhausting efforts of the Fishwife, so he would not have been burned. But he was accused of 'sowing thorns and obstacles to the very clear truth of faith in the field of the Church' and 'working to produce harmful thistles and poisonous thorn bushes'.*

*His life's work was declared a poison.*

*So no burning; but with his reputation savaged, the repression of his teachings would follow, he'd seen it done before. He would be as one who had not existed on this earth, his words suppressed or destroyed for the greater good. His own Dominican Order, as Henricus de Cigno had explained at their final meeting, would have to disown him, drop a veil of silence around his activities.*

*'My activities? You make me sound like one plotting evil!'*

*It had been a meeting of some haste, and some distance, physical and otherwise, Henricus behaving as though Eckhart was a leper, as though he carried some disease. But the Order needed the support of the Pope, he must understand that, papal support against the Franciscans – he knew how it was, surely? The Franciscans couldn't be allowed to win, he must understand, you do understand, Eckhart? You do understand that we can't be seen to be supporting people like yourself?*

*'People like myself?'*

*So when the stranger entered the deep and silent dark, he'd left his cell, left his Order, left his status in the world ... but he'd not left faith, whose origins were found beyond the Church's creeds. True to himself, he'd been a free man within his Order, but now he must be true again, and find freedom in the oblivion beyond. No Dominican habit, no holy orders, just an old man and a road heading south, precarious and uncertain. But what other road was there?*

*'He knows God rightly who knows him everywhere.' How often had he said that? He'd find freedom now in different clothes, his life's calling over and only just begun.*

*Life begins when you want it to.*

*I like the ephemeral thing about theatre, every perfor-mance is like a ghost – it's there and then it's gone.*

Maggie Smith

# Author's Notes

Meister Eckhart was a real historical figure, of course, as were those with smaller parts in his story told here: William of Paris, Marguerite Porete (who deserves a book of her own), Henricus de Cigno, the Archbishop of Cologne and Pope John XXII – who, ironically, was condemned as a heretic himself by his successor, Pope Benedict XII. And they all played the roles attributed to them in this story, though the Archbishop was not Eckhart's prosecutor at the trial.

It is not known whether Eckhart ever met Porete, whether Johannes ever met Marguerite, but it was quite possible; they could have been in Paris at the same time and they certainly shared many ideas.

Eckhart was a Dominican monk. But the Dominican authorities, wary of Franciscan influence in the papal court, had been concerned about his teaching. The Dominican General Chapter held in Venice in 1325 had spoken out against 'friars in Teutonia who say things in their sermons that can easily lead simple and uneducated people into error'. And so it was that the Dominicans, his own people, conducted an investigation into Eckhart's orthodoxy.

Eckhart had the support of local Dominicans, however. On 13 February 1327, faced with the Archbishop's inquisitors, he preached a sermon in the Dominican church at Cologne, and then had his secretary read out a public protestation of his innocence. Eckhart translated the text into German, so that his audience could understand it.

The verdict went against him, however. The Meister responded by denying competence and authority to the inquisitors and the Archbishop, and appealed to the Pope directly. So in the spring of 1327, when our story starts, this 66-year-old man set off for Avignon, a walk of over five hundred miles.

On 30 April 1328, the Pope wrote to the Archbishop of Cologne that the case against Eckhart was moving ahead. But the Pontiff added that Eckhart had already died; 28 January 1328 is the date sometimes given for his death.

Yet his end remains a mystery to this day: for there is no known date of his death, no record of his funeral and no evidence of a grave, which is strange for such a public figure, for one with such an outstanding employment record in the Church. He simply disappeared from the face of the earth, silently and without record, which has led some to wonder if, for whatever reason, he was allowed to wander quietly into the night, stripped of his old identity.

PS. If you would like to discover more about the man and his words, I dare to recommend my own book, *Conversations with Meister Eckhart,* published by White Crow. He's a deep well, but the water is fresh.

PPS. You can follow Abbot Peter on Twitter @AbbotPeter.

*A series of macabre murders in a bleak English seaside town, each with cast of suspects with secrets of their own to protect.*

*But who can hide from the man who sees our inner truths?*

ABBOT PETER
A HABIT FOR CRIME

'Abbot Peter is a true original.' *Daily Mail*

**Coming soon**

ISBN: 978-0-232-52997-5

ISBN: 978-0-232-53061-2

ISBN: 978-0-232-53020-9

www.dltbooks.com